TAMING OF THE RAKE

The Gentleman Courtesans Book 4

VICTORIA VALE

PROLOGUE

Benedict Sterling paced the length of the dressing room, hands folded behind his back. His entire body thrummed with nervous tension, making it difficult to stand still. His patience was paper thin, but snatching his watch up and noting the time, he realized there was no reason to rush. He had over an hour before his assignation. If only that knowledge could ease his mind. As it was, he hadn't slept the night before and couldn't stomach a bite of food. He was a powder keg ready to explode at the slightest provocation.

He flicked his gaze at the woman preening before the cheval mirror, hands braced on her hips. Wearing a riding habit of navy blue, Lady Celeste Browning, Dowager Countess of Langford, was dressed for an afternoon of being seen in Hyde Park. Driving down Rotten Row with her at his side, the hood of his landau lowered for all the world to see, was typically one of his favorite past-times. Firstly, because he knew word of his every move always reached his father—and if there was one thing Benedict enjoyed, it was annoying the viscount. Secondly, there was the appeal of Celeste herself, who had become as close to him as his male friends over the years. Few were privy to the secrets he kept close to the chest, but he trusted the woman the entire *ton* thought of as his mistress.

If only they knew the truth. As a gentleman courtesan, he was in no position to keep a mistress—not that he particularly wanted to. *He* was the one who did the servicing, along with the dozen other men he had hired to join the agency. Only he, Celeste, and two of his closest friends knew the entire truth of their arrangement. Most had no idea what *really* went on when he visited the countess's townhouse three nights a week. His role as proprietor of the agency was only one aspect of Ben's secret profession. It wasn't necessary for the others to know what he was up to, and Celeste offered the perfect smokescreen.

However, it had begun to wear thin. While he had never been more financially secure, and was glad to have helped his friends achieve the same success, Benedict was beginning to regret founding The Gentleman Courtesans. What had started out as a means to make money had become an enterprise fraught with dangers. The threats of exposure and scandal had always hung over their heads, but they were now exacerbated by a gossip columnist with a penchant for unearthing the most salacious stories.

How could Ben have guessed she would latch onto the notion of male courtesans in London and make it her personal mission to unmask them?

Really, it wouldn't have bothered him so much if not for the other things he wished to keep hidden—secrets so damning that 'ruin' would be too mild a world to describe the consequences of their discovery. Aside from that, there were his friends to consider. Out of the original five men who had founded the agency, three were retired and settled with wives. One was even expecting his first child. They had families to protect, and Benedict would never forgive himself if his downfall led to their shame.

It was up to him to ensure the protection of not just his own secrets, but theirs, as well. His mother and brothers were dead, and he abhorred his father. For all intents and purposes, the other gentleman courtesans were all the family he had, and he would be damned if the devious London Gossip trifled with them.

Celeste turned away from the mirror, her cat-like blue eyes

following his progress—back and forth, back and forth. "Ben, do relax. Have a drink."

Benedict waved her off. "I need to be sharp when I meet her. I cannot afford to be addled with drink."

"You mean, when *we* meet her," she corrected, turning to lift two hats into the light. Celeste inspected them with a critical eye—one a sedate design matching her habit, the other a deep violet with an array of flamboyant plumes. "Which hat? I think the blue would be best, to help us avoid too much scrutiny."

"No, wear the feathered one," he muttered. "A little attention might not be a bad thing. The Gossip obviously wants us to be seen. She chose the fashionable hour for our meeting, and I will not have her think she has intimidated me into trying to go unnoticed. Either she plans on making a spectacle of me, or she wants to use the crowded park as a safeguard."

"She fears you would wring her neck otherwise," Celeste quipped, setting the blue hat aside and settling the violet one over her dark brown hair. "Not that anyone could blame you if you did."

Benedict was known for his lethal fists, but he would never use them against a woman. However, the author of *The London Gossip* tempted him sorely, and at times he couldn't help but think he would like to make her choke on the pen she used to slander everyone who crossed her path.

"I don't want you involved in any of this," he grumbled. "As I've said countless times, anyone caught—"

"Associating with you may also be ruined," she interjected, rolling her eyes. "Yes, I did hear you the first ten times you said it."

"This is no laughing matter."

"Of course it isn't. If you think I will allow that shrew to scare me into shunning you, you do not know me at all."

Benedict sighed. He *did* know Celeste, and one of the things he admired most about her was the unflinching strength and bravado with which she faced the world. The gossip about her ran rampant, with all of society speculating that she had murdered her husband to earn his fortune. Like Ben, she wasn't interested in anyone's approval, least of all acceptance into a world where a friend could become an enemy with nothing more than a whisper in the right ear.

When he had come to her with his proposal that she pose as his mistress, Celeste had laughed in his face. But, when he explained *why* he needed her to do it, she embraced him and agreed to help him for as long as he required it. He had come to her aid once, and though he insisted she owed him nothing, Celeste asserted that she most certainly did.

"It will cost me nothing to do it," she had said when he'd made the suggestion three years ago. *"Besides, I think it should be quite an amusing lark."*

Now, it would seem his machinations *would* cost her something. The rumors about her notwithstanding, for Celeste to be tangled up in his eventual ruin would see her ostracized.

No, Benedict would not let it come to that. The London Gossip had dealt a few blows, but nothing they couldn't recover from. This had not spiraled too far out of his control.

The minutes passed far too slowly, but once Celeste announced it was time to leave, all that changed. It seemed he entered his waiting carriage only to blink and find himself strolling along a footpath with Celeste on his arm. The late afternoon air held a biting chill, and he faintly noticed the smell and taste of coming rain. Nevertheless, Hyde Park was as crowded as could be for this time of year, where those who only journeyed to London for the Season had taken their leave. The dismal gray of the sky fit his mood. He fairly vibrated with unease, eyes darting as he sought out his enemy.

He had never seen her face, of course, but would know her when he saw her. Benedict could picture her as he had last seen her—dressed in black from head to toe, with a veiled hat obscuring her features. He recalled the scent that tickled some buried memory in the back of his mind—one that had him reaching up to finger the scar on his right temple. The thin line was only visible when his hair was combed back and someone stood close enough to notice. Many had tried to draw him into conversation about the injury, but it was his habit to spin some outlandish story about where it had come from.

"Did she specify where you were to meet her?" Celeste asked, interrupting his convoluted thoughts.

"She only mentioned the Serpentine, but if I haven't missed my guess, she will want to be visible to as many people as possible. From here, anyone walking the footpaths or riding Rotten Row will be able to see us. She's close."

The plumes in Celeste's hat brushed his jaw as she craned her neck to look around, her grip on him tightening. "There?"

He followed her gaze to where a woman stood near the edge of the Serpentine. Awareness prickled the back of his neck as he spotted the lonely figure dressed in somber gray instead of black. But, everything else about the London Gossip was the same, right down to a wide-brimmed hat with a veil. Benedict narrowed his eyes as he noticed the four hulking men standing in loose formation around her. After being accosted and assaulted by two of them, he had expected this. She had planned it all perfectly—ensuring he would not be able to unmask her without causing a scene.

"That's her," he confirmed, guiding Celeste along the path toward them. "This is your last chance to back out. Go home, Celeste. Let me face this alone."

"I think not. I am as much a part of this as you and your courtesans. You cannot be rid of me so easily."

Benedict patted her hand and said nothing. In the absence of the other courtesans, there were few people he could rely on. He grudgingly allowed himself to feel comforted by Celeste's presence as they drew nearer to the figure in gray.

The Gossip turned to face them, and the four men edged forward to box them in—though they were careful to keep their gazes fixed elsewhere. Their presence was a tangible threat radiating at Benedict with the promise of violence if he made one false move. He could have taken one of them in his sleep with a hand tied behind his back. Two of them wouldn't be a problem even on his worst day. But, four? Too risky, even in such a public place.

"You aren't very good at following directions," one of the men barked. "That's close enough!"

Celeste flinched, but Benedict held his ground, glaring at the man standing just before him and to the left. He was the only one looking at them, his beady eyes narrowed under a heavy, prominent brow. He had a jaw like an anvil and huge, meaty hands.

Come alone, the note had said. *Don't look for me, I will come to you.*

Benedict looked to the Gossip, searching for her eyes behind the sheer gauze of her veil. "In case it has escaped your notice, I do as I please. You wanted me, and here I am. Either we talk now, or I walk away."

The Gossip inclined her head but said nothing. Aside from that small motion, she did not move, appearing as if she weren't even breathing.

"M'lady was very clear—"

The Gossip raised a gloved hand, and it was enough for the brute to snap his mouth shut.

Lowering her hand, she then proffered something to Benedict with the other. Celeste advanced before Ben could make a move. The Gossip remained where she stood, allowing Celeste to take the offering. Paper rustled as she returned to Benedict, face blanching while she read what looked like a copy of *The London Gossip*. If it was today's issue, Benedict did not understand her reaction. They had read it together over tea—an account of a mysterious woman who'd had an affair with one of his courtesans. The details were too exact to be a fabrication, and after finishing it Benedict had been certain the man described was Dominick Burke—who had just eloped and escaped to Paris with his bride following a magnificent scandal. Nick hadn't been named outright, and that was enough to bring Benedict comfort. For now.

When Celeste reached him, her head tipped back and wide eyes peered up at him, filled with trepidation. He glanced down at the paper with a frown. It was, in fact, a copy of today's issue of *The London Gossip*. However, sitting atop it was a slip of paper, upon which was written a list. Benedict turned it over to read the words. His entire body went numb, his hands shaking as he realized what he was looking at.

There were names written on the scrap of paper, at least a dozen of them. He found his own name at the very top, but that wasn't what made bile rise up in the back of his throat. It was the four others written beneath his that made Benedict feel as if he might be sick.

The Hon. Dominick Burke

The Hon. Hugh Radcliffe

Mr. David Graham

Mr. Aubrey Drake

He recognized the other names as well, but it was those four that struck dread in him.

Benedict wanted to tear the page to shreds and hurl them at her feet, but understood the futility of such an act. Destroying it wouldn't change that his nemesis had unearthed the names of nearly all the men in his employ, including those who were his closest friends.

Swallowing past the acidic taste of defeat on his tongue, Benedict squared his shoulders. He was not beaten yet. If she played this hand so openly, it had to be because she couldn't prove what she knew. Perhaps she had enough to implicate him and Dominick, but not the others.

"Why?"

It was the one question that had haunted him from the moment he realized the woman was on to him.

The Gossip's tinkling laughter emitted from behind the veil, grating and familiar. Benedict flinched, something within him reacting adversely to the sound. His suspicion grew as she pressed a slender hand to her middle, laughing as if Ben had told the most humorous joke.

He knew her. There was something about her that nagged at his memories, making him dizzy from trying to puzzle it out. Whenever he prodded at the persistent thought that she felt familiar, he brushed up against other recollections better left alone. Things he had endured that he never wanted to think of again.

"Because I can, of course," the Gossip replied. "Being the cause of your destruction gratifies me more than you will ever know, Mr. Sterling."

Benedict wrinkled his brow as the sound of her voice jabbed through his eardrum like a needle. It went deep, piercing his mind like a lightning strike. A flash of light illuminated the mystery for half a second before he was once more cast into the dark.

Celeste frowned, concern written all over her face. "Ben?"

"I know you," he rasped. "How do I know you?"

"That isn't important now, and if you cannot puzzle it out for yourself, that is of no consequence to me," the Gossip replied, an acerbic bite in her tone. "All you need to know is that I have everything I need to take you down. Unless you give me exactly what I want."

Benedict shook his head to clear it, determined to keep his composure. Where he had been chilled before, he was now burning up within the confines of his greatcoat, a sheen of sweat breaking out along his skin. His insides churned, and his eye twitched—whether due to lack of sleep or his unraveling self-control, he wasn't certain.

"And just what *do* you want?" Celeste asked, moving to stand between Benedict and his foe. "What have you to gain from targeting someone who has done nothing to harm you?"

"Mr. Sterling, you will inform your strumpet to keep her silence, or this interview will come to an abrupt end."

Celeste's voice raised sharply, "*Strumpet?* Why you—"

"Enough." Benedict just barely managed to take hold of her arm before she could advance on the Gossip. He then gently tugged Celeste back to his side. He could feel the hostility thrumming through her. If he turned Celeste loose, she might murder the Gossip with her bare hands. "Will you answer me, then? What do you want?"

"We aren't here to discuss that."

"Like hell, we aren't!" Benedict roared, forgetting the other occupants of the park.

A group of women bundled in furs and hats paused to stare at them before walking on, shaking their heads in disapproval. One of the Gossip's men edged closer, knuckles cracking as he curled his fists. The Gossip laughed again, and this time it held a note of irony to it. She was toying with him, the little bitch.

Benedict drew in a calming breath and tried again, keeping his voice level this time. "If you didn't summon me to tell me what you want, why are we here? I hardly needed you to deliver me a copy of your ridiculous paper, as I have already read today's outrageous fabrication."

The Gossip scoffed. "My source was a reliable one, and we both know it."

Benedict ground his teeth, the scandal sheet crumpling in his fist. Damn her, she had him over a barrel. He had already spent the morning rifling through his documents and contracts, trying to decide which of their former clients had betrayed them. He was fairly certain he knew which woman had gone running to the Gossip with her story, and was prepared to deal with her in due time.

"I simply asked you here today to make certain I have your full attention, Mr. Sterling. As you can see, I have been made privy to every so-called gentleman *selling himself* as part of your organization. If you do not wish for me to publish those names, you will give me what I want."

"I am still waiting for you to tell me exactly what that is."

There was a slight movement behind the veil, and Benedict detected the flash of white teeth when she smiled. "We will get to that when I'm good and ready, and not before. Think of this as a prelude of sorts, Mr. Sterling. Until recently, I believe you thought of me as nothing more than a minor nuisance. Today, I have come here to inform you that if you don't fear me yet, you ought to. You *will*."

"Will I? Where is your proof, your evidence?"

"Oh, but I do have proof. It isn't much, but it is a start, I am sure you will agree. There's a collection of distinct calling cards—"

"Which could belong to anyone with the initials G.C.," he countered with a dismissive wave. "Is that all?"

"There are accounts of a secret office in the back of Madame Hershaw's dress shop."

"And when you visited there, what did you find?" Benedict felt bolder now, realizing that what information she did have was now obsolete. He had taken great pains to make sure of that. "I'd wager absolutely nothing."

"You are awfully brash for a man whose back is against the wall."

"And you are as stupid as you are arrogant if you think I can be intimidated by names on a list, and an outlandish story you could have spun out of thin air. Unless you have something more substantial than that, we have nothing else to discuss."

It was a wild gamble, and he knew it. But Benedict had never been one to back down, even when faced with insurmountable odds. Defiance seemed threaded through the very fabric of his being.

The Gossip issued a labored sigh and folded her hands. "I had so hoped we could avoid such unpleasantness, but I can see you are determined to do this the hard way. Very well, then. If you will not give me what I want—"

"Will you come to the point anytime today, or continue beating around the bush?"

She issued a derisive sound. "You know, I don't believe I will. You seem to be itching for a fight, Mr. Sterling, and I do not want to disappoint you. If it's war you want, so be it. You cannot say you weren't warned … more than once."

Benedict bit back a string of curses as he realized this woman had never intended to bargain with him. She was like a cat playing with a wounded mouse—only, she seemed to expect him to grovel and plead. Apparently, his impudence had only exacerbated her need to toy with him before swallowing him whole.

"Goddamn it, who are you?" he snapped, unable to keep the desperation out of his voice. Thus far, she had been beating him at their little game, and it infuriated him to be at such a disadvantage. "What have I ever done to deserve this?"

She made to walk past him, her guards falling in step behind her. Her shoulder brushed his and she paused, staring up at him. Through the gray fabric of her veil, he made out a round face and large dark eyes. His belly clenched with the urge to vomit as her scent assaulted his nostrils.

"Now you're finally asking the right questions, Mr. Sterling."

Before he could form the words to respond, she was gone, leading her pack of dogs behind her. Benedict couldn't give chase, because at that moment the meager contents of his stomach rose swiftly up his throat. He stumbled to the nearest tree, one hand braced on the trunk as he leaned over and retched. His face flushed hot from the exertions, and he nearly crumpled to his knees.

When he straightened, Celeste was at his side, offering a handkerchief and a mournful expression. He avoided her gaze while wiping at his mouth and drawing in deep breaths. He trembled as some darkened corner of his mind unlocked and began spilling memories out into the light. That scent, that voice ... he was beginning to suspect he knew very well how he recalled them.

He had to be sure. Without having seen her full face he had only his faulty recollections to fall back on. They came from a time in his life he had actively worked to forget, a period too intimately tangled with his past. If she was who he suspected, Benedict could hardly fathom why he would be the object of her vendetta. She'd do better to turn her anger on his father, who had been the force driving them into each other's lives.

You don't even know if it's really her. You have managed to anger and annoy half the ton *in the last few years. It could be any number of women.*

In order to be certain, he was going to have to call on another of his friends. He hated to involve anyone else he cared about in this mess, but found he now had no choice. He could not fight his enemy blind.

"Are you certain it was wise to provoke her?" Celeste asked as he tucked her soiled handkerchief into his pocket. "And what are you going to do now?"

"First, I'm going to go home and scrub my teeth," he said with a cringe. "And then I need to visit a friend. I think I know who the Gossip is, but I want to be sure."

"Really? Who is she?"

He shook his head, refusing to draw Celeste any deeper into this web. Bringing her here had been a mistake, no matter how much better it made him feel to not have to face this alone.

"It doesn't matter yet ... not until I can prove it. Come, I need to send word if I want to meet her tonight."

Celeste took his arm again. "Who?"

"Lady Millicent Dane."

· · ·

They called her The Ravishing Widow, and it was never difficult to see why. Lady Millicent Dane was known for her beauty and a scandalous reputation. Being widowed at a young age had freed her from the control of any man, and she'd cast off the expectations and strictures of society to live as she pleased. Like Benedict, she was amused by the hypocrisy of the *ton* and delighted in giving them something to talk about.

However, some things were better kept secret; which was why tonight he chose to meet her in the one place the London Gossip wouldn't follow him. His obsessive reading of her columns had revealed something very telling about the woman. Self-righteousness and piety were her weapons, and she used them against the people she maligned in her writing. She would never risk following him into the White House in Soho Square, a brothel catering to a wide array of tastes with its themed rooms and variety of available whores. Her own reputation could be ruined by such an act, and Ben had a feeling she wasn't willing to go quite that far to bring him down.

So, as he entered The White House to find himself overwhelmed by whores offering to guide him into the room of his choice, Benedict waved them off. He inquired after Millicent's location, and was promptly led into a room known only as 'the dungeon.'

He found his old friend within the dark interior, which was illuminated by only a few tapers. The effect heightened the menacing look of the various implements arranged along one wall—things made of leather and metal and wood that promised pleasure or pain depending on the mood of the person wielding them. An array of tables and benches with buckles and straps filled the space, while a St. Andrew's cross acted as a proud centerpiece.

Benedict raised his eyebrows when he noticed the nude woman strapped to the cross, spread wide and tethered to its beams. Her pale skin glowed in the meager candlelight, her back, buttocks, and legs left on full display. On either side of the cross stood Millicent and the man who was presented to the world as one of her footmen, but whose role in her household was of a more intimate nature. Peter was a large man, broad through the shoulders and chest—which were proudly exhibited by the absence of a shirt. Arms crossed, he watched Benedict in silence as Millicent came forward to greet him.

She was the only one fully clothed, in a pair of black breeches, shirt and waistcoat, a pair of boots clicking against the rough floor. Tumbles of white-gold hair fell loose down her back, and her lovely face was fixed in an expression of amusement at Benedict's reaction to the scene.

"I'm sorry to interrupt," he said, lips quivering with coming laughter.

Millicent waved one hand, displaying a riding crop held in a small fist. "No apologies necessary, darling, we simply grew bored waiting for you. But Peter and I have only just begun, and I think it will heighten Lily's anticipation to be made to wait. What say you, Peter?"

The manservant gave the whore a lascivious glance, running his fingertip down her spine. The woman whimpered, but remained still.

"Whatever pleases you, Mistress."

She thrust the crop toward Peter without a glance in his direction. "Hold this until I return, pet."

Peter reacted to the command in her tone and hurried across the room to do her bidding. Instead of taking the crop in hand, he bent down to clutch it between his teeth.

Millicent grinned and reached back to pat his bare chest. "Good boy. Come, Ben, we'll speak elsewhere."

Benedict followed her from the room, where Peter took up a silent vigil beside the cross, eyes fixed on the opposite wall as he remained docile with the crop in his mouth.

"As always, you manage to both impress and astonish me," he quipped.

Millicent's deep, throaty laughter floated back toward Benedict as she guided him down the corridor as if she lived in The White House and knew its every square inch. Throwing open a door, she guided him into an innocuous sitting room that had a fire going in the hearth.

"You know how easily I grow bored," she said, dropping into an armchair and crossing her legs. "Peter is always finding such inventive ways to keep me happy and I adore him for it. Now ... your note seemed rather urgent. I take it you are here about today's copy of *The London Gossip*."

Sitting across from her, Benedict stared into the fireplace. He described his meeting with the Gossip in a monotone voice, relating the details as if he had observed it all from a distance.

Millie's back snapped straight, and her fingers dug into the arms of her chair as she stared at him open-mouthed. "Dear God."

"Yes. She knows our names, though the fact that she hasn't published them yet brings me some modicum of comfort."

She tapped her finger against her chin and narrowed her eyes. "If that woman had anything other than a list of names, she would have gone public by now. Aside from her so-called 'anonymous' source and the story she published this morning, I daresay she has nothing of any substance."

Benedict shook his head and sighed. "She still knows far too much for my peace of mind. I worry that today's story is going to rattle the other courtesans as well as our clients—both past and current. If one of us can be betrayed by a former lover, we are all in danger of exposure."

"Then you came to the same conclusion I did? This morning's column was about Dominick."

"So it would seem. There are two courtesans with dark hair who have earls for fathers. But only one of them had a nine-month affair with a widow with enough gall to go running to the Gossip with her story."

"Lady Thrush," Millicent spat, upper lip curling with derision. "I have always disliked that woman. She never stopped wanting him, you know, and only ended their arrangement because of her husband's jealousy. The moment he died, she began plotting her course back to poor Nick. She hardly waited until her time of mourning had passed."

"Dominick told me she accosted him at Viscount Barrington's house party. She was quite ... aggressive. Of course, he refused her and went on to elope with Miss Barrington a few weeks later. So, Lady Thrush certainly seems to have a motive—however maniacal it may be."

"Only an insecure woman makes such a cake of herself over a man."

Benedict grinned. "No ... some of you would much rather have the men make cakes of themselves over you."

"It *is* ever so much fun," she replied with a laugh. "But, enough about that, darling. Tell me what I can do to help. Shall I handle Lady Thrush for you? I do have some information I could hang over her head to ensure her silence. She won't cross me."

"*I* will deal with her. There is no dirt you can hold over her like the things I am privy to. No, I have a different request to make of you. One that will require the utmost discretion."

"Discretion is something of a specialty for me, as you well know. Tell me what you need."

"The London Gossip. I think ... no, I *know* she must be one of us. A member of high society."

Millicent wrinkled her nose. "Do you really think so? Her writings have always struck me as being rather biased *against* the *ton*—as if she were an outsider looking in, writing such horrible things out of jealousy."

"You and I both know one doesn't need to be an outsider to be made to feel as if they do not belong."

Her face softened as a hundred confidences floated on the air between them. Over the years, the circle of people he could entrust with the truth had widened a bit. Included among them was Millicent because, like him, she had experienced her share of loss, pain, and darkness. As well, her secret inclinations would make her a pariah if word ever spread, and Benedict knew such a burden well.

"I think I know her," he whispered, uncertain why he had such a difficult time saying the words. A cold sweat broke out on the back of his neck as he recalled that nauseating scent and the sound of her grating voice. "In fact, I'm almost certain we've met before and perhaps ... you are going to think I'm mad."

She furrowed her brow, leaning forward to rest a hand on his knee. "Ben, you've gone white as a sheet, and you ... you're shaking. What on earth?"

"My father," he ground out, fighting to regain control of his senses. "He has something to do with this. Not the column, of course, but *her* ... when I saw her today, when I heard her voice, I *knew*."

He felt as if he would be sick but didn't want to face *why* he felt this way. It required jabbing at the parts of himself he thought had healed. Apparently, the wounds had merely festered, and now he was going to have to rip them back open.

Millicent rested a hand atop his. "Say no more. I will make a few inquiries and see if I can turn up anything pointing to her identity. Would that help?"

"Tremendously."

"Consider it done," Millicent said, giving his hand another squeeze before pulling away. "I will send word when I have something to report."

Benedict cleared his throat, annoyed with himself for almost falling apart in front of her. It didn't matter that she was part of the small circle of people he trusted. He had worked long and hard to turn himself into the man he was now—to cultivate strength and stoicism, and exercise control in everything he did. The scar at his temple served as a constant reminder of the night he had, in a sense, been reborn. He had stopped allowing things to happen to him and started shaping his own life as he saw fit. Uncompromising, he was often called. Relentless. Cold.

But those traits had saved him and seen him through the darkest times of his life. They would not fail him now.

Sitting up straight, he squared his shoulders and clenched his jaw. The Gossip was nothing more than a bothersome fly, and he would have the last laugh once he had effectively swatted her away.

For the sake of the people he loved, the family he had formed not of blood but of a different sort of bond, he could not fail.

CHAPTER 1

"Rumor has it that the Honourable Mr. B—and I confer such a title on him out of formality, not because I actually believe him to be possessing of actual honor —has absconded with a certain runaway bride to Scotland. It is the least he can do after thoroughly destroying her previously unblemished reputation, not once but twice. Time will tell whether marriage might prove enough to tame one of London's most notorious rakes."
-The London Gossip, 25 November 1819

David Graham had died and gone to heaven. Surely that was what had happened, because he'd climbed into a large, plush bed and was now surrounded by his favorite creatures in the world. Heavenly beings, women. He had sampled enough of them to realize there was something to love in each and every one. His insatiable appetite for them was a straightforward fact of his existence, stitched into the fabric of his character. He reveled in their sweet scents and tinkling giggles, loved the sight of a trim ankle and a dainty hand as much as he did a well-formed bosom or a pair of spread thighs. He wasn't a selective man, and was often accused of being *too* indiscriminate. But David believed one could find the beauty in anything if they looked close enough.

Some men prided themselves on their titles and social standing, or the immaculate tailoring of their clothes. Others were connoisseurs of fine horseflesh, quality spirits, or excellent cigars. *His* expertise involved the fair sex.

David derived much satisfaction from his ability to appreciate women in the manner they most deserved: with the full force of his charm and amiability ... and a talent that had earned him a reputation as 'the most skilled tongue in England.' Of course, there had never been any official contest to be won, but he'd pleasured enough ladies to earn himself that unique title, and it was one he guarded with fierce pride.

It was his notoriety which had led him here, to heaven. Two hands caressed his bare chest, soft and searching, while another made its way up his thigh. His cock pulsed with a need that was promptly met by a fourth hand wrapping around him and taking up a slow, measured stroke. He groaned against the wet, silken flesh pressed to his lips, working his tongue in the rhythm this lady seemed to like best. It had taken years of meticulous calculation to develop this particular skill, and just now it rewarded him as it always did ... with musical moans of ecstasy and a pair of thighs clenching his head in a shuddering, forceful grip.

He peered up at the woman riding his face as if she sat astride a bucking stallion, clawing the headboard as she screamed her release. David refused to let up, even when she insisted she couldn't take anymore. They all said that, and he was always happy to show them otherwise. It was another one of those things about women he found so utterly fascinating—their ability to reach climax over and over again, when someone actually took the time to learn what made them tick. As it happened, puzzling them out was his favorite past-time, which made his present efforts more fun than work.

Lady Rebecca Grant fell from atop him with one last moan, which melted into a satisfied sigh as she went limp at his side. Raising up on his elbows, David peered at the two others awaiting their turn with him. Lady Frances Beeton was the one working his cock, a knowing smile curving her lips as she observed the state her friend was in.

"Didn't I tell you, Becky?" she purred before bending her head to run her tongue along his shaft. "He's exquisite."

David hissed at the velvet wetness stroking the length of his cock, biting back a grumble of regret when it was gone. Frances had always been a little tease; it was what he liked most about her. That, and her adventurous nature.

The lady had hired him as her courtesan while between marriages. Her first husband died a mere six months after the wedding, leaving Frances a grand fortune. In the year that followed, she kept David as her personal plaything, parting with an exorbitant sum to have him at her beck and call. Frances cut him loose upon getting engaged to her second husband, who had been thirty years her senior. Predictably, he had also died, freeing her to once more live her life as she pleased.

Thanks to her, David could now indulge in one last round of debauchery before he was obliged to face the reality of his situation. Being forced to leave London was a dire prospect, but Frances and her friends were giving him one hell of a sendoff. He had been paid to entertain Frances and her friends for three days and nights, but David would never tell them he might have done it for free had they only asked. Benedict would insist that simply wasn't good business.

"He's the best present I could have asked for," Rebecca managed between labored breaths.

David cupped the nape of her neck, drawing her to him for a kiss. "Happy birthday, sweet."

She whimpered against his mouth, arching and writhing as he plunged his tongue in deep. The taste of champagne mingled with the flavor of her juices on his palate.

His attention was quickly stolen by the third woman, who moved up his body to have her turn. He flopped to his back and licked his lips, offering Lady Elinor Howe a welcoming grin.

"My lady ... your saddle awaits."

She giggled, then moaned when his tongue darted into the seam of her mons. Just as he found her clit and began teasing it in a playful prelude, Frances fit her mouth around his cock, and David fell headlong into hedonistic paradise.

Time seemed suspended as the cares of the outside world became a distant afterthought. David had never been one to take anything too seriously. However, present circumstances left him with no choice but to confront the responsibilities he'd been outrunning his entire adult life. There were some things he simply had not been ready to face, so if he could immerse himself in the delights of the moment a bit longer, he certainly wasn't going to turn down the chance.

Frances had just sheathed him with a condom and tied its ribbons when a sudden knock on the door echoed through the room. David gripped Elinor's thighs to keep her from rolling off him, then raised his hips to encourage Frances to go on. She had made it clear they weren't to be disturbed, so David saw no reason to stop. The tight clench of France's cunt enveloped him, and Elinor's moans came muffled from behind the hand she held over her mouth. Rebecca lay in repose beside them, content to watch as she absently reached out to fondle one of Elinor's breasts. The distraction of the knock faded away as David thrust up into the welcoming grip of Frances, who had begun to ride him with slow, agonizing surges of her hips.

The three of them had been toying with him for the past hour, and he was so near to spending it was almost embarrassing. Nevertheless, he had a reputation to uphold, so he fought off climax with a great deal of effort, concentrating his energies on Elinor.

The knock came again, more insistent this time, followed by the voice of a servant. Frances pulled away, leaving him hovering on the edge of near release.

"Oh, for the love of Christ," she grumbled, the mattress shifting as she shot up from the bed. "When I say I do not wish to be disturbed ..."

Then, Elinor was gone, she and Rebecca reaching for dressing gowns while muffling their giggles. David draped himself with the bed sheet, though he needn't have bothered. Once properly covered, Frances merely pried the door open a crack. Curiosity mingled with his annoyance as David listened in, catching only snatches of her conversation with a servant.

"Apologies, my lady ... insisted it was urgent ..."

"I don't care how urgent, my orders were quite clear ..."

"... must speak with Mr. Graham right away ..."

He frowned, realizing there was only one person who would have known to come here looking for him. Dread poured through him like ice water, snuffing out his arousal. Benedict was the consummate professional, and would never interrupt a courtesan on the job unless he felt it necessary. Something must be very wrong.

By the time Frances returned, David was on his feet and searching for his clothes. Elinor and Rebecca looked on in silent disappointment, while Frances gave him a look filled with equal parts irritation and curiosity.

"Mr. Sterling has come here looking for you," she said while he stepped into his breeches. "He insists the matter is of the utmost importance, and will not leave until he's spoken with you."

With a sheepish smile, he yanked his waistcoat on, not bothering with a cravat or coat. "Sorry, sweet. I'm sure we will only be a moment. I'll see what he wants, and then ..."

Frances preened beneath his promising gaze. "We'll be waiting."

The titters of the women followed him into the corridor. His irritation had been replaced by a sinking feeling that turned his stomach, making his footsteps slow and heavy. The last time he met with Benedict, David had been told to quit London and lay low. Ben had even informed him of his intention to stay away to keep from incriminating him. That his friend now chose to act against his own plan couldn't mean anything good.

He told himself he was being ridiculous. Benedict had only come to him for lack of anyone else to turn to. Two of the courtesans were gone on wedding trips with their wives, and the other was busy painting portraits. It was simply a fact that whenever someone needed a problem solved or a sympathetic ear, David was the last person they would consider. It didn't bother him to be the most frivolous and light-hearted of their set, because it was how he preferred things. If someone needed to be distracted from their melancholy with a night of drinking or cards, David was their man. His skills included being able to break through tension with jokes and innuendo, and making people forget their troubles for as long as they were in his company. He did not deal well with conflict or adversity, and had a penchant for making matters worse.

Benedict must be truly desperate.

The footman awaited him at the bottom of the stairs. The man kept his expression stoic, giving no hint that he knew what had gone on in Frances's bedchamber. He simply extended a hand toward the drawing room door, keeping his gaze averted.

David entered to find not only Benedict, but two other men. One of them was Warin Lyons, the young man who worked as Benedict's apprentice. With the demand for gentleman courtesans growing by the day, Ben had hired Lyons to learn the ins and outs of his job as proprietor and orchestrator of contracts. David didn't encounter him often, but he had always seemed out of place among the other courtesans. His looks were sharp and severe, his frame slender, and his bearing could only be described as cold. He was the last man David would have pegged as courtesan material. But who was he to question Benedict, who had an uncanny skill for this business?

David frowned when he noticed the third man lingering near the window, wearing a grave expression. It was Gilbert Wren, steward of his father's estate in Lancashire. For the past few years, David had ensured the family country pile received an influx of funds through Mr. Wren—who assured him they would be put to good use. Typically, the steward wrote if he needed more money. The sight of him in a London drawing room heightened David's anxiety.

"What's going on?" he asked, tearing his gaze from Wren and fixing it on Benedict.

His friend had an odd expression on his face, one David didn't think he had ever seen before. The hard slash of his mouth was softened into something like pity.

"David …"

"What are *you* doing here?" he added to Wren, who flinched at the sharpness in his tone.

"Perhaps you ought to sit down," said Lyons, his dark eyes betraying nothing. But then, the man was always as somber as an undertaker.

"I don't want to sit. Ben?"

Benedict approached, resting a bolstering hand on David's shoulder. "Mr. Wren came looking for you last night. When he found you weren't at home, a servant was sent to fetch me."

David's throat clenched as he glanced about the room, as if the walls might speak and offer some insight into this mystery. But then, David realized he already knew. He hadn't wanted to acknowledge Mr. Wren's grim expression, or the stark black band wrapped around the man's upper arm—standing out against the gray worsted of his coat.

"It's your father," Ben said.

David blinked and gave his head a little shake, certain he must now be in Hell. The Heaven of a few minutes ago seemed to have happened to someone else entirely. The world tilted beneath his feet.

"My father?"

"I'm so sorry, David. He's dead."

A WEEK LATER, DAVID SAT ACROSS FROM MR. WREN IN THE carriage that had been sent to fetch him to Lancashire. The conveyance was an ancient one that had given them trouble and delayed their journey by two days. Making matters worse, the wheels seemed to find every rut and bump in the road, exacerbating the pounding sensation between his eyes.

Gritting his teeth, he stared through the parted curtains at the bleak countryside covered in gray, misty fog. They had been on Graham lands for some time now, and David did not like what he'd seen thus far. He hadn't visited home in over a year, and it would seem the family estate had fallen even further into disrepair in that time.

He was by no means an expert on anything having to do with farming or the care of sheep, but the sorry state of cattle enclosures and barren fields were certainly a sign that something was amiss. It made no sense. David had sent thousands of pounds into the care of his family, to be used for revitalizing their heap-of-shite farm and breathe new life into a house that had fallen into disrepair. Even without being able to see every acre from the carriage, it was plain to David that the money had been mismanaged.

The house. That was it. Perhaps his father and Mr. Wren had decided to put the money toward renovating the manor and updating the wardrobes of his mother and sisters. But even that made no sense when David considered the amount of time that had passed and the fortune he'd parted with.

As they neared the house, David pinned Wren with his gaze, suspicion narrowing his eyes.

"What happened here? I sent money each month without fail, and I was assured it would be used for the benefit of the estate."

Rather than squirm under his scrutiny, the steward drew himself up with a delicate sniff. "I've done my best, Mr. Graham. You must understand that your father—God rest his soul—hardly ever heeded my advice. As his steward, I could only counsel him as best I could. The managing of the funds themselves was left in his hands. As you can see …"

David bit back a string of epithets at the evidence of his father's negligence and lack of sense. While he wasn't known as the most practical of men, he had at least learned to make the best of every situation. Upon realizing that the farm was no longer enough to support his family, David had become a courtesan to not only help them but cement his own future. He might have shunned learning anything substantial about the land he was to inherit, but he never forgot that it would all belong to him someday. 'Someday' had arrived far sooner than he'd anticipated. His father was gone, and it appeared that all David's efforts had been for naught.

The late Noel Graham had not been known for his business sense, but neither had he been a fool. How could he have squandered the opportunities that David's money would have provided?

Perhaps it isn't as bad as you think. At least wait until you see the house before you decide all hope is lost.

His optimism lasted as long as it took for the carriage to pull around the drive. Once the footman opened the door and placed the steps, David was confronted with the sorriest sight he'd ever beheld. The beloved family home, where he and his sisters had grown up— where he was expected to someday raise his future children—was in shambles.

Overgrown hedges obscured the ground-floor windows, while those of the upper floors displayed dirty panes and shabby curtains. The stone was crumbling on the edifice of the west wing, and when he squinted he noticed a massive hole in the roof.

"Bloody fucking hell," he muttered under his breath as he stared up at what had once been one of the finest homes in Lancashire.

He cringed when the front door creaked and groaned like an old man's bones as it was pushed open, revealing Caruthers—who had been serving as the butler since David was in leading strings. He'd grown thin, and his gait was slower than David remembered. What hair remaining on his head had turned a snowy white, offering a stark contrast to his somber black attire.

"Welcome home, sir," the butler said with a stiff bow. "Mrs. Graham had begun to worry at the delay."

"There was trouble with the carriage and we had to stop for repairs," he said, peering past the butler and into the entrance hall. Dark, dusty, and uninviting, it loomed like the maw of some hellish nightmare. There was an odor wafting from within—that of death and decay. "Where is she?"

"In the blue salon with your sisters."

"Very good." He had nearly made it inside before a sudden thought had him turning back to Caruthers. "We *do* still have footmen, do we not? No one's come to see to my things."

"A few, sir. I will send for one right away."

Well, that was a good sign, he supposed. If they could still afford to pay servants, they might not be as bad off as he had first supposed.

Yet again, his optimism was overshadowed by even more evidence that the Graham estate and house grounds were on the brink of complete ruin. Exhaustion made it difficult to manage a blank expression as he took it all in. With the housekeeper sweeping into a curtsy and watching him with an anxious expression, he studied every detail. Faded wallpaper and dull wood wainscoting. A checkered pattern of black and white tiles that could use a good polish. Tarnished brass sconces hanging askew, and the tell-tale patches on the walls showing where paintings had once hung.

Craning his neck, he took stock of the skylight, which ought to allow in a great deal of natural light, even on a dreary day such as this. However, a thick coat of grime obscured the panes—which was probably for the best. More light would only better display the disgraceful state of the space. He was loath to take a step beyond the entrance hall, but the welcoming smile of the housekeeper bolstered him a bit.

"Welcome home Master David!" gushed Mrs. Moffat. She was as much a fixture in this house as Caruthers, having served the family for as long as David had been living. "Oh, but it's so difficult to remember that you aren't a mischievous little boy anymore. Forgive me, *Mr. Graham.*"

Plump and ruddy-cheeked, she had to gaze up to look him in the eye. Her endearing face and kindly brown eyes offered a modicum of succor as David took hold of her shoulders.

"I'm not sure I like the sound of that," he teased. "Mr. Graham sounds far too serious, and we both know I'm as much a mischievous boy as I ever was."

She giggled like a woman half her age, reaching up to cup his cheek with one doughy hand. "Still as incorrigible as ever, I see. Master David, it is."

"I wouldn't have it any other way."

Mrs. Moffat's cheerful expression gave way to a pitying one, and she darted a look down the corridor. "I'm so glad you're home. Your poor mother has been inconsolable, and your sisters ... they need you."

He patted the housekeeper's back as she began to blubber and sniffle. "I'm here now. I will take care of them."

Someone had to. He had done his part, thinking that the people he loved were secure because of his efforts and thoughtfulness. Now, it seemed that wasn't the case. He would get to the bottom of the condition of the estate and what had been done with his money; but not before he had comforted his mother and sister.

Clearing her throat, Mrs. Moffat inclined her head toward the door across the entrance hall, leading into the drawing room meant for receiving visitors. Its doors were fastened tight.

"Mr. Graham is within, if you wish to see him."

David flinched, his gorge rising as he envisioned a shriveled corpse on the other side of the closed doors. Now he realized what that nostril-singeing smell was. "You mean to say he hasn't been buried yet?"

"Mrs. Graham wouldn't allow it until you had arrived. Besides, as the man of the house, it falls to you to represent the family at the funeral since none of them can attend."

He grimaced at the reminder that he had now stepped into his father's shoes, something he hadn't anticipated doing for another decade or more.

"You needn't worry, Master David ... we've taken pains to preserve him as best we can with ice. And, well ... flowers help."

Mentally counting the days that had passed since his father's demise, Wren's journey to London, and David's delayed return, he cringed. While he was certain Mrs. Moffat and the staff had done the best they could, he had no desire to set foot inside that room.

"I'll see to Mother first."

"Of course, of course. Dinner will be ready soon, but I suppose after such a long journey you must be hungry. Can I send for refreshment?"

"I can wait for dinner."

He headed for the drawing room then, avoiding another glance in the direction of the chamber holding his father's corpse. It was another matter he must attend to, and quickly, but his remaining family required his attention. The darkened corridor held the odor of mildew, which meant there was a leak nearby. The floor runner was bare and worn, and his boots echoed on the boards beneath, rendering it all but useless.

The door hung open a crack, and when he pushed it wide he found three women shrouded in black and clustered on a sofa.

His mother came to her feet first, crossing the distance between them with a ragged sob. "Oh, David ... thank God!"

David hardly registered her face—tight with strain—before she was in his arms and sobbing against his waistcoat. She was thinner than he remembered, trembling as if shaken by a mighty wind. He tightened his hold on her and rested his chin atop her head.

"I came the moment Wren delivered the news. We were beset by trouble on the road, but I'm here now."

His sisters came next, throwing themselves into the widening arc of his arms. Three watery pairs of eyes peered up at him from faces ravaged by grief—his sisters' a deep brown, his mother's the same vibrant blue as his.

Theodora Graham was where he had inherited his own looks, though at the moment, her classical beauty and riveting eyes were made dull and lifeless by sorrow. Her deep olive skin held a concerning pallor, and a few wisps of silver hair had begun to show at the edges of her lace cap. They hadn't been there the last time he had visited, striking David with just how fast time seemed to be passing him by.

Petra and Constantia were identical twins who had inherited nothing of Theodora but her swarthy skin and thick head of black hair. Aside from that, they were matching mirror images of their father, with soft pleasing features. Mourning garb made them look older than their twenty-one years.

Was this what his neglect had caused? David had thought himself doing the right thing, sending his monthly bank drafts and telling himself that the money was being put to good use. But the shabby state of the drawing room and the outmoded attire of his mother and sisters told him otherwise. While he had been living in opulent excess, enjoying a never-ending string of soirees, dinners, and nights on the town, his family had been scraping together whatever existence they could manage.

"He called for you before he went," Petra said, clinging tight to his arm. "We told him you were coming but might not make it in time. And he said—"

"He had faith in you," Constantia put in, finishing Petra's sentence that uncanny way of siblings who had shared a womb. "He knew you would take care of us, David."

He held Petra as she began to weep, burying her face in his shoulder. His mother's chin trembled, and her eyes brimmed with a fresh wave of tears. In the depths of those blue irises, he found the same hope he'd heard in the voices of his sisters. It was the same expectation Mrs. Moffat had leveled at him. The weight of such responsibility was already bearing down upon him before his father was buried, before he'd even opened a single ledger to take stock of their financial situation.

As the man of the house ...

The housekeeper's words echoed in his mind, reminding him that every duty befitting that of a landed gentleman and head of a household had just been thrust upon him. His own grief had been compressed, pushed into some deep part of him until he could get home. But now, as he blinked back tears and swallowed through a throat burning with grief, he realized it would have to wait. The time to grieve his father wasn't now, with his mother and the twins looking at him as if he were their savior. He wasn't certain he would ever have that time for himself, because now there was work to be done and there were hundreds of people counting on him—from his mother and sisters, to the servants of the manor, down to the tenants who worked land that now belonged to him.

The man of the house, Mrs. Moffat had called him. Funny; just now, he felt like a lost little boy.

CHAPTER 2

*"News of the death of gentry landowner, Mr. G has reached London, forcing the
ton to part ways with one of its darlings. The young Mr. G will likely be short
on time to spend social-climbing now that he's inherited a crumbling country
pile. One does wonder when a marriage of convenience might follow. This
writer would be willing to bet a proper period of mourning will not have passed
before the gentleman has nabbed himself an heiress."*
-The London Gossip, 4 December 1819

His father's steward was a charlatan. After only a few days at
home, David could clearly see the signs of Gilbert Wren's
perfidy. How had his father gone about blind to the truth
for so long? David might not be the smartest of men, nor had he
always been the best at managing his own funds. However, when
considering how much money he had sent home over the years,
there was no reason for the house and farm to be in such a sorry
state.

Burying his father had been the first order of business, which he
had achieved with a small, modest funeral. Now he could see for
himself that things were not as they should be, he couldn't return to
London and leave his family to fend for themselves. As well, there was

the threat of scandal in London and his promise to lay low. So, he had set about taking control of the family holdings.

With each passing day, David grew more aware of how woefully unprepared he was to accept so much responsibility. He spent the first few days after his father's burial in Mr. Wren's office. Stuffed into the cramped space near the back of the house—which suffered from a terrible draft and an irking dampness—he had pored over the steward's ledgers and records. Wren was a meticulous man, having kept all of David's correspondence, as well as a record of each bank draft he'd sent. Three hundred pounds here, five hundred there ... and after a particularly lucrative contract in which a duke had paid him to pleasure his duchess while he watched, three thousand pounds. It all amounted to an astronomical amount of money, which ought to have the estate running smoothly and generating income for his parents and sisters to live on.

"Your father made a number of poor decisions with the funds, I'm afraid," Wren told him. "He insisted on investing a large sum into some scheme or another. Only, it turned out that the man he trusted with the money was a thief. He never invested it at all, and the money was lost."

It sounded like something his father might have done, so at first David did not question it. He had made a number of poor choices himself, which led him to servicing women for funds. However, the deeper he dug, the more confused he became, and the more he began to realize that Wren had been the real problem here.

The steward's records showed purchases for much-needed materials for repairing the mill, mending fences, and sprucing up tenant cottages. Only, the amounts spent had not been nearly enough, and David suspected the supplies hadn't been of the best quality. However, Wren insisted that everything had been done on his father's orders.

The man was so confident in his ability to pull the wool over his eyes that David was content to allow him to go on thinking he'd managed to get away with it. It was a common fact of David's existence that most people didn't think he possessed anything between his ears but air. Perhaps he had not made the highest marks in school, and he certainly did not help matters with his propensity of making a joke of absolutely everything. It could now work to his advantage that the steward thought him an imbecile. If Wren really had embezzled funds meant for his family, David intended to see him prosecuted. He could not do that without evidence, and it would be easier to gather proof if Wren went on thinking him oblivious.

When the steward was dismissed for the day, David interviewed what remained of the household staff and searched his father's things for any hint to what had gone on in his absence. The house once boasted an army of maids, footmen, and gardeners, but many of them had been let go over the years. They were now down to a butler and housekeeper, two footmen, two chambermaids, a cook and a scullion, a stable groom, and a single ladies maid shared between his mother and sisters. It was a pitiful staff for a house of this size, which meant keeping most of the rooms closed off. The gardens and grounds were overgrown and unsightly, and the west wing was on the verge of collapse.

The cook reported receiving a pittance with which to purchase food to feed the Graham family, while the chambermaids had gone long stretches of time without pay. Those who complained had been dismissed, and others simply left after deciding not to countenance shabby treatment by their employer any longer. The house's most costly objects d'art had been sold off piece by piece, and once those were gone his mother's jewels had been the next to go. Tenants complained of miserable living conditions, and those who petitioned Wren for help were put off by either empty promises or cold dismissal.

And just where had his father been as the estate began falling down around his ears?

Drinking, according to Caruthers and Mrs. Moffat. The faithful servants had been reluctant to speak ill of his father, but David assured them he wanted the truth—however difficult it might be to hear.

"Mr. Graham grew morose in his final years," Caruthers told him. "I often overheard him lamenting that he'd let you down, sir. He would leave a tarnished legacy for his only son, and you would come to hate him for his ineptitude."

"I never resented him," David replied. "He inherited an estate that was already on its last leg. He did his best."

"He was ashamed that he'd reduced you to something as common as *work*," Mrs. Moffat added. "That he and your mother and sisters must live on your charity ... he loathed it, he did. Drove him to the bottle."

It had been difficult to keep a straight face after hearing *that*. He had been very cryptic with his parents regarding the occupation which earned him the funds to send home. They had not delved beyond his fabrications, likely because they hadn't wanted to admit their only son was driven to seek employment to support his family. A gentleman did not sully his hands with actual work, and it had probably been a relief to have David so far away in London. It was easier not to have to tell their friends and neighbors that their son had wasted a gentleman's education on a lowly *job*.

David had a difficult time remembering the details of his last visit home, as he'd spent much of it carousing. He had been invited to a string of dinners and card parties, and a rather persistent widow intent on having him warm her bed. Between keepers at the time, he had seized the chance to do what he pleased for a change. Had he been so absorbed in his own affairs he hadn't noticed his father becoming a drunk right before his eyes?

"The accident," Mrs. Moffat hedged. "No one will say it and I beg your pardon, Master David, but ..."

"Go on," David urged.

She traded glances with Caruthers, who picked up where she left off. "He fell off his horse ... you knew that. Broke his neck. But, the decanter in his study was empty, and I'd only just filled it that morning. Your mother and sisters don't imbibe strong drink, sir, and Wren doesn't partake when he is here. There is only one person who could have emptied it."

"Christ," David muttered, resting his head in his hands. "He had to have been absolutely soused. No wonder he lost his seat. I'd wondered ..."

His father had been a country gentleman familiar with every horse in the stable. There was no reason for him to have died in such an accident unless the horse had been spooked ... or, the rider had been dipping too deep.

It all made sense now. If his father had taken to drink, it would have been easier for Wren to steal from them. The fiend had likely been taking advantage of his father's trusting nature for years, and began ramping up his efforts once he realized he could get away with taking more.

The final shred of proof came as David rifled through a stack of journals from his father's study. He'd been reading over them since his arrival, but had found mostly dull tidbits regarding matters of the estate. His father had kept a record of everything, from tenant disputes to crop yields. However, he was convinced that the truth would reveal itself if he kept sifting through the meticulous records.

His mother entered just as he reached the volumes covering the past few years. David glanced up to find her approaching him with a tray, a shaky smile on her face. She was wrapped in her dressing gown, her white-streaked dark hair hanging down her back. Without her caps or pins, that voluminous hair made her look younger, softening the sharpness of her features.

"I hope I'm not disturbing you," she said while placing the tray near his elbow. "You have been working so hard. I noticed you didn't eat much at dinner."

On the tray, he found a teapot with two chipped cups in saucers, as well as a sparse offering of biscuits.

"You could never be a bother, and this looks wonderful. Thank you."

She poured the tea, squeezing a wedge of lemon into his. David sipped and turned the page as she slid a biscuit onto his saucer. When he glanced up at her again, she'd taken the chair facing his father's desk, her own cup held in both hands.

No, not his father's desk. *His* desk. Remembering such details was going to take some getting used to.

"Your father was so fastidious about his records, wasn't he?"

His mouth twitched with a smile that never quite manifested. "He was. Did you know he named the lambs? Every lambing, he would tally how many had been born ... and he gave them names."

His mother chuckled, giving a little shake of her head. "I did not know that, but am hardly surprised. That sounds like my Noel. Are you ... looking for something in particular?"

He paused, a biscuit halfway to his mouth. "Why do you ask?"

She peered into her teacup. "I did my best, David. I truly did. But you know how your father was. He claimed my place was as lady of the house, and I shouldn't worry myself over matters of the estate. He disliked being made to feel as if he didn't know what he was about."

"Yes, I remember. I don't think he meant to imply that you did not have the head for the numbers."

"No, only that it would shame him as a man to admit he didn't have it all well in hand. But I did try ... when he would listen to me. I managed to get through to him on occasion, but never when it came to that *man*."

"You mean Mr. Wren?"

"Yes. You've noticed it, too ... the discrepancies in his records?"

"*You* noticed them?"

She raised her chin and gave a delicate sniff. "Do you know how easily a hat pin can be used to pick a lock? The day after your father's death, I went into Mr. Wren's study and read through his account books. I saw the letters you sent and the amounts that were enclosed. It would have been enough to at least get us out of debt. The profits from the farm would have taken care of the rest."

That was precisely what he'd thought, and it didn't surprise David that his mother had come to that conclusion as well. She was smarter than his father had given her credit for.

"When I said I was glad you are here, I didn't only mean so that you could be a comfort to us, David. I knew you would see what your father could not. I realize Noel's death was sudden and you didn't expect to inherit so young, but we need you. Not just the twins and I, but everyone who relies on our lands for their living."

He knew that well enough. The mountains of ledgers and reports stacked around him served as proof.

"I will do my best," he mumbled, flipping another page in the journal with a sigh. "There isn't much here for me to work with, and what we need is an influx of funds from ... somewhere. I will manage it. I can let go of my townhouse in London, sell off some of my things."

"And Mr. Wren?"

"Will be dealt with the moment I have ... proof."

His half-eaten biscuit dropped to the desk as a line in the journal caught his eye. He took up a pen and dipped it in the inkwell. Under his mother's watchful eye, he circled the passage that had sent alarm bells ringing through his mind.

She leaned forward to watch him scan the page, finding another entry and circling it, as well.

"David? What is it?"

"I've found something, I think. Wren kept records of the money I sent, but so did Father. I don't think the man counted on that, otherwise he would have never ... well, I'll be damned."

She didn't bat an eyelash at his coarse language, standing to round the desk. David was frantic, his jaw winding tight as he circled line after line of his father's handwriting.

"This doesn't add up," she said, echoing his thoughts. "The amounts Mr. Wren recorded are easily two or three times what your father has written here."

The page snapped as David turned it, his movements stiff and jerky from the rage winding through him. He'd had his suspicions, but here it was right in front of him: proof that his father's steward had been stealing from them for years.

"Son of a ... apologies, Mother."

"Oh, hang niceties. If you will not say it, I will. That bastard ... damn his eyes!"

David's pen flew over the page as his gaze caught sight of the figures. At times, the funds were barely enough to keep the family fed and the hearths stocked with wood. It was no wonder the house was crumbling around them and the farm had been nearly bankrupted.

"Oh, Noel ... you fool."

David glanced up to find his mother backing away from the chair, hands balled into fists. She did her best to keep her composure, but he could see her chin quivering and her eyes blazing with fury. He came to his feet just as she burst into tears, sobbing into her hands and slumping against the wall. Pity lanced through him at the sight she made, so broken and worn down. His mother had always been a force of nature—strong and stiff-backed, able to weather the worst of times with poise and dignity. It would seem she had reached the end of her forbearance.

He took her into his arms and let her weep on his shoulder. "It's all right. I will make this right, Mother. Give me time to make it right."

David could not allow Wren's treachery to stand, but there was still the matter of his family to consider. They didn't just need his presence, they needed money ... and despite a gentleman's education and a wealth of high-society connections, David only knew of one surefire way to get his hands on a large amount of capital in a short period of time.

THE MORNING AFTER THE UNEARTHING OF HIS FATHER'S JOURNAL, David sent for the nearest constable and took the ride across the estate to the small plot and house intended for the steward. There was no time to waste if he wanted to ensure Wren paid for his crimes. Then, David could mend what had been broken.

They found the modest cottage vacant—save for a household staff comprised of a housekeeper who also functioned as a cook, and a chambermaid.

"Mr. Wren took himself off in a hurry early this morning," the housekeeper informed them, wringing her hands around her apron. "Before the sun was even up, if you can believe that."

The evidence of the man's flight showed itself from what he could see of the interior of the house. The walls had been stripped, every surface cleared.

"I assume he took just about everything he owned with him?" he asked through clenched teeth, trying his damnedest to keep from releasing a volley of epithets. He'd only just taken over managing the estate, and had already bungled his first important task. "And, I take it he made no mention of where he was going?"

The woman's eyes went wide as if she hadn't given the matter any thought. "Why, yes sir, you're right! He set off in a wagon heavy with trunks and such. Made no mention of when he would return or where he might be headed."

"Goddamn it," he whispered, spinning away from the housekeeper and pacing across the small entrance hall.

The constable merely stood near the door, glaring at David and pursing his lips. The man had been awakened from the sort of sleep induced by too much gin, and his breath still reeked of the stuff. He'd been coerced into doing his duty, but made his displeasure clear—grumbling all the way here about the breakfast he had been deprived of as well as his pounding head. Now, it seemed David would be the recipient of his ire and not the actual criminal who had absconded with thousands of pounds of his money.

"Is there something amiss, sir?" the housekeeper asked. "Begging your pardon, but you coming with the constable cannot mean anything good. Has Mr. Wren been up to some kind of mischief?"

"Mischief is a rather mild word for what he has done," David snapped. He paused, took a deep breath and gentled his tone. The poor woman had no idea what was going on, and none of this was her fault. "You should not expect him to return. Another steward will be hired to replace him. In the meantime, we could use you at the manor. The maid, too. Your pay will be the same, and you can work there until there is a need for you to return to serve the new steward."

The woman ceased wringing her hands and beamed at him. "Thank you, sir. Marjorie will be glad to hear it. She worried what would become of us if Mr. Wren never returned."

"Gather your things and report to the manor. Mrs. Moffat will receive you and see you settled."

"Bless you, sir. I just know things will turn around now that you are here. Everyone says so."

At the sharp look he leveled at her, the woman seemed to shrink several inches, lowering her head and blushing.

"That is to say ... we were that sorry to hear of your father. Forgive me, sir, I meant no offense."

Of course she hadn't, and who could blame her—or everyone within a thousand acres, apparently—from hoping things might change now that he had taken matters in hand. Though, this housekeeper must not have heard much about David if she could so readily place her faith in him. His reputation did him no favors. As well, David wasn't sure he had much faith in himself. He already felt like an utter failure.

"Wren must have been onto you," the constable offered with an apologetic shrug. Apparently, the man had decided to now have pity on him. "But don't worry ... I'll have the word spread to every other constable and magistrate in Lancashire. If anyone lays eyes on him, you can be sure we'll bring him in."

David highly doubted that, but said nothing. If Wren was smart—which he'd proven to be thus far—he would put as much distance between himself and Lancashire as possible. Assuming he hadn't spent all the money he had embezzled from the estate, he would be flush enough to get himself out of David's reach.

He held himself together long enough to part ways with the constable. Shoulders slumped, David began the ride home.

Halfway there, he had to pause and dismount, unable to take it any longer. He felt as if his skin were pulled too tight over muscle and bone, his hands shaking and itching to destroy anything within reach. Wrath tangled with helplessness inside him until he felt sick with it. Stalking away from his horse, David lashed out at the first object in sight. A length of fencing that had seen better days was the recipient of several kicks, the impact radiating up his hips and back as he shouted obscenities to the empty stretches of field beyond. His throat burned with the effort and his entire body ached from the exertion, but damn if it didn't feel good to give himself over to the toxic emotions roiling in his gut. He had spent weeks trying to maintain a stiff upper lip, to appear as if he was in complete control for the benefit of his family. Never could he allow anyone to think he was in over his head.

One of the fence posts splintered, and he had to catch himself on another to keep from toppling over. The ridiculousness of his position struck him as he glanced down to find his best boots scuffed to hell and a hole torn in the left leg of his breeches. Turning to lean against a precariously leaning post, he took a deep breath and let it out on a laugh. For, it was the one thing he could do to keep from weeping like a baby.

This was how Warin Lyons found him as he rode up the lane on his way to the house—doubled over and cackling like a lunatic. To his credit, the man simply sat astride his gelding and stared at David with his implacable expression, waiting for him to finish.

"Rough morning?" he drawled, his voice as flat and expressionless as ever.

David swiped a hand over his face to find it damp. Apparently, his hysterics *had* included tears. Thank God no one but Lyons had seen him like this. His friends would make a fuss and insist he needed their help, and his mother would tell him he ought to drink tea and lie down. He didn't want anyone's pity, nor did he relish being made to feel as if he needed to be led about by the hand. He was a man, goddamn it. This was his land, his home, his problem to solve.

"You could say that," he replied, crossing the road to retrieve his mare. "You're a long way from London."

"I'm here on behalf of Mr. Sterling, with a contract for you to consider."

At last, a reprieve from the dry buggering life had been subjecting him to. Just then, he might have kissed Lyons square on the mouth at the news that his prayers had been answered. A new keeper meant money, and if she were willing to pay what he was worth, his outlook might not be so dire.

"There's also a note," Lyons added as David swung up into the saddle and nudged his mount back onto the road. "Mr. Sterling bade me remain until you had written your response."

That meant Benedict had received David's letter—which he'd regretted the moment it was posted. Benedict had problems of his own, and the last thing he needed was David heaping his problems on top of the matter of the London Gossip. However, there was no one else and he'd been wallowing in his grief and desperation, needing someone to understand what he had come home to. Whatever help Benedict offered—for that was simply in his nature—David would decline. As the master of every blade of grass, tree, or shattered fence post for a thousand acres, *he* was responsible for cleaning up his father's mess.

"Come, ride to the house with me and we'll discuss the contract."

David calmed during the ride, feeling better than he had in days.

His problems were far from solved, but a lucrative contract would certainly help matters. Aside from that, he hadn't been feeling like himself since leaving London. Death and the drudgery of wading through his ruined inheritance had turned him into a morose, brooding heap of bones and skin. Trying to untangle the complicated situation filled him with a sense of ineptitude that had shaken his confidence.

He wasn't used to being horrible at things. Only, the things he excelled at were of no use to him here ... unless he could secure this contract. If he could get back to the business of servicing some willing woman with the full range of his carnal skill and be showered in money for it, he wouldn't have to feel so incompetent.

By the time they arrived to the stable, not even the lonely groom and ramshackle state of the structure could rob him of his good mood. This contract felt like a lifeline being thrown just before his head went under. Clapping a hand on Lyons' shoulder, he began guiding the man toward the house.

"Now then..."

David quickly dropped his hand when Lyons stiffened and gave a cool look that somehow spoke volumes without even the slightest shift in expression.

"Right," he muttered, clasping both hands behind his back. "We are short on staff at the moment, so you needn't worry we'll be overheard. I take it this client resides in Lancashire."

"About an hour's ride from here," Lyons confirmed. "I've just come from calling on Mrs. Regina Hurst—a widow who lives on a neighboring estate. She is amenable to meeting you tomorrow afternoon, during which she would like to discuss the terms of your agreement."

Regina Hurst. The surname was familiar to him—another local landowner, he was certain. Was this woman Hurst's wife or daughter? He had never been introduced to a Regina Hurst during his years of living at home.

"Perfect. Is she beautiful? No, don't answer that, I want to be surprised. Did she mention how long she wished to contract me? Did she request me specifically, or have I been assigned to her based on proximity?"

Lyons reached into the satchel slung across his body, retrieving a sheaf of papers and offering them to David.

"Her looks, as I'm sure you know, are irrelevant. Though I cannot see that you will have cause for complaint. Mr. Sterling received word from an acquaintance of Mrs. Hurst that the lady wished to contract a courtesan. That she happens to reside in Lancashire is a coincidence proving convenient for your situation."

David shuffled through the contract as they walked and frowned. "There's no amount here, nor any indication of a time-frame."

"Those have been left blank at Mrs. Hurst's insistence. It is her wish to negotiate payment and duration with you directly. Mr. Sterling was content to allow it."

That was certainly unprecedented. David never went into an arrangement metaphorically blind. Benedict usually arranged the pairings himself, using his skill for reading people to match a client with her ideal courtesan. David was always assigned to one of two types of women—unhappy wives who wanted the kind of pleasure their husbands couldn't deliver, or seasoned widows who knew what they wanted and appreciated a man who knew how to provide it.

"Please tell me she isn't married," he groaned. He had never balked at servicing someone's wife, but just now found he lacked the fortitude to climb through windows and run from the ominous shadow of a jealous husband.

"Widowed," Lyons replied as the house came into view. "She has very few requirements. Only that her courtesan be a man with a pleasing face and form, and that he make himself available to her a few nights a week until the arrangement has ended."

David didn't know whether to feel dread or excitement over such cryptic terms, but then decided it was of no consequence. If this woman wanted him to lick her toes while calling her Empress of the Universe, he would do it as long as she was paying.

"Her direction," Lyons informed him before they mounted the front steps. "She'll be expecting you tomorrow."

They entered the house, and David sent for refreshment for himself and Lyons, hoping their larder wasn't depleted to the point of bareness. They could hardly afford to host guests, but Lyons was one man. That his saddle wasn't loaded down with baggage meant he had his own lodgings for the night. It would not be seemly for them to host anyone while in mourning, anyway, but if it was the last thing David did, he would restore the house to its former glory. His mother had once been fond of entertaining, but Mrs. Moffat had confided that she ceased once the house fell into disrepair. He would give her a grand home she could be proud to open to visitors if it killed him.

Petra and Constantia would have new clothes and dowries. They weren't too long in the tooth to make good matches, and their pleasing looks would work along with the dowries to catch acceptable husbands.

By the time they reached the study, David was grinning at the hope such plans inspired. All was not lost; not while there were still women in England who were willing to pay for the attentions of a man like him.

While Lyons stood at one of the windows overlooking the lawn, David sat behind his desk and opened Benedict's note. It had been hastily written and lacked Ben's typically neat penmanship. Squinting to make out the words, David read:

D,

Burn this note after you have read it. The shrew has been mollified for the moment, and I am working on a more permanent solution. I am sorry to hear of your trouble, my friend. I offer my assistance in whatever manner you require. You have but to send word of whatever you might need. The new contract is yours to benefit from and I will take no percentage. Take care of your family. I will send word when there is more to report.

-B

David sat staring at the words in slack-jawed silence for a moment. Never had Benedict offered to give up his portion of any courtesan's earnings. As the proprietor of the business, he was entitled to a cut, which he gleefully accepted as his due. Of course, his financial circumstances had vastly improved since the founding of the agency, so Ben could well afford to forgo his commission on what might be a lucrative contract.

It was more than he would have ever asked of his friend, but David was not too prideful to accept such a gift. He would need every penny he could get his hands on in the coming months.

"How is he, really?" he asked while rifling about for a scrap of paper to pen his response. "You probably have more contact with him than anyone these days."

Lyons turned away from the window. "As well as can be expected given the circumstances. The matter of Lady Thrush has been taken care of. The Gentleman Courtesans need not worry that she will cause trouble for us ever again."

"How did Ben manage that?" David murmured while penning his response.

"With a bank draft and a very pointed threat." At David's raised eyebrows, Lyons added, "One of social ruin, of course."

Interesting, that the woman had been willing to oust them in a fit of jealousy but didn't want her own name dragged through the mud. If she had any sense, she would take the money Ben had offered and disappear from London for a good, long while.

"The Widow Dane has been charged with unearthing any substantial evidence pointing to the Gossip's identity. As well, she is exerting her influence to ensure past clients maintain their silence, but also that they understand we are doing everything we can to silence the rumors. If this goes on much longer, we run the risk of losing business."

David paused, pen hovering over the page as he glanced at Lyons. "The other courtesans often joke that you are Benedict's long-lost son … you're so much like him. You are suited for this work, Lyons."

Amusement danced in the man's eyes, but he didn't so much as crack a smile. "Mr. Sterling has been a good mentor and an even better employer. I count it a compliment to be compared to him."

"I meant it as one."

Finishing off his letter with the one request he would make of Benedict, David signed it with his initial and folded it closed. After all Ben had done for him, he would not make a burden of himself. But because of Wren, he would find it difficult to trust anyone. He could not manage without a steward for long and could trust Benedict to recommend someone beyond reproach.

That done, David turned his mind back over to his new client, letting himself fantasize over what she might look like, smell like, taste like. He hadn't had a woman since his interlude with Frances and her friends, and he'd been interrupted before finishing. David had never been one to think of the duties of a courtesan as actual *work*. This arrangement would serve as a pleasant distraction, something he could look forward to when the drudgery of his days became too much.

Whoever this new client was, he was going to seduce her out of her clothes as well as a great deal of money.

CHAPTER 3

"The notorious lady known as the Ravishing Widow has been seen about Town much these past weeks, visiting with those who are bold enough to call her 'friend.' One wonders why such illustrious persons of the beau monde *are happy to take such a viper into their midst. She has been rumored to be connected with those disreputable debauchees known as The Gentleman Courtesans. Though, knowing the truth of her scandalous background, that should come as no surprise to anyone."*
-The London Gossip, 6 December 1819

Firelight cast an ominous glow over the room in which Regina Hurst paced like a caged animal, projecting oblong shadows along the floor and against the wall. The clock on the mantel had just chimed three o'clock, which meant her expected caller might arrive at any moment. She ought to have specified a time for this meeting. That would have kept her from jumping at every sound beyond the drawing room door.

There was nothing for it now. She had told Mr. Lyons to have her prospective courtesan call upon her at his leisure, and that could not be changed. The rest of her arrangement would be carried out with far more control. Her nerves required—no, demanded—rigid adherence to a list of protocols. Otherwise, she might never be able to go through with this.

Steady Regina. It is the only way ...

Swallowing past the bundle of nerves lodged in her airway, Regina rested one hand on the mantelpiece. As a young woman she had been foolishly idealistic, and such folly had cost her dearly. Older, wiser, and battered to cold, hard steel by experience, she had learned to adjust her expectations and take comfort in what she *could* have. A happy life with a man who loved her? Impossible after what she had been through. Passion and romance? Randolph had ensured she could never have them.

Love ... she didn't think she could ever come to feel it for any man. This courtesan would simply be a channel through which she might gain the one thing she wanted most in the world. It was a gamble, especially when she was not certain how she might react to his touch.

However, Regina would be willing to endure it if there was even the slightest chance fate might finally decide to start smiling on her. It was her due after the torment she had lived through and the resulting emptiness that festered within her—a wound that refused to heal. Wasn't she owed something good after all that had been taken from her? Yes, she was owed, and rather than lament that she might never come to have the life she wanted, Regina had decided to take matters into her own hands. After all, Randolph's death had left her with more money than she knew what to do with. A terrible husband he might have been, but no one could accuse him of neglecting his duties to matters of business and his estate. Regina was now the sole owner of everything that had belonged to her late husband, though she was still uncertain how that had come to be. At times, he'd even seemed to hate her. Why would he leave her everything when there was a male cousin next in the line of succession?

When Randolph called to his solicitor from his deathbed, she had feared the worst. Regina expected to receive nothing, not even a dower's jointure. However, her otherwise predictable husband managed to shock her during his last days, altering his will so she gained everything the moment he'd taken his last breath.

Perhaps staring death in the face had forced Randolph to confront the truth about himself. He had been a surly, ruthless bastard who made the lives of everyone around him miserable. Maybe it had been his way of atoning for all the pain and degradation he'd subjected her to during the eight years of their marriage. Or perhaps agony and laudanum had taken him out of his right mind.

Whatever the case, Regina chose to think of her unexpected inheritance as a blessing. It had given her the freedom to avoid a second marriage, to walk about the corridors of this house without cowering in fear, and to heal as best she could.

Glancing down at her shapeless mourning attire, she frowned. It wouldn't be seemly to be seen wearing anything else, though Regina despised the idea of Randolph exerting any modicum of control over her even in death.

It will not be forever, she reminded herself. *The day you cast off these horrid black rags is the day you are finally free of him.*

The ghastly black did nothing for her fair complexion and bright red hair, nor did the heavy bombazine complement her figure. Her courtesan was sure to think her a sorry sight, but then she did not require him to desire her. Her husband certainly hadn't suffered any hardship subjecting her to his attentions, no matter how poorly she looked or felt. For what Regina was hiring her courtesan to do, the man needn't think her beautiful. He only had to make his cock rise to the occasion when she required it, and if a male whore couldn't be counted on to achieve that, who could?

Regina had told herself that nothing was worth submitting herself to the unwanted attentions of a man ever again. She now enjoyed autonomy and wouldn't surrender that for anything. However, to get what she wanted, there was no choice but to allow this courtesan into her bed for however long it took. And she would do it while maintaining possession of herself in every sense. If this courtesan wanted to earn the money she was willing to part with for his services, he would abide by her rules or she'd find someone else.

A scratch at the door preceded the entrance of Powell, his hulking frame taking up the entirety of the opening. His craggy features, overshadowed by a mop of dirty blond hair and made sinister by eyes so dark they appeared black, had intimidated her at first. Over time, she had come to think of his face as one of the dearest sights in the world. To call him a footman would be an insult, despite the livery he wore and the position he'd held in this house since before she had become its mistress. However, he meant so much more to her than a mere servant—a confidante, a friend, a protector.

"He has arrived, ma'am," he informed her, his voice deep and rattling as if a handful of nails was lodged in his chest.

Her hand tightened on the mantel, but Regina straightened her spine. "Very good. His name?"

"Mr. David Graham."

"What do you make of him?"

Powell shrugged one colossal shoulder. "Pretty."

She wrinkled her brow, though not due to Powell's curt answer. He had always been a man of few words. No, it wasn't that he had answered with one word, but that 'pretty' was the one he used. She had never heard a man described that way before, which left her with an image of some effeminate fop.

"I see," she murmured. "Very well. Show him in, and ... you'll remain, will you not?"

Powell's hard face softened, and he gave her the barest hint of a smile. "Always, ma'am."

That offered some relief. At times, Powell's strong presence had been the only thing keeping Regina alive. While the danger had passed, it was still reassuring to know he was there.

She turned to face the door, hands folded before her just as Powell returned, leading her new courtesan. The instant she laid eyes on Mr. David Graham, Regina realized why her servant had referred to the man as 'pretty.' There was, quite literally, no other description that would have fit. The picture of some thin, pasty dandy was burned to ash by the tall, broad-shouldered specimen standing before her.

Hair black as pitch fell over his brow in a glossy tumble, and matching brows might have been considered too thick on any other face. Not *this* face. They were a perfect match for his headful of hair, enhancing features that looked as if a sculptor's loving hands had molded them. Aquiline nose, strong chin and jaw, slashing cheekbones, and just the hint of a dimple in his left cheek when he offered her a warm smile. A flash of perfect, white teeth was a startling contrast to skin that held a swarthy, olive cast. Even more astounding were his eyes—the brightest blue she'd ever seen, rimmed with a heavy fan of dark lashes.

Regina hadn't realized how long she stood there silently appraising him until he spoke.

"Mrs. Hurst, I presume?"

His voice was deep and silky, holding cultured tones those could rival those of any highborn peer.

"Y-yes," she stammered. "Thank you for coming, Mr. Graham."

His smile widened as he approached, long legs carrying him toward her far too fast, the ripple of muscle and sinew beneath his clothes both an enticement and a threat.

"That's close enough," she blurted in a shaky but forceful voice, one hand raised to ward him off.

Mr. Graham nearly tripped over his own feet at the vehemence in her tone, but halted just short of arm's length from her. Regina took a step back, but could go no farther unless she wanted to incinerate her skirts in the hearth. A wave of calm rushed over Regina at the ease with which she'd been able to command him. As she had thought, hiring a professional was the best way to achieve her goal. If the man wanted his money, he would dance to her tune and then leave when he was finished.

His smile faltered, but Regina—now bolstered—raised her chin. "I take it as a good sign that you know how to follow orders."

He huffed a little laugh and braced his hand on the back of a nearby chair. "I enjoy a woman who knows what she wants and how to demand it." His gaze darted to Powell, a strong and silent sentry pretending he could neither hear nor see them. "Is your footman going to remain in the room while we discuss ... terms?"

"Powell is here for my protection and will almost always remain near enough to hear us, Mr. Graham. If this arrangement is going to work, you will need to grow accustomed to his presence."

The courtesan's brow furrowed as he studied Powell, then swiveled his gaze back to her. Regina waited for him to balk, or demand to be left alone with her, but he gave an acquiescing dip of his head.

"I aim to please, Mrs. Hurst."

The statement might have been innocuous, if not for the silken way he caressed the words with his voice, giving them a completely different connotation. Other women might have responded to the seduction dripping from those words, but Regina was too aware of the difference in their sizes, how easily he could overpower her if he ever decided...

No, she berated herself. *There is no room for fear if you are determined to go through with this.*

"Please, sit down, Mr. Graham. We have much to discuss."

He sank obediently into the chair, while Regina remained on her feet. Odd; she had thought making him sit would somehow diminish his presence, yet it did nothing of the sort. He crossed one leg over the other and watched her expectantly. When she didn't immediately begin, he wrested the reins from her.

"Many of my past clients have found these beginning stages awkward, but they needn't be between us. It might help if you begin by telling me what your needs are. Being a courtesan isn't all about bedroom matters, you know. It is my duty to ensure that you are made happy, though of course that is a relative concept, is it not? I can be your lover, but I can also be your companion, your confidante, an escort—though, I can see you are in mourning so perhaps you will not require that. Simply tell me what you need, Mrs. Hurst. I am more than up to the task of pleasing you."

Regina was taken aback, though not at his words. She had more or less expected such a speech from a man who made a profession of selling himself. It was the way he was looking at her, his gaze caressing a path from the top of her head to the hem of her skirts—a slow, leisurely perusal that made her feel as if she stood before him in nothing but her skin. Was it the act of a man skilled at seduction, or did he really find her worthy of such heated regard? He stared at her as if she stood before him in rich, flattering silk or satin as opposed to the heavy, amorphous bombazine; as if she were a smiling, simpering chit vying for his attention rather than a sulking, scowling widow who might otherwise have never given him the time of day.

Clearing her throat, she paced away from the hearth, unable to meet his gaze when he watched her so intently. She studied the wall-paper as if it were the most fascinating thing she had ever seen and forced herself to speak.

"You will not find me demanding or unreasonable. As you've already noticed, I am recently widowed ... less than a month ago."

"I'm so sorry to hear it."

She looked at him then, one hand clenching her skirts in intuitive reaction. "We were wed for eight years, and now he is gone. I will not stand here and pretend my mourning attire is anything other than a formality."

Now she had truly shocked him. He tried to hide it, but Regina noticed the flicker of surprise in his eyes before he quickly snuffed it out, uncrossing his legs, then crossing them again, as if uncertain what to do with himself.

"I see."

"If you decide to go forward with this arrangement, I will require you to come to my bed as many nights a week as you can manage. Mr. Lyons informed me of your usual rate, and I have agreed to pay it, though ... I do think you might wish to negotiate once I have informed you of the specificity of my need. That is why the contract you were offered had a few unfinished sections. I need to be certain you under-stand what I would ask of you before you agree."

"Mrs. Hurst, there is nothing you could ask that I would hesitate to offer. Your every wish is my command, and I do mean that. Why don't you come sit, and tell me exactly what it is you need? I've been doing this long enough there isn't likely to be a request I have not heard."

Ignoring the hand he waved toward the chair near his, Regina paced back to the hearth, hands clenched before her. Taking a deep breath, she prepared to deliver the most important requirement of her offer—the reason she had sent for him in the first place.

"Mr. Graham, I have only one goal and I am hoping you can be the man to help me achieve it. You see, I ... I wish to have a child. Unfor-tunately, the late Mr. Hurst was unable to give me one. His loss has only renewed my desire to become a mother, and so ... I need you to do your utmost to impregnate me."

. . .

Mrs. Regina Hurst was a madwoman. There was no other explanation for the outrageous words that had just fallen from her lips, yet the longer David stared at her in slack-jawed disbelief, the clearer it became that she was not only in her right mind, but also quite serious. In the past, David's first instinct would have been to laugh and search behind the curtains for one or several of his friends. He might have pegged this as some childish prank pulled by Benedict, with Nick as an accomplice. He could imagine sharing a good chuckle about it over drinks, laughing until he cried at the absurdity of such a lark.

But he was acutely aware that this was no laughing matter. For one thing, Benedict was busy trying to single-handedly stop the London Gossip's reign of terror. Pulling David's leg would be the last thing on his mind. As well, he could clearly tell by the way Mrs. Hurst fidgeted with her hands and shifted from foot to foot that she had meant every word of her absurd request.

David snapped his mouth closed while searching for the words to respond. His assertion that she couldn't demand anything that countless others hadn't already asked of him had just been rendered false. Yet, he had not known she would ask him for something so far outside the realm of his usual repertoire. Over his years as a gentleman courtesan, David had been faced with all manner of lascivious tasks, all of which he'd accomplished with relish. Taking pains *not* to get his client of the moment with child had been at the center of each arrangement, and he was always prepared to take the necessary precautions. Thinking of the cedar chest filled with lambskin condoms and sea sponges hidden away in his bedchamber, David nearly laughed to realize he would not have use of them here.

He couldn't actually go through with this, could he? It was ridiculous, outrageous, and completely out of the question.

"I can see I've shocked you, and I am sorry for that," she offered, her expression one of cool composure despite her trembling hands. "There was no way to ease you into it, I'm afraid."

No, he supposed there was no way to tell a man you wanted him to help you make a baby other than to simply come out and say it.

"Before you refuse, I would like the chance to plead my case.

Perhaps a walk in the garden? You look as if you could use some air, and the weather is pleasant enough today."

David tried to smile but found his lips uncooperative. "I wasn't ... I would never refuse without ... yes, I think a walk would be good."

"Very well. Come along."

Feeling as if he watched this entire scene from outside his body, David came numbly to his feet. Mrs. Hurst gave him a wide berth on the way to the door, and he followed with slow steps. Was this truly happening? Had he really come to call on his newest client only to find that she wanted to use him like a high-priced stud? Or, had he never awakened this morning? That would make this entire meeting nothing more than a very disturbing but lucid dream.

The massive footman dogged his steps, remaining far enough that David realized he meant to be unobtrusive, but close enough to convey every intention of leaping to his mistress's defense if necessary. Another queer aspect of the day that left David's thoughts in a jumble of confusion. This Mrs. Hurst certainly did not act like any keeper he'd ever had. He wasn't sure what to make of the woman with her prickly manners, brusque speech, and staunchness. Most women meeting him for the first time were either aware of his reputation and eager to have him, or enraptured by his looks, charm, and easygoing nature. Not so, this woman.

Though, he had to admit she was certainly one of the loveliest of the lot. On first glance he might have mistaken her as a sallow, washed-out creature in a shapeless dress. Experience had taught him to look beyond the surface, and a few minutes in Mrs. Hurst's presence had called his attention to her attributes. Her skin was the creamiest shade of porcelain he'd ever seen, smooth and unblemished. Amid so much black, her red hair was a startling splash, scraped back in a severe knot that put her delicate features on full display. There was something almost fairy-like about her, and he found himself tracing the graceful arch of titian brows over pale green eyes, down the slope of a button nose to a plush, narrow mouth the color of pink rosebuds. The gentle line of her jaw angled to a dainty chin. The slender column of her throat was the only part of her body that wasn't hidden by black bombazine and lace, though the heavy garment did little to disguise a petite but pleasing figure. Amid the rustling fabric, he made out full breasts and slender hips, and could imagine the soft stretch of pale stomach, the sinews of supple thigh and calf. She was a tiny thing, her head barely reaching the center of his chest. Something about that appealed to him in a way that wasn't entirely lascivious.

David shouldn't be thinking of how lovely she was, or how diverting it would be to peel her out of all those starched, black layers to bare that perfect skin to his view. He ought to start considering how he was going to get out of this mess without insulting Mrs. Hurst or annoying Benedict. Surely his friend could not know this client's true aims, or he never would have sent Lyons with the contract. If anything, her proposal spat squarely in the face of the rules of the gentleman courtesans—one of which barred complications that would put the integrity of their agency at risk. David was fairly certain that purposely impregnating someone counted as such.

She pushed open a door leading outside, revealing the stone pathway to a garden enclosed by a wrought-iron fence. Many of the plants had gone to sleep for winter, their bare branches brown and uninspiring beneath a dreary gray sky. But here and there, the winter-blooming hellebore, pansies, and crocus offered bursts of color against some still-green shrubbery. Between the rows of blossoms, earthen paths led the way to a massive evergreen growing up from the center. The shade lowered the temperature by several degrees, but David found the air milder than it had been in days and was glad for a reprieve from the wet and fog.

He could no longer see Powell, but felt the man's presence and decided it was prudent to keep his distance from Mrs. Hurst. The giant footman looked as if he could rip both his arms off with a single tug, and David quite *liked* having use of all four of his limbs.

This time, he remained on his feet while Mrs. Hurst settled on an iron bench, staring up at him with pleading eyes. She looked so forlorn that David wanted to give her whatever she needed to erase the sadness from her eyes and turn that frowning mouth into a smiling one. But that would require surrendering a part of himself he wasn't certain he wanted to give.

A child, by God. His seed purchased in what felt like a far too mercenary and heartless transaction.

"I should explain myself," she murmured. "Though, I am not certain where to begin. If you have any questions ..."

Running a hand over his jaw, David emitted a sarcastic snort. Questions ... he only had about a hundred of them. He settled on the first one that came to mind.

"You were married for eight years. If your husband could not get you with child, what makes you think someone else can?"

Twin spots of pink appeared on her cheeks, and she jerked her gaze away from him. "I was led to believe that our inability to conceive was my fault. However, anyone of importance in Lancashire can attest that my husband was a man of ... voracious appetite. His conquests numbered many, and he did not cease after he married me. None of his mistresses ever came up with child. I investigated the matter myself, because I had to know whether I berated myself for my failures all this time when the affliction was his and not mine. Not a single child was ever born of Mr. Hurst. I've been inspected by no less than five doctors who have assured me there is no reason I cannot carry and birth a healthy child."

Now David was the one pacing, hands folded behind his back as her words began to sink in. Whenever he thought of a life that included children, he imagined some faceless woman as his wife. David hadn't envisioned himself settling down for at least another ten years, if that. But he'd taken the hour's ride to meet this woman and discuss the contract. The least he could do was hear her out.

"I see," he replied. "If you are able and desiring to have children, why hire a courtesan? Why not take a discreet lover, or marry again, or—"

"I *never* intend to wed again."

Mrs. Hurst's fervor drew him up short, and David found her fairly vibrating with a mixture of fury and indignation. She flushed to the roots of her hair, and her small fists were clenched. Her eyes had gone wide, dark pupils expanding to eat away at her sea-foam irises.

"I was not fond of the bonds of matrimony," she added. "Another marriage is out of the question."

There was definitely something more behind her vehement opposition to remarrying, but it was none of his affair. She didn't look as if she would appreciate him prying further. "Understood. I assume you would have no qualms about subjecting your hypothetical child to the scorn they're sure to experience as a bastard."

"Mr. Hurst has been dead less than a month, and news of his demise is not yet widespread. It is my hope that I might become pregnant quickly enough to pass the child off as his. If I can manage that, there would be nothing to worry about."

He shook his head in disbelief. "But *why*—"

"Why a courtesan?"

"Yes!"

She lifted her chin, the gesture almost defiant. "Because paying you ensures there can be no complications or entanglements. Your profession alone leads me to believe that you are not on the hunt for a wife? You have no immediate plans to settle down and begin a family?"

David could hardly afford to feed himself, his mother, and sisters, let alone a wife and children. "No."

"There, you see? I need someone who is willing to give me what I want with no strings attached. You should not worry that I will make any demands of you. As Mr. Hurst's sole heir, I am more than capable of caring for a child on my own, and have every intention of doing so. Were I to take a lover without such parameters in place, the risks would be too great. He might come to expect something I would rather not give. He might think I intend to entrap him and get cold feet. You are a professional, Mr. Graham, and that is what I need. Someone whose business is ..."

"Fucking?"

"Precisely," she replied, without even batting an eyelash at his crudity. "This need be no different than your usual liaison, except that you will neglect to use whatever methods you prefer for avoiding conception."

"That's *all*? Forgive me if I find it difficult to be as blasé about all this as you, Mrs. Hurst. What you are asking goes far beyond simply failing to sheath my cock."

"It can mean exactly that if you could only choose to see it that way. When you think about it, siring a babe is a risk you take every time you enter into an arrangement with any woman."

She was right, damn it, but David was still wrestling with the part of himself that wanted to cave to her wishes and the part that wanted to find his horse and ride back home as fast as physically possible. This was utter madness, and he had entertained it long enough. And yet ...

"You must realize there is a chance *I* cannot sire children? I have always been careful, but even so ... as far as I'm aware there are no consequences of my past affairs, of which there have been many. What then?"

She came to her feet, hands folded neatly before her. She was calm again, the befuddling reaction caused by mention of her dead husband melting away. The man must have been a right bastard for her to react to the mere thought of him with such disdain. Thinking back to her mention of numerous affairs, David decided it made sense. No woman wanted to be made a fool of, and it sounded as if Mr. Hurst had had little regard for her feelings in the matter.

"I understand the risk, but it would be no different were I to take a lover in the hopes he could see the job done. I am willing to put my money and my best efforts into it if you are."

"And if not me, then someone else, obviously."

"I ask you not to judge me too harshly, Mr. Graham," she said, her voice low but bolstered with a steely edge. "You cannot fathom what I have endured, what I have lost over the years, and what I have been deprived of. A child of my own is the one thing I want most in the world, and I will not be made to feel as if there is something wrong with me doing what I must to have it."

David's shoulders sagged, and he was struck once more with what a pitiful, lonely sight Mrs. Hurst made. The haunted depths of her eyes held a thousand secrets, lending truth to her assertion that he had no idea what she had endured or the reason for her desperation.

"I would never judge you, Mrs. Hurst. I am only taken aback by your request, as I'm certain you can understand."

She came to her feet, but took care not to get too close to him—something that was beginning to press on his curiosity as well as his annoyance. The woman was inviting him into her bed while acting as if he were a viper.

It was certainly a departure from what he was accustomed to.

"If you need any further inducement, consider that I am prepared to offer you a very generous bonus of five thousand pounds if we are successful. I cannot pretend to know what drives a man to become a courtesan, but I suppose money must have something to do with it? If funds are any enticement to you at all, perhaps that might help you push any reservations aside. I am quite desperate, Mr. Graham."

He blinked, uncertain he'd heard her correctly. Five thousand pounds on top of his usual monthly rate was nothing to turn his nose up at. In fact, even if it only took him one month to impregnate Mrs. Hurst, the bonus would be more than enough to pull the estate back from the brink of ruin. It would give him the sort of security he so desperately needed. He could refuse her offer, but there was no guarantee Benedict would be able to secure another arrangement so close to home. There would never be an opportunity like this one, and David was as desperate as she.

Was he really considering going through with this? The proposal was about more than the use of his body for a short time. In the past, there had only been pleasure and a parting of ways with David confident he'd done his best to satisfy the client. Never had he finished an arrangement knowing he had left something behind—something tangible and real, with ten fingers and toes and his blood coursing through its veins.

"Would you permit me time to think it over?" he asked. "I understand time is of the essence, so I promise not to take too long. I'm sure you understand that this is more than I was expecting when I arrived today."

Her placid expression underwent a slight shift, sympathy and understanding showing through. "Of course. It is a lot to ask."

That was a gross understatement. Thankfully, he had just bought himself a few days, at the very least, to consider the ramifications of such an agreement.

"You may send a message with your response," she added. "I will understand if you refuse. Thank you for listening, at least."

"You're very welcome."

At a loss as to what else to do or say, he executed a stiff bow and then turned in the direction of the house. Mrs. Hurst remained where he'd left her, but Powell fell in step with him. The servant guided him through the house and to the entrance hall, where he called for another footman to send for David's horse. While they stood waiting for the beast to be brought from the stables, Powell turned to David, pinning him with a hard, dark gaze.

"A word, if I may, sir?"

David was surprised that the man had thought to ask permission to speak, but then remembered a footman was addressing him. Livery aside, Powell's size and bearing struck him as decidedly authoritative. That, and the fact that he looked as if he could crush David like a grape.

"Erm ... of course."

"My mistress deserves whatever happiness she can get after what she's been through. It isn't my place to divulge the details, but you should know ... no one would be a better mother than Mrs. Hurst. You are in a position to help her, and better your own circumstances while you're at it. What have you to lose?"

A groom arrived with David's horse, freeing him from having to respond. And what was he to say to that? The man made it clear he wouldn't give voice to whatever had happened to Mrs. Hurst under the thumb of her late husband. However, it was abundantly clear that she was a miserable sort of person. If having a child would change that, could David be the one to provide that for her? Could he knowingly sire a child on someone and then walk away without a look back?

His head had already begun to pound as he set off for the ride home, and he had a feeling it would get no better. It seemed he was damned no matter what he decided.

CHAPTER 4

"Mrs. Hurst?" Petra murmured, peering at David over the rim of her teacup.

She and Constantia gave him matching looks of curiosity at his query concerning their neighbor—the woman who might potentially become his new client and the mother of his child.

No, not *his* child. The transactional nature of their arrangement meant he was, in essence, selling her a part of himself. David would have no claim on the babe, and wasn't certain he would want to if given the choice. He was barely hanging on by a thread, hands filled with matters of the estate and caring for his family. The last thing he needed was another mouth to feed.

That led him down his present course, in which he tried to push his reservations aside to give Mrs. Hurst what she wanted. While taking tea with his sisters, he had casually dropped her name, hoping not to arouse their suspicions.

"Mrs. Hurst," Petra said again, drawing out the name as if tasting it. "Can't say I've heard of her."

"Yes you have," Constantia chimed in. "Her estate is just down the road, you know."

"*Her* estate?"

"Oh, yes. Remember? She's the one whose husband died and left her everything, just a few weeks ago. Apparently, her husband called for his solicitor in the eleventh hour. It is thought that he made the change to his will to bequeath everything to his wife ... even though he has a male cousin everyone assumed would inherit."

Petra snorted. "Oh, yes ... I remember the rumors if not the lady herself. Never laid eyes on her."

"Hardly anyone in the county has. She is reclusive and prickly, and never attends dinner parties or soirées. Of course, now she is in mourning she cannot socialize."

The twins sighed in unison, casting mournful looks at one another. They wore matching gowns, their hair concealed by coordinating lace caps. Since no new clothing could be afforded, his mother and sisters had resorted to dying everything black, using lace and other trimmings to cover worn patches and holes.

"How boring Christmas will be this year," Constantia murmured while absently stirring her tea. "No parties ..."

"Or parlor games," Petra filled in with a childish pout.

"No visiting or merriment at all. Why *do* you ask about Mrs. Hurst, David?"

He shook his head, taken aback by his sister's abrupt change of subject. "Erm ... I met her by chance during my morning ride yesterday and am simply curious. Like you, I knew nothing about her."

"What does she look like?" Petra asked, eyes bright at the idea of being privy to anything happening outside their house. The twins were used to spending their days calling on neighbors and indulging in the latest *on dits*. While he knew they missed Father sorely and that they grieved him, David also realized how difficult the mourning period would be. Virtually cut off from the world, they would miss out on the festivities of the holiday season. Then there were their dwindling chances at snaring appropriate husbands.

Next year, David promised them silently. *You'll have new wardrobes and dowries, and you may have your pick of any man you please.*

"Mrs. Hurst is ... lovely," he mumbled, holding his cup out to Constantia to be refilled. "Red hair. Fair skin. Very petite."

He took care to keep his tone light and even, though something in him reacted to the memory of those doll-like features and the contrast of vibrant hair against skin like Devonshire cream. Regina Hurst was beyond lovely, even if she was a bit haughty.

"Red hair," Petra said with narrowed eyes. "How unfashionable."

"What of her husband?" David pressed.

Constantia wrinkled her nose. "Never heard a favorable word about the man. One of those with a high opinion of himself that is most decidedly unearned. You know the type."

"Mama encountered him on occasion, I believe," Petra chimed in. "I do not think she liked him very much."

"Mama is the best judge of character. If she disliked him, we would have also."

"Indeed."

David glanced up just as Caruthers entered the drawing room, his mouth twisted in a worried frown. Coming to his feet proved a great chore, as David had been walking about all day feeling as if the weight of the world were on his shoulders. Whatever the butler needed to tell him was sure to compound the burden.

"I will see you at dinner," he said to the twins before following Caruthers from the room. "What's wrong?"

"There's a Mr. Stone here to see you, sir."

David frowned. "I don't know a Mr. Stone."

"He's a tenant. He and his sons work as farmhands. Before Mr. Graham's passing, Mr. Stone became rather vocal about the state of the tenants' cottages. Several requests had been put to Wren, but ..."

"The blighter put them off with claims that the repairs couldn't be afforded."

"So it seems, sir. I informed Mr. Stone that you couldn't possibly see him so soon after you'd gone into mourning and urged him to return at a later date, but he was most insistent. In fact, he has stated his intention to await your convenience. I'm terribly sorry, sir, but I did try."

He patted the butler's shoulder. Caruthers really had gotten too old to go on working, but would hear nothing of retiring. His loyalty to the Grahams was absolute, and he refused to leave them until he was certain all had been set right. Yet another matter for David to consider; one more thing his father and the damned Mr. Wren had left on his overflowing plate.

"It's all right. I cannot avoid these unpleasant matters forever. Pretending they don't exist will not make them go away. I take it he is in the drawing room?"

"Yes, sir."

"Then I will see him. We aren't to be disturbed."

David set off to meet his tenant, the sense of unease growing worse with every step. He had been surprised to discover that so many of their tenants had remained, given Wren's neglect. If every last one of them had packed up and abandoned their cottages as well as their work, David wouldn't have been the least bit surprised. However, he didn't know how close they might be to such a mass exodus. He supposed Mr. Stone was here to enlighten him.

He found the older man pacing near the windows overlooking the overgrown front lawn. He was nearly David's height, and thick with the sort of brawn honed by manual labor. Work-roughened hands twisted a worn cap, which he must have removed upon entering the house. Without it, his head was as bald and shiny as a billiards ball, while his jowls were speckled with silver stubble.

"Good afternoon, Mr. Stone."

Stone's jaw clenched as he perused David from head to toe, nostrils flaring as if he took in a noxious odor. His clothing was stark black save his shirt, his plainest and least remarkable pieces. However, he was aware of how it looked for him to stand here, fresh from London in the first stare of fashion while the house and estate were in shambles around him.

"Didn't think you'd see me. That butler of yours seemed to think you wouldn't."

David glanced to the console where a collection of decanters was neatly arranged, glad to see that one of them was half-full. Crossing to it, he lifted the lid on what his nose told him was a decent brandy.

"Caruthers simply wanted to ensure I had adequate time to hear your concerns. Drink?"

Stone scowled at the tumbler David offered him but accepted it anyway. When David gestured toward a chair in invitation, Stone opted to remain standing.

"I ain't come here to exchange pleasantries."

"Of course not. I understand you have some concerns, and I am here to listen."

Stone scoffed and glared down into his brandy. "Concerns be puttin' it mildly. I been up to this house every week for months askin' to speak to Mr. Graham, but that bounder Wren always claimed he were too busy. Said he was the man to see about estate concerns and such."

David bit back a curse, despite having already known what to expect. He could place the blame on Wren until he was blue in the face, but his father had been no better, wallowing in self-pity and drowning himself in drink. A man like Stone didn't look as if he would appreciate a string of excuses from his previously absent landlord.

"Mr. Wren is no longer in my employ, and I am currently on the hunt for a new steward. In the meantime, I will manage estate matters myself, so you may bring your concerns straight to me. Caruthers will be informed to admit you when you call."

Stone made a gruff sound of derision, swirling his brandy about his glass. He had yet to take a sip. "Sure, I can come and you'll hear me out. But what'll you actually *do* about any of it? You got thousands of acres of land what's been worked to death, herds of cattle we can't feed through winter, and enclosures that won't keep them penned long enough for it to matter. Most our cottages have started fallin' down around our ears, and it's a wonder the lot of us haven't said to hell with it and taken ourselves off elsewhere."

"Why haven't you? I am genuinely curious, and might I add baffled, that you haven't done just that."

"'Cause before he was a pitiful drunken heap, your father was a good man. Most of us been here our entire lives, have raised our children here. A few decided to try their luck, but the rest of us ..."

David raised an eyebrow when Stone trailed off, giving him a measured look. "Yes?"

"The rest of us is content to give you a chance to prove you're more than a pretty London fop in a nice suit."

The insult struck as intended, but David bit his tongue around a retort. He would be within his rights to throw Stone out on his ear, but figured the man could be excused for being in a dudgeon. Because of the mismanagement of the estate, Stone and his family would see a bleak Christmas along with an understandable amount of worry over what the coming spring might have in store. David's pride was of no consequence here.

"By God, this is good." Stone had finally sampled the brandy, and his expression of scorn had been replaced by one of shock. The brandy was probably the finest thing the man had ever tasted in his life.

"There's plenty more. Have as much as you like."

Stone seemed content to take him up on the offer, downing what was left in a single swallow before going to the console to help himself to more. David's lips twitched in amusement, but he wiped the coming smile away. Time to get down to business.

"Caruthers tells me you've visited often in the past several months. He made no mention of any other tenants, so I take it you speak for the others as well as yourself and your own family."

"I do," he grunted out after another healthy swallow of brandy. "S'pose I ought to tell you ... some think we ought to refuse to work or pay the Christmas rents till our demands are met. I haven't cast my lot with them as of yet, but am thinking that all depends on whether you do more than fix your mouth to spout off empty promises."

David set his tumbler aside and considered the clear, underlying threat in Stone's words. Tenants who wouldn't pay rents was one matter, but to refuse to work would cripple the last leg David had to stand on, and Stone knew it. So did all the other hands, who he suspected would abandon their work with nothing but a word from Stone.

"We have our own to think of, after all," Stone went on. "I've five mouths to feed myself ... six come summer."

"Congratulations. I, too, have a household to think of, which is why I'm sure you know the loss of labor would be untenable. Without you all, the problems you just outlined cannot be fixed, and the farm cannot sustain enough to support even my family, let alone yours."

Stone folded his arms over his chest, the glass balanced in the crook of his elbow. "What do you reckon we do about it, then?"

"Well," David said slowly, tapping his chin as he measured his words. This was new territory for him, and he had no idea what he was doing. He did, however, understand what was right and fair, and what his tenants were owed. "What if we were to come to an agreement? If I forgo collection of the rents until Lady Day, I imagine that would help ease the burden. Perhaps, enough that you might help me make right the matters that have gone neglected for far too long."

"Forgo the ... you'd really do that?" Stone's jaw had gone slack, and he was looking at David as if he'd suddenly grown a third eye in the center of his face.

"I would, if you give your word that you will convince the other hands not to abandon their work. In exchange, I will also ensure that the materials for repair of cottages are made available at the earliest opportunity. That will take me time, mind, but you have my word that it will be done."

"Wren gave me his word lots of times."

"I'm not Wren, nor am I my father. Look, Mr. Stone, I realize you have no reason to trust me. After I came of age, I left Lancashire without a look back and did very little to secure my inheritance. I was unaware of Wren's deceit, but that is no excuse. I do not expect you to forgive me the oversight, or to trust me right off. But you did say you were content to give me a chance, so that is all I'm asking for now—a chance to make things right. No rents until Lady Day, the materials to mend your homes, and an eventual improvement on all the rest—the enclosures, the tools and the mill. I do not yet know everything that needs to be accomplished, but I haven't been idle since my return. I am taking stock of what needs doing. I could certainly use your help convincing the other tenants, and ... well, advice you may have on any matter that I am ignorant to, I would be glad to hear it. It does nothing for my pride to admit that I am woefully unprepared to assume my role, and without a steward I am quite at a loss. I'd wager I could learn a lot from a man like you."

Stone looked as if he would faint, but quickly recovered with a shake of his head. "I ... me, sir?"

Now, he was 'sir', instead of 'a London fop in a nice suit.' They were making progress.

"Yes, you. In fact, if you would return in two days' time, I would like to tour the fields. My father mentioned in one of his journals that that forest bordering the south pasture might make for prime farmland once slashed and burned. I'd like your opinion on the matter."

Stone looked as if he might smile, but then smoothed his face back to inscrutability. "I been tellin' Wren we should slash and burn that land for over a year. He wouldn't listen."

"Well, *I'm* listening. What do you say, Stone? Neither of us has anything to lose, and I'll admit to being desperate here."

The man surprised David by extending a hand toward him with a hint of a grin. "You have yourself a bargain, Mr. Graham."

Taking Stone's hand, he winced at the bear-like grip, but gave it a firm shake. "Then I will see you again on Thursday, as early as is convenient for you."

"Of course, sir."

"My pleasure. Oh, and Stone? See Caruthers on your way out and inform him that I want you to have a bottle of that brandy ... to share with your sons. I'm sure they'll like it as much as you seemed to."

Stone was really smiling now, slapping his cap onto his bald pate as he backed toward the door. Their stores were nearly depleted, but it was less than David would be willing to part with to get the man on his side.

"That'll be fine, thank you, Mr. Graham."

The moment Stone was gone, David began to pace, hands clasped behind his back. He had just made a promise he couldn't afford to keep. Refusing to take up Christmas rents meant making life harder on his mother and sisters. Perhaps it wouldn't be unbearable, but they had already been through so much. The last thing he wanted was to inform them that they would live like paupers for half a year at the very least, while he worked to get the farm profitable again. Even if he sold every valuable thing he owned—which he fully intended to do—there were still unpaid debts to be considered as well as the collapsing roof of the east wing. Yet, he couldn't go on collecting rents from tenants who had not been given what they were owed. The people who worked his land had families to care for, just like him, and he refused to sacrifice them to keep his own family comfortable. It seemed one would have to suffer for the care of the other.

Nothing needs to be sacrificed if you take Mrs. Hurst up on her offer.

With a frustrated grunt, he pushed a shaking hand through his hair. There seemed to be no other choice. Until the farm began generating enough income, David had only one thing to fall back on. Serving as some woman's courtesan was far easier in London, where he'd had his pick of wealthy ladies outbidding one another to take him as a lover. But here in Lancashire there was only Mrs. Hurst, and the money she was willing to pay would be enough to keep them afloat until spring—perhaps longer if he could earn the bonus she was offering.

Of course, that bonus was contingent upon him successfully getting her with child.

The longer he thought on it, the more David began to see her offer as the perfect solution to his problem. Mrs. Hurst wanted a family, and he wanted to save his. By mutual agreement, they could both get what they wanted with no one the wiser.

Pleasing women had always been his forte, something he enjoyed as much as when women pleased him. If planting a baby in her womb improved Mrs. Hurst's life in some way, turned that solemn expression into a contented one ... well, what could be so wrong about that?

He practically ran to his study, keen to make the decision final before he could change his mind. Short of the sky suddenly opening up to rain thousands of pounds upon him, David had no other recourse.

Unlocking the safe where he had stashed the contract, he carried it to the desk and signed it, hands shaking as he waited for the ink to dry. He steadied it long enough to pen a short note to Mrs. Hurst.

A smidgen of relief stole through him once both had been sent off, and the tension clenching his joints and muscles eased. Upon delivery of the contract, he would be owed a substantial payment from Mrs. Hurst up front. He would put that toward the most necessary of needs around the house, and the rest would go into supplies to repair the tenants' cottages. It was enough for now; he would earn the rest.

And he would eventually convince himself that walking away from a woman pregnant with his child was necessary to the well-being of everyone and everything he cared about.

Two nights later, David was ushered down the darkened corridors of Regina Hurst's house by her massive footman. He had spent the entire day on edge, despite having the distraction of hours in Stone's company. In fact, he should be tired after a long day of riding and taking note of the improvements and changes he would begin implementing in the coming months. However, his exhaustion had lasted as long as it took to bathe and change clothes before sending for the carriage. All the way here his mind had run in a hundred different directions.

This was unprecedented. He had never been nervous to meet with a client, nor had he suffered any anxiety about taking one to bed for the first time. But, even his limited interaction with her had told David that Mrs. Hurst would be unlike any woman he'd ever serviced. She had made it clear that his charm and easy smiles would have no effect on her.

But then, those weren't the only tools in his arsenal. David smiled at Powell's broad back as he thought of getting the lovely Regina Hurst naked and spread out on a bed. He would have weeks—at least—to discover all the treasures hidden beneath her stiff bombazine; to discover the weight of her breasts in his hands and learn the contours of her waist and hips. His cock began to stir at the thought of spreading her legs to find curls the same vibrant hue as the strands on her head. Would she be a quiet lover, muffling the sounds of her plea-sure behind pinched, quivering lips? Or, would she scream and cry out her release, hips bucking and body writhing? His smile had widened by the time they reached the door to what he assumed must be the lady's bedroom.

When Powell turned to face him with a dark scowl, David quickly wiped his grin away. "She is expecting me, I presume? Shall I just go in?"

Powell's fists clenched as he glared at David, jaw working as if he chewed a mouthful of pebbles. When he finally spoke, it was with a cold precision that prickled David's spine.

"I'll be standing right outside this door until you leave. If she calls for me, I'm coming in and you will suffer an unfortunate accident resulting in the separation of your head from your shoulders."

David's hand went up to his throat before he could control the gesture, and for a split second he wondered if it might not be too late to back out of this arrangement. He had never been subjected to such a thing in his life. A bloody footman standing guard outside the door? And just *why the hell* would Mrs. Hurst have cause to call out for her servant while she was in bed with him? If David did his job well—which he always did, thank you very much—it was his name she'd be screaming, not Powell's.

But, he remembered the footman's protective stance when he had first come to meet Mrs. Hurst. There was also the concern and care Powell had conveyed when asking David to consider her offer. The man obviously wanted to be assured he wouldn't do his mistress harm, and since he was a virtual stranger David could hardly fault him for that.

"I can assure you, your lady is in the best of hands."

Powell gave a stiff nod and then rapped on the door three times before stepping aside. David took that as his cue to enter. He found the room dark save for the fire in the hearth and a solitary lamp near the shadow of a large tester bed. He made out the outlines of more furniture, but couldn't see much beyond the circle of yellow light illuminating the figure standing near the bed.

And suddenly, David didn't want to see anything else, for he had laid eyes on his new client and he very much liked what he saw. Curiously, there was nothing titillating about her attire, which consisted of a heavy dressing gown—one that likely covered a white nightgown or chemise like the countless others he'd seen. And yet, she made a most alluring sight. The severe knot of hair he remembered from their first meeting was gone, and the coppery mass fell in a thick braid over one shoulder. The cinch of the robe's belt around her waist offered a tantalizing preview of what was hidden underneath. Her face was as pale and luminous as the moon, her eyebrows bright slashes of red over the dark orbits of her eyes.

"Mr. Graham. Thank you for accepting my offer. You cannot know what this means to me."

David wanted to approach, pull her against him and ease the stiffness from her back with a kiss. He could melt her with a single touch of his lips, and he knew it. Still, he held himself in check. There was something unnatural about her rigidity, as if she were using stillness as a means by which to keep herself grounded and present. The wide set to her eyes told him she wasn't ready to be touched.

"There are no thanks needed. While I will obviously benefit from the arrangement, I truly want to help you."

She dipped her head in a nod but refused to look at him. "I take it you received the bank draft I sent after signing the contract ... your first payment?"

"I did."

David remained where he stood, sensing there was more. Despite the dim lighting, he noted the twitch of her lips as if she wrestled over her words.

"Before we begin, I have a few guidelines I'd like you to observe."

He raised his eyebrows at that, and not for the first time he found himself at a loss when it came to Mrs. Regina Hurst. It wasn't uncommon for a new client to have a few limits, though with the women David had serviced those had been few and far between. Mrs. Hurst's tone led him to believe he would be dealing with something grave. In fact, she sounded as if she anticipated facing the hangman's noose rather than a night in bed with her courtesan.

"I'm listening."

At the gentleness in his tone she glanced up, then started when she realized he had extended a hand to her. He hadn't come any closer, leaving the choice of skin-to-skin contact completely on her.

"Mrs. Hurst ... may I call you Regina?"

She hesitated only a moment, her gaze lifting to meet his. "I suppose that would be all right."

"And you should call me David. We will be spending several nights a week together. I want you to feel comfortable with me. Whatever limits you wish me to skirt, I will gladly do so."

That seemed to reassure her, and she took the few steps to close the gap between them, placing her hand in his. It was ice cold and shaking, so he laid his other atop it and lightly chafed the chilled skin.

"David," she said, his name nothing more than a strained whisper. "I think it would be best if we established that this arrangement is strictly for the purposes of procreation. Mr. Lyons was most adamant about your ... um ... experience. However, you need not worry that I will require any ... prolonged ministrations. Truly, the faster it is over, the better."

David's hold on her hand went slack and he felt certain his eyes were about to fall free from their sockets. It would seem this arrangement was set to introduce him to a wide range of firsts. Never in his life had he encountered a woman who wanted him to rush through bedsport.

"You cannot be serious."

"I'll remain in my nightgown, and I'd like you to be clothed save for ... well, you know."

She waved her free hand in the general direction of his pelvis, as if she indicated a vase or a heap of horse manure. David wasn't certain if he should be affronted on behalf of his cock.

"We shall always lie face to face," she went on, talking faster now, as if the first words had freed her. "And ... and the lamp is to be doused."

"Regina, do you really want me to take you to that bed and rut on you like ... like some sort of ..."

"Stud?" she offered with a little shrug of one shoulder. "With all due respect, Mr. Graham—"

"David."

She gave him a brittle half smile. "David ... our contract specifies that you are to be exactly that."

"But, I'm a courtesan. Pleasure is my business, and at the risk of sounding arrogant, I'm very good at what I do. Wouldn't you prefer to actually enjoy the conception of your child? It needn't be so ... impersonal."

Her plush lips set into a firm line, and she fixed her gaze somewhere south of his chin. "This is the way I need to go about it. Do you understand?"

No, he didn't understand this woman at all. But for what she was paying, David did not need to understand her. He simply had to fulfill the contract, which meant giving her what she wanted, exactly how she wanted it.

"Very well. I will insist on removing my coat, at least. The tailoring is too exact for me to have full range of motion."

She gave a silent, stiff nod in response, then turned away. David peeled off his coat as she went to the bed, slowly and carefully turning down the coverlet. Then, with her back still turned to him, she shrugged out of her dressing gown. The heavy damask fell away to reveal a prim, white nightgown. As he laid his coat over a chair near the hearth, she climbed up onto the mattress, offering him a glimpse of a dainty foot, a slender ankle, and a taut calf. The small peek of skin was enough to get him moving. He approached the bed as she went onto her back, legs straight and pressed together, arms at her sides.

As he neared the bed, dousing the lamp before climbing on over her, it struck David that she looked more like a corpse laid in a coffin than a woman waiting to be fucked. It was the worst sort of luck. As he crouched over her, knees spread on either side of her thighs and hands bracketing her shoulders, he became very aware of her scent—crisp, clean, and slightly floral. Womanly. The dim light of the fire cast shadows over her eyes, but he could clearly make out the plump lips, the darling little chin, the column of her throat, the swells of high, firm breasts.

He would have gladly spent the night kissing and toying with her until she begged him for the pleasure she claimed not to want. And there was the rub. His cock was already eager, ready to be taken into her body. More than that, his fingers itched to loosen the row of buttons running between her breasts, to caress her bare skin and find out if it felt as satiny as it looked. His mouth watered to kiss the patch of skin just below her jaw, take her nipples into his mouth, kiss his way down her belly until he was making love to the valley between her thighs with his tongue.

He swallowed, having worked himself into a state with nothing but his wandering imagination. David felt her eyes on him, registered the anxiety thrumming through her tensed limbs as she waited for him to begin.

Keeping his movements slow and deliberate, he began lifting the hem of her gown. He paused at her knees, hooking his fingers behind each soft cleft to urge them to bend. David held his breath as what little she would allow him to see was revealed. Shapely calves, soft thighs, rounded hips, and—sweet God above—the downy curls between her legs. The slash of moonlight illuminated alabaster thighs, and right between them, a contrasting thatch of hair like a sunburst. Copper and ivory; an appealing combination that had him wanting to sink to his belly then and there so he could press his lips to the hidden, pink flesh of her cunny.

There would be none of that, so he pushed the thought aside before it could root itself too deeply in his mind. He slid a hand down one thigh, gently pressing it open, then the other. She lay beneath him unmoving and, it seemed, hardly breathing. Regina wasn't even looking at him. He could not make her eyes out clearly, but could tell they were fixed on the ceiling. Her hands gripped the bunched fabric of her nightgown as she remained silent and waiting.

One hand still braced on her inner thigh, he slid a thumb through the nest of curls, whispering over sleek folds and the taut circle of her opening. She sucked in a sharp breath when he moved upward, seeking the bud of her pleasure, then flinched when he offered the gentlest press of his thumb.

"I ... you shouldn't ..."

"Shh," he crooned, lightly working his thumb over her clit once more. "It'll be easier if you're wet. You aren't ready yet."

He had a feeling she might never be, but David would do what he must to keep from making her uncomfortable. It was a ridiculous notion when she was lying like a plank of wood beneath him, obviously wanting his attentions to come to a swift end. She was nothing if not uncomfortable.

It was so odd, being near this woman—so warm and seemingly vibrant, yet somehow cold and shuttered. Had her husband never offered her pleasure? He couldn't have, if Regina could lie there with him stroking her clitoris without wanting him to linger there.

David withdrew long enough to lick the pad of his thumb, then was caressing her again, slow and steady. She tensed, then went loose-limbed, her thighs widening as he stroked her, coaxing forth her natural wetness. He delved his first finger into her sheath, finding her dewy and soft, gripping his finger with unwitting spasms. Her fingers flexed convulsively around her nightgown, and when he peered at her face again, he found her jaw clenched tight, nostrils flared as she took slow, deep breaths.

"Now, David," she whispered, still not looking at him. "Please."

That wasn't exactly what he wanted to hear, not when a few more seconds could have had her saying 'please' for an entirely different reason. But she was clearly intent on hurrying him through the encounter and David didn't want her to call out for the footman. He liked his head just where it was.

He had his fall open in a matter of seconds, his cock hard and already wet at the tip. The sight of her bared from the waist down, the feel of her on his fingers, her scent ... it was enough. He hooked her thighs over his and guided his prick toward her, carefully nudging his way in. She let out a choked sound as he lodged half his length in her with one stroke, her breaths becoming rapid and harsh as he withdrew and plunged, giving her the rest. His arms nearly buckled from the strain of holding himself up, when the tight clench around his cock made him want to collapse into her.

He gritted his teeth and rolled his hips, surging deeper, grinding against her as the stroke of her velvety sheath caressed him. Her body had gone pliant, accepting him. Yet, her arms remained at her sides and the same preternatural stillness held her in its clutches. His instincts cried out for more stimulation, for the taste of her lips, the rasp of her tongue against his, the hard bud of her nipple in his mouth. Closing his eyes, he imagined being allowed to do this properly, conjured up the sounds she would make when he licked her throat, pinched her nipple, worked a hand between them to stroke her clit in time with his thrusts.

His hips jerked and he increased his rhythm, clinging to his fantasy and letting it run wild in his mind. She would come alive for him, panting and writhing and clawing his back, chanting his name. Her legs would wind around his waist, drawing him closer and deeper, urging him on.

David's eyes flew open as climax slammed into him, and instead of pulling away, he drove in and released with a shudder, his teeth clenched around a hoarse groan. It was jarring, foregoing his usual methods of avoiding conception of a baby. But this was what Regina wanted from him—*all* she wanted from him.

She was trembling again, finally looking at David as he slowly withdrew from her body and sat back on his heels. He could see the whites of her eyes, flared wide in the dark, as if she were just as surprised by what they'd done as David. His hands were clumsy as he worked to close his fall, and Regina looked away from him as she eased the hem of her nightgown down her thighs. He fumbled for words ... any words. What was he to say to her now that it was over? He was out of his depth here, when cuddling a satisfied woman against his chest typically followed his beddings. Perhaps a few kisses and caresses, another tumble if she were up for it.

However, Regina Hurst had retreated into herself, seeming to want nothing to do with him now that he'd done his job.

"Are you ... all right?" he ventured, hating the uncertainty threading his words.

"Fine."

She didn't sound fine. Her voice had trembled on the solitary word.

"Regina ... can I do anything for you? Get you something? I could—"

"No, thank you, David. I just want to sleep now. You may return at your convenience to try again. Thank you."

Thank you. It was the coldest dismissal he'd ever been treated to.

"Of course. I will return tomorrow."

"Very well."

He climbed off the bed, turning the coverlet up over her before backing away. Regina remained where he left her, head turned toward the window. As he took up his coat and shrugged into it, David frowned, a bitter taste flooding his palate. Despite achieving release, he had never left a woman's bed so dissatisfied in his life. Glancing down at himself, he cringed to realize he hadn't even removed his boots.

It was what she wanted, he reminded himself as he turned for the door.

The thought did nothing to make him feel better, because David could see that what Regina wanted was based on what she thought intercourse ought to be. Who had taught her that? Had her wretch of a husband visited her bed this way—in the dark and still wearing his clothes—to take from her while giving nothing in return? Was that why Regina wanted it done with quickly? Of course it was. No woman wanted some panting, sweating beast of a man rutting on her with no care to her needs. She fathomed no other way because no one had taken the time to show her otherwise.

Rationalizing all of this in his mind, David ignored the questioning stare of Powell as he made for the stairs without a look back.

His skin crawled with the need to immerse himself in a hot bath. Not once over his years as a courtesan had David felt like an object, something to be used and then discarded once he'd fulfilled an obligation. He had reveled in the feeling of being desired and wanted, being able to put a smile on the face of the woman in his bed. There was nothing he found more beautiful than a woman flushed with passion, stretching and grinning like a cat lying under the warmth of the sun.

Tonight, however, he left the home of his new keeper feeling filthy and low, and wondering how he was ever going to make himself go through with this night after night for God knew how long. Better for them both if Regina turned up pregnant sooner rather than later.

CHAPTER 5

"This author happened to spot the Honourable Mr. R and his wife about Town the other day. The artistic gentleman was engrossed in selecting pigments for his craft while Mrs. R lingered over the most darling items meant for an infant. Dear reader, if you took my advice and wagered that the newlywed lady would be breeding by Christmas ... I do believe it is time to collect your winnings."
-The London Gossip, 7 December 1819

Regina turned onto her side, staring sightlessly through the drapes parted to the moonlit night. Drawing her knees up to her chest, she made herself as small as possible and wrapped her arms around herself. Despite her best efforts, she could not seem to stop shaking. It wasn't that she was cold—quite the opposite. The warmth of her courtesan's body still clung to her nightgown, as well as his scent. It flooded her nostrils with every inhale—sandalwood and musk. Her throat constricted, and she forced herself to swallow and breathe while reminding herself why this was necessary.

David's seed was slick and sticky between her thighs, her only comfort in the aftermath of what had just happened. Tonight, they might have conceived the child she wanted so badly. Enough to part with several thousand pounds. Enough to allow a man back into her bed after so many years of loathing the act of intercourse. Randolph made certain she could never enjoy it, though for years she had lain still and tolerated him with a single hope burning in her chest. If his attentions would bear fruit and give her someone to love and call her own, she could bear it. She could part her legs and do her wifely duty and swallow her revulsion.

Only, time and the fruitlessness of his affairs had proven her husband unable to sire children, yet another cruel circumstance of a life that had heaped nothing but misery on her.

Pressing a hand against the flat stretch of her belly, she silently prayed.

Please ... please ... please ...

Please let her plan work so she would not have to spend the rest of her life alone and mourning what never was. Please let her womb quicken sooner rather than later, so she wouldn't have to withstand the attentions of her courtesan any more than necessary.

It would have been funny if Regina still possessed a sense of humor. Randolph had stomped that out of her, too, along with her hopes, her youth, her passion. There was nothing amusing about hiring a man who specialized in erotic pleasures, while taking no joy from the act of lying with him.

And yet ... it hadn't been quite as unpleasant as she had expected. Unnerving, that. She had been prepared to grit her teeth and bear it, to disconnect her mind from her body long enough to endure his attentions. Regina's strategy had been a good one, thought up to protect her from anything that would conjure unwanted memories of Randolph.

Dim lighting, layers of clothing between them, a restriction against unnecessary touching, a position that would allow her to open her eyes at any time and be reassured by a face that was not her dead husband's.

However, it hadn't worked quite as well as Regina had hoped. She had not expected him to insist that he could give her pleasure. Nor had she anticipated the gentleness with which he'd handled her, the slow and methodical attempt at ensuring she was ready to accept him into her body. Randolph hadn't cared whether she wanted him, had never done more than flip up her nightdress and force his way into her.

Regina shuddered, recalling the touch of David's long, slender fingers on her thighs, the press of his thumb against a part of her body that had set off sparks between her legs and pangs of ... *something* deep in her belly. No one had ever touched her that way, and she'd never realized her body was capable of such a response. Her cheeks flushed hot as she remembered the slick sounds of him stroking her, one finger plunging in and out of her channel.

His touch had produced the most befuddling sensations, as well as a most embarrassing phenomenon. As he'd stroked and touched her quim with efficient skill, Regina had become *wet*. Was that what he had meant by claiming she wasn't yet ready? She had to admit, the expected discomfort of his invasion into her body had been made easier by the slickness, which had increased with the friction of him moving in and out.

How very odd.

Regina still couldn't understand any of it. Not his careful treatment of her, or the baffling war of sensations that had raged within her from the second he first touched her to the moment it had ended. The self-imposed isolation of mind from body had been shattered despite her best efforts, and the man on top of her had ceased being a mere vessel for her use. He'd become *David*.

When Regina closed her eyes, she saw him with uncanny detail—the moonlight glinting off his hair, illuminating the contours of his perfect, plush mouth, the intriguing ripple of his arms through his shirtsleeves, taut and strained from holding his weight over her. Biting her lip, she shook her head to blot out the echoes of the only sound he'd made, right at the end as his cock jerked inside her and spilled. The deep, throaty growl had taken her by surprise in its rawness and vulnerability. Regina had dared a glance, finding herself enraptured by the sight of him. Head tipped back, jaw wound tight, nostrils flared and eyes squeezed shut. She had been the most intrigued by the view of his jaw and chin, tilted at an angle she might not otherwise have viewed. The man was ridiculously beautiful, almost godlike, and yet the moment of his completion had brought him down to the mere plane of a mortal. It had exposed a part of him she would rather have not witnessed.

A soft rap on the door preceded Powell's deep voice, muffled through the wood. "Are you all right, ma'am?"

She wanted to tell him to go away and leave her alone with her thoughts, but the faithful servant wouldn't go away until he was reassured.

"I'm fine," she called out.

A short hesitation, and then, "Are you certain? Mr. Graham didn't … I just want to know you aren't hurt, or …"

The uncertainty in his voice made her chest constrict, her heart aching for the man who'd stood by for years with no choice but to keep his silence while Randolph treated her like a possession to be toyed with, broken, pieced back together, and shattered anew. He had shown her kindness whenever he could—offering cold compresses for her bruises, finding ways to distract Randolph when it could be managed so she could escape to her rooms, ensuring the other servants kept their silence about what went on within the walls of this house.

"He did his job and I am no worse for wear," she said, trying to inject strength into her voice that she didn't feel. Powell would never leave her be otherwise.

That seemed to satisfy him, because he merely bid her goodnight. As his heavy footsteps carried him away, Regina released a sigh of relief and resumed her fetal position in the center of the bed.

Sleep eluded her for near an hour, as each time she closed her eyes she saw David on top of her, arching and groaning, the thick column of his neck stretched taut, lips parting to reveal his clenched teeth. That sound echoed in her mind in a continuous refrain that left her both confused and intrigued.

The last thing she needed was to become intrigued by her courtesan. He was here for one reason only, and she would not lose sight of that. He was, after all, a man. From her father and brother, to the husband who had tormented her every day of their eight-year marriage, those she had trusted most had turned out to be cold creatures incapable of love. She would not let her courtesan's air of politeness and veneer of gentleness fool her into trusting him. Randolph had been courtly and chivalrous, tricking her into falling in love with him—or rather, what Regina had thought to be love. Time had proven her wrong, and her infatuation with a man she'd barely known had been shattered mere hours after the wedding. She would never make such a mistake again.

All she wanted or needed of David Graham was his seed, and the sooner it took root the sooner she could put him out of her life, and her mind, for good.

REGINA HAD JUST SAT DOWN TO HER BREAKFAST THE NEXT MORNING, bleary-eyed and fatigued from a night of tossing and turning, when a footman announced a visitor. Spoon hovering over her teacup, she sucked in a sharp breath when she realized who had intruded upon her peace and solitude.

She exchanged glances with Powell, whose fists had clenched at his sides as he glared at the open door as if sensing the threat lingering beyond.

"Should I get rid of him?"

Staring longingly at her breakfast, Regina decided she wouldn't be able to enjoy it until she confronted the intruder. "That will not be necessary, Powell. Though, I would be grateful if you'd accompany me."

He fell in step behind her without a word, palpable tension radiating from him. Regina tilted her chin up and straightened her back, pasting a serene expression on her face before entering the morning room, where Tobias Hurst awaited her. He whirled away from the mantel, where he had been inspecting a collection of porcelain figures. The breath was knocked from Regina's lungs as their gazes clashed, the cold, dead eyes of her late husband boring into hers.

No ... not Randolph's eyes. Randolph is dead.

Still, the resemblance was uncanny and it always unnerved her to stand in the presence of a man who could have passed for Randolph in his youth. Dark hair not yet kissed by silver at the temples, rigid features, a short yet broad-shouldered frame ... her cousin-in-law should have been a handsome man. But, cruelty and malice were too apparent around his mouth and eyes, just as they had been in Randolph's. A shudder of revulsion washed through her, and her stomach turned.

"Tobias," she murmured, keeping her head held high and her tone cool. "How ... surprising it is to see you this morning. I had not expected to see you again so soon."

He sneered while reaching into his coat, coming out with a crumpled sheet of paper—a letter. She raised an eyebrow in silent question, though she could very well guess what had brought Tobias to her doorstep.

"Do you think to make me a laughingstock?" he demanded, the letter rustling as he waved it through the air.

Regina blinked, pretending to be confused by his outrage. "Why, Tobias, I don't understand. We are family, even if only by marriage. Why would I ever want people to laugh at you?"

He advanced on her, but a low, warning snarl from Powell drew him up short. Tobias sputtered and reddened, glaring at her servant, though he was careful to maintain his distance.

"This must be some kind of joke. Surely you cannot think a man of my status should live on such a pittance each year. It's preposterous."

Regina ground her teeth, wishing Randolph had left her penniless. She might not have had anywhere to go or a penny to her name, but at least she wouldn't be saddled with Tobias, whose funds she was now responsible for.

"Considering what your allowance was under Randolph's management, I would think you might consider my offer a boon. It is more than you were getting before."

And more than you deserve, you graceless brute.

As if he had plucked her unspoken words out of thin air, Tobias held up the letter from her solicitor and ripped it in two. "Don't think for a moment I cannot see what has happened here. You inheriting everything he ever owned makes no sense, and we both know it."

"I was his wife."

Tobias snorted and rolled his eyes. "And how much did that mean to him if he couldn't even bother to keep to your bed?"

Powell sucked in a swift breath, and Regina felt as if her molars would be ground to dust if she didn't stop clenching them. It seemed the only way to keep from telling him just where he could shove that letter, as well as his opinions about her, her inheritance, and her miserable marriage.

"If you are unhappy with your yearly stipend, might I suggest finding employment?"

Tobias's face went as red as an apple, the destroyed remnants of the paper falling from his hand. This time, Powell wasn't quick enough to stop him before he took hold of Regina, one hand wrapped around her upper arm. A cry of alarm died in her throat as he hauled her toward him.

"You forged that will, or you twisted his mind while he lay dying," he snarled, spittle flying from his mouth. "I don't know how you did it, but I'll expose you for the lying—"

His words broke off on a gurgle as Powell's large arm appeared from over her shoulder like a striking snake, his palm slamming into Tobias's throat. Regina shrank away from the pair as Powell backed the other man toward the door, nearly lifting him off his feet. Her blood had frozen to ice, and she was numb everywhere except for where Tobias had touched her. The scorching brand of his fingers seemed to have burned away the sleeve of her gown and the flesh of her arm straight to the bone. However, when she stared down at herself, everything was intact. He might have left a mark, but then her fair skin had always been easily bruised.

It took her half a minute to breathe through the darkness encroaching on her vision as a flood of memories overwhelmed her—of being grabbed that same way just before a palm cracked against her face, of being shoved against walls and over pieces of furniture. Another half a minute passed before she realized that if she didn't find her voice and stop Powell, he was going to murder her cousin-in-law.

"Powell, that's enough," she managed, though she could not look at either man just now. Violence hung heavy in the air around them, and Regina wanted nothing more than to escape it. "I think Tobias understands now that his behavior was unpardonable. We should give him the opportunity to take his leave while he still can."

The gurgling sounds of Tobias being strangled died away. Regina kept her eyes fixed on the wallpaper, controlling her breathing and doing her utmost to keep from collapsing into a sobbing heap on the floor. She was stronger than that, could endure a raised voice and a hand gripping her arm. She had lived through far worse; Tobias didn't have the strength to break her.

"Both my solicitor and yours have agreed that the contents of Randolph's will were sound and legal. There is nothing for you to contest, and you risk making yourself look even more the fool if you continue on this course. Might I suggest you be content with the generous stipend I have offered and move on with your life? Oh, and now that the matter is settled to my satisfaction, I must inform you that I'll not receive you in the future. Should you need to communicate with me, a letter will suffice. Good day."

Tobias's protests fell on deaf ears as the sound of scuffling indicated that Powell had begun to see him out.

Regina sank into the nearest chair once they were gone, releasing the breath she'd been holding. To keep from bursting into tears, she turned over the matter of Randolph's will. Like Tobias and everyone else in the Hurst family, Regina had been shocked by the revelation that Randolph had left her everything—the house and estate, every penny of his money, and all his valuable possessions. The house had been passed down through generations, and over the years had been filled with expensive furnishings, not to mention the safe in the study which held a collection of jewels previously owned by several Hurst women, including Randolph's mother. In one fell swoop it had all become hers, and she could hardly fathom how or why.

Her husband suffered a slow and painful death after his horse had spooked and thrown him. The beast trampled Randolph before bolting, leaving him a pulpy heap of broken bones and purpled, bruised skin. He was carried back home by servants and tended by a surgeon who had not been optimistic regarding his chances of survival. Regina had stood at his bedside, stoic and silent as the physician explained the extent of his injuries. The man seemed to think she was in shock as she stood there staring at Randolph without truly seeing. Instructions for his care had been related to a maid, and the surgeon even left a tonic for her 'delicate nerves.' He had tried to shoo Regina from the sickroom, supposing that the sight of her husband's broken body was surely more than a gently bred woman could bear.

What a ridiculous idea. But then, the doctor had not understood why she could only stare at Randolph in a silent stupor. The sight of her husband's swollen and discolored face had hypnotized her, the devastating beauty of mangled limbs and a chest that struggled for every breath holding her in their thrall. She wondered then how he had ever been able to make her afraid of him. Randolph had seemed so large before, so terrifying—an indestructible force of nature hellbent on crushing her. But, as she'd listened to the wheezing of his breaths and studied the broken fingers and crooked nose, it had surprised her to find him pitiful.

Ordering everyone from the room except Powell, she had stared down at Randolph for a long while without moving or speaking, taking stock of all his injuries, counting them in her mind. Interestingly, they didn't even come close to matching the ones he had inflicted on her over the years. Yet, there he was, brought low and at the mercy of her and the servants who had witnessed his abuse, and often been on the other end of it themselves. There wasn't a soul within this house who would care if Randolph died a slow, excruciating death.

Regina had edged closer to the bed where he lay, a pitiful heap beneath the coverlet. He stared up at her with wide, pleading eyes, chin trembling as if he might weep. He hadn't uttered a word, but Regina clearly saw the truth in his stare. He had known his life rested in her hands—that she could press a pillow over his face right then and he wouldn't have the strength to fight her off. The temptation had proved nearly irresistible. The intent must have radiated from her, because even Powell acted accordingly, closing and locking the door so no one would witness her sin.

But then, a sudden sense of calm had washed over her, and Regina could only laugh. She'd had the power to snuff out the sputtering flame of Randolph's life, but it would never be enough to repay his abuse or change the past. If anything, it would riddle her with guilt for the rest of her life, and she had no desire to live with Randolph's ghost after he was gone. She would be free of him, completely.

"I wouldn't waste the energy it would cost me to end your pitiful existence," she had whispered without breaking his gaze. "I think I would rather allow God to decide your fate. But you should know that whether you live or die ... you will never lay a hand on me again."

Those had been her last words to him, though Randolph survived for several days after. She had charged a collection of servants to see to his every need and send for the surgeon if necessary. Regina then went about her life as if Randolph did not exist—which was easy to do when he could not leave his bed and dog her every step. His solicitor had been called for suddenly, but the matters of the estate and money meant nothing to her. If she was to be granted a jointure, so be it. If not, she would find some other way to get by. One thing she had been determined to avoid was crawling back to her family, who had abandoned her to Randolph despite knowing the extent of his mistreatment.

If learning that her husband had been trampled to death by a horse had shocked her, it was nothing to what she felt a few days later when learning of her inheritance. While another woman might have been elated to have such welcome security, Regina saw her fortune as the burden it was. Not that she minded caring for her tenants and lands. She had Randolph's agent to take care of such matters on her behalf, and thus far she had no reason to doubt his competence. However, while Randolph had alleviated some of her worries, he'd created others —in the form of his family. Tobias had been the most persistent, unable to accept that the will was valid. As Randolph's closest living male relative, he had expected to take everything and now felt as if he'd been cheated.

"He's gone, ma'am," Powell said, reentering the room. "I'm sorry he got close enough to touch you. It won't happen again."

She forced a smile for his benefit, but doubted Powell was fooled. "Think nothing of it."

"Begging your pardon ma'am, but it's all I can think about most days. You've been terrorized enough, with me impotent to stop it. No, not impotent ... cowardly."

Regina came to her feet and closed the distance between them. Taking Powell's big, rough hands in her own, she stared up into his dark eyes.

"If you had acted against Randolph, he would have had you

arrested and taken away from me. Who would have been here to help me stand when I was low, or make me feel safe? Where else would I have found the will to live when I wanted to curl up and die? No, Powell ... you did what I needed you to do by remaining close, helping me where you could, and giving me a kind face to look upon every day. Randolph might have hated me and my neighbors never really knew me, but you were the only person in the world who cared for me, and I owe you everything."

His throat undulated with a forceful swallow, and for a moment he looked as if he might actually shed a tear. Regina would have counted it a miracle if he had, because the man rarely showed his emotions. True to form, he pulled himself together and squeezed her hands.

"And I owe you the same. I suppose that means we are beholden to one another."

This time, the smile she gave him was genuine—a rare expression, but one he brought about easier than anyone else. "At least, until you meet the future Mrs. Powell."

The tips of his ears went red and he shook his head. "No ma'am. I'm happy here, if it's all the same to you."

"Then you should remain. But you must promise to inform me the moment that changes, no matter how you think it might make me feel."

She could see the defiance in his eyes, but he merely nodded and released her hands. He then trailed her from the morning room back to her waiting breakfast. Another footman had refreshed her tea, and now set a new plate before her, steam rising from the coddled eggs.

Her appetite returned now that the unfortunate business with Tobias had been settled, so she laid her napkin in her lap and took her first bite with relish. The rest of the day would be better, Regina would make certain of it. The future was hers for the taking, and her plans were set. All there was left to do was hope she could finally have that final missing piece, the thing that would make her whole.

Buttering a third slice of toast, she decided it couldn't hurt to begin eating for two right away.

CHAPTER 6

David stepped from his carriage, having just arrived on the fringes of Seven Dials. He had arrived a few days ago on the business of selling everything that would fetch a price. His solicitor had been busy in his absence, finding a buyer for his townhouse. Taking rooms in a modest hotel, David had seen to the transfer of the deed into its new owner's name. From there, he spent two days selling off his phaeton and pair, as well as every piece of jewelry he owned, and scraping together quite a tidy sum to help see his family through winter. He didn't intend to remain in London long, as there were affairs back in Lancashire requiring his attention—not the least of which included Regina Hurst.

However, the note he received last night had urged him to make haste meeting Benedict in Seven Dials before dawn. Not wanting to drive his carriage into the center of one of the most dangerous neighborhoods in London, David opted to walk the rest of the way. Hands in his greatcoat pockets, head lowered and chin dipped into the warmth of his muffler, he traversed a veritable minefield of puddles—most of which weren't composed entirely of rain. The stench of human and animal excrement and unwashed bodies made his throat simmer with nausea, but he choked it down and pressed on. Keeping his eyes forward, he did his best to pretend he did not hear the shuffle of feet, coughs, and groans of suffering from the shadows. He wasn't certain if he was in danger of being set upon by pickpockets, beggars, or disorderly drunks, but David would rather not find out.

What the devil was Benedict doing in Seven Dials? Even with his less than stellar reputation, the man was a future viscount who had no need to go about rubbing elbows with prostitutes and drunks. Having been away from London for weeks, David had no notion what was going on or how matters of The London Gossip were being handled. He had to assume that was what this was about.

His assumption was proven right when he followed the glow of distant light down one of the seven narrow streets converging into the circular center of the slum, where a single column thrust up toward the grayish sky with six sundials adorning its peak. At the foot of this spire stood a circle of broad-shouldered men, many of whom held torches. The flickering flames cast their light upon Benedict, who stood in their midst staring down at something in his hands.

As David quickened his steps to draw closer, the men parted and he caught sight of a collection of young boys. Grubby, dressed in worn clothes and tatty caps, the lads likely ranged in age from seven to thirteen, each one busy loading something into a large wagon under Benedict's watchful eye.

They were bundles of broadsheets, David realized as he paused in the gap left by two of the men. By his estimation there were hundreds of copies of *The London Gossip* here, every last one being stowed in the vehicle. Glancing up to notice him standing there, Benedict grinned and waved him over.

"There you are. Come ... witness the genius of my plan."

Stepping around a lad in a threadbare shirt and patched trousers, David made his way toward Benedict. On his way, he noticed a second wagon, this one overflowing with rough gunny sacks bulging with mysterious contents.

"What's going on? You know my opinion about any time of the morning preceding daylight. It's unnatural to be awake at this hour."

With a hearty laugh, Benedict shoved one of the scandal sheets at him. "Trust me, friend, this was worth waking up early for. It's not every day one thwarts a madwoman with nothing more than a handful of sovereigns and a cart full of food."

David darted a glance at the boys running about to do Benedict's bidding, most of whom looked half-starved. Glancing down at the copy of *The London Gossip* marked with today's date, he began reading. His brow knit and his mouth fell open as he absorbed a rather accurate description of the way the Gentleman Courtesans had been doing business—from meetings in the back of a modiste's shop, to clandestine encounters, contracts and raucous parties where the favors of the men could be had for a night at no cost.

"For the love of ... she isn't making this up, Ben. It's all true."

Benedict tossed his crumpled sheet onto the growing pile of others. "Not anymore it isn't. I am going to find the person who told the Gossip bitch about that and break his jaw if it's the last thing I do. The last thing I wanted was to bring scrutiny upon her."

David issued a sarcastic huff. "If there's one thing Millie is used to, it's scrutiny."

"You're right. Still, if I stop these details from becoming public knowledge, I can protect everyone involved until I uncover her identity and shut her up."

Handing his copy of the paper off to a passing boy, David frowned. "Nothing yet?"

"Millie is still making inquiries, but I am a patient man. In the meantime, I have my friends here."

Just then, one of the aforementioned friends came to stand before them, tufts of dirty blond hair peeking out from under his hat.

"That's the last of 'em, me lord!"

"Well done. David, may I introduce my good friend Oliver? He and I set off on a rocky start, but we have settled our differences and decided to work together."

For a second, David was flabbergasted at Benedict's claim. But then, he remembered Ben's story about being attacked in an alley by a collection of thugs working under the command of the London Gossip. He'd gotten himself into that mess following a boy working as a deliverer of the gossip column.

Before he could respond, the other boys surged around them with hands open and arms outstretched.

"All right, one at a time," Benedict chided as he reached into his coat pocket and came out with a purse heavy with coins. The boys scampered away in twos and threes, stuffing the money away before helping themselves to one of the stuffed sacks from the other wagon.

David watched all this in silence, until the last of the lads was gone, save for Oliver, who tipped his hat to Benedict with a grin sporting two missing teeth.

"Same time tomorrow, me lord?"

"Yes, and remember—"

"Aye, me lord! We got no idea what 'appened to the papers once we delivered 'em."

"Good lad."

Once Oliver darted off in the wake of the other boys, Benedict turned to David. "Those lads and their families are living in squalor and starving. The Gossip pays them a handful of shillings a week to deliver her papers. Is it any wonder I was able to buy their loyalty with the promise of filled bellies?"

David stroked his jaw. "So ... they bring the papers to you instead of delivering them. For how long?"

"Until she figures out what they're up to."

"What then?"

"Then, I help those boys find other employment. And if it isn't enough to stop her, I have other means at my disposal."

Shaking his head in disbelief, David grinned. "Ben, you're a genius. You're as mad as a March hare ... but a genius nonetheless."

Benedict slapped his back with a chuckle. "Leave it to me, and this will all be over soon. When do you return to Lancashire?"

"Today, I think. I have matters to attend."

Guiding him far enough from the other men that they wouldn't be overheard, Ben lowered his voice. "And all is well with Mrs. Hurst? If not, say so and I will find you someone else right away. Or rather, I'll get Lyons on the job. He is certainly earning his wages these days."

David avoided Benedict's gaze at the mention of his keeper. He had visited her three more times since that first night, and had promised to return to her bed the moment he made it back to Lancashire. Each appointment had been much the same as the last, with her lying under him all but motionless without looking at him, and David trying his damnedest to pretend it didn't bother him. In truth, it haunted him, knowing that the woman neither wanted nor enjoyed his attentions.

It wasn't a question of his pride so much as the reason for her reticence. When he began to think on the matter, the conclusions his mind led him to were distasteful. For, surely there was more to the matter than he'd first thought. Randolph Hurst had certainly been a philanderer and a brute. But, David was beginning to suspect he'd hurt Regina in ways that went beyond the emotional. Such thoughts had made the night before his departure for London difficult, with David counting the seconds until it was over so he could escape the room and scrub himself clean with the hottest water he could stand.

"Regina and I are getting on well enough," he hedged. "She's lovely, if a bit quiet and withdrawn."

Benedict's grin turned wicked, his eyes knowing and bright in the torchlight. "If anyone can draw her out of her shell, it would be you."

In the past, David would have wholeheartedly agreed. But, how was he to do that when Regina had made it clear she wouldn't appreciate any such effort?

He forced a smile of his own. "Quite right. Thank you for sending for me. I knew you had things well in hand, but I feel better knowing there's a plan in motion. What of the others?"

"Hugh and Evelyn left for Norfolk just before you arrived. He has an architectural landscape to paint, and you know he doesn't like to go anywhere without Evie. Nick and Aubrey are still away on their wedding trips and will be for at least a few more weeks. Perhaps longer for Nick. I received a letter from him. Apparently, word of the column in which he was mentioned made it to him in Paris."

David winced. "I'm certain Calliope didn't take that well."

"According to Nick, not well at all, but she is angrier with the Gossip and the woman who leaked the information than she is with her husband. They'll likely remain in France through the New Year, though when I wrote him back, I assured him there was nothing to worry about. I will not allow his name to be connected to the agency. I won't let it happen to any of you."

If David could have faith in anything without question, it was the ironclad truth of Benedict's words. They were always sure to be followed with swift and decisive action.

"Let me know if I can do anything to help."

"I think not," Ben said. "Go home, David. Take care of your family. Leeds, see him back to his carriage, would you?"

One of the torch-bearing men pulled away from the others. Hands shoved into the pockets of his greatcoat, David went back the way he'd come with more confidence in his gait and a small weight lifted off his shoulders. There was, of course, plenty for him to concern himself with back in Lancashire, but the journey home would be less nerve-wracking with the security of the funds he was bringing with him. It wasn't much, but there would be coal in the hearths, fabric for his mother and sisters to have mourning garments that weren't falling apart, and food that wouldn't make him want to slit his own throat from lack of variety.

During the drive back to his hotel, David's thoughts landed back on Regina. Try as he might, he couldn't stop the trajectory of his mind. It was a damned problem. He would have much preferred to pretend she did not exist until the time came for him to visit her bed again. Aside from being a problem, it was also an aggravation, because he couldn't think of a time when having a new keeper did not fill him with expectation and excitement. The courtship phase had always been his favorite—learning a new client, coming to understand the inner workings of her body and mind. There was none of that with Regina.

In a few weeks he would know whether their efforts had been successful, and if she would require him for another month. Needing the promised income, he was torn between wanting the arrangement to last until spring and praying she would turn up pregnant as soon as possible.

Resting his head on the squabs, he closed his eyes and tried to steal as much sleep as he could before it inevitably became time to face the world again.

. . .

REGINA STARED UP AT DAVID, WHO CROUCHED BETWEEN HER PARTED knees in the dimmed lighting of her bedchamber. After ten days away from Lancashire, David had returned, ready to resume his obligation. He had arrived an hour later than their established time, citing the rain as his excuse and apologizing profusely. Despite being annoyed with him for keeping her waiting and sharpening the edge of the anxiety she'd been wrestling with all day, Regina had accepted his apology and led him to her bed. Several valuable opportunities for him to get her with child had already been wasted during his trip—though she wanted to be understanding that the man had a life outside her needs of him. He was here now, and she would take advantage of it.

There was a crisp layer of cold winter air clinging to him tonight, tangling with the sandalwood and his natural, masculine scent. He had towel-dried his hair, but the damp strands had begun to curl about his neck and forehead in a way she found intriguing.

Regina closed her eyes and waited for him to begin. He was taking his time tonight, a departure from the last few nights he had visited her. Instead of casually flipping up her nightgown, he slowly drew it up, his fingertips skimming the inside of one thigh. She shivered, goose bumps rippling along her bared skin. Yet, she wasn't cold—quite the contrary. Heat flared low in her belly as he stroked his way toward her quim, his breath slow and steady in the silence of the room.

Regina's parted legs began to tremble, her breasts heaving beneath the drape of her nightgown, her breath quickening at the whisper-soft stroke of his touch along the seam of her lower lips. What was he doing? There was nothing efficient about his ministrations, and she could hardly make sense of it. His visits had taken on an almost comforting monotony, and Regina had come to expect certain things from him. However, there was something different in his touch tonight, as if he wanted to *savor* the moments leading up to the actual act. She had never experienced anything like it. Weren't men accustomed to speeding through the pleasantries so they could sink their prick into a warm, dark hole?

Her mind turned into mush when he finally found what she'd come to think of as her 'pleasure spot.' He never lingered there more than a few minutes—just long enough to coax that embarrassing wetness from deep inside her. Tonight, however, he took up a slow, circular rhythm, sending the most unnerving flutters through her. Her gut clenched when he pressed down, and her eyes flew open, lips parted to ask him to stop. He would hurt her. His touch was too … oh, God. It didn't hurt. The pressure was unlike anything she had ever known or imagined. A ragged breath tore from between her parted lips, but nothing else came forth as he quickened his circling thumb, rubbing and sending sparks jumping along her nerves.

David's gaze was focused intently between her legs, a forelock of hair tumbling over his brow. The shadows hid his expression from her, but she could see his lips, parted and slick as if he'd just licked them. Her sheath clenched around air, the involuntary spasms of muscle both shocking and confusing. It was as if a part of her was coming alive, one she hadn't known existed until David prodded at it with his skilled fingers.

He kept up his stroking while opening his breeches with his other hand, never breaking the rhythm. Regina bit her lip until she tasted blood, wrestling with panic, fear, and something that felt a lot like … arousal. Was that what this was—this hot, flushed sensation stealing over her entire body and making her limbs melt? Her nipples ached, and each breath made the fabric of her nightgown rasp against them, further agitating the sensation.

The broad crown of David's cock touched her opening, gently prodding its way in. Regina held her breath, wanting to clamp her legs shut to keep him out, even as her traitorous sheath throbbed and pulsed in response to the invasion as if welcoming it.

He didn't push all the way in, keeping his thrusts shallow and giving the barest few inches of him. Her chest and throat burned from lack of air, and her heart pounded. The angle and shallow depth of his cock made his swollen head press against a place inside Regina that heightened the confusing sensations tearing through her. Her breath came out on a surprised cry as light flutters began rippling through her, growing stronger with each slow, deliberate thrust. The pressure on her bud increased, sending a sharp burst of almost painful pleasure through her. It spiraled from the point of contact and pene-trated her womb like the savage thrust of a dagger, twisting and penetrating parts of her she'd never intended to open up to this man. To *any* man.

David withdrew and thrust to the hilt, the collision of his pelvis against hers and the deep plunge of his cock setting something off within her. Regina's lips parted on a shrill cry, one of her hands coming up to clutch at his waistcoat as the entire world began to spiral away.

"Regina," he groaned, his hips moving in swift thrusts that heightened the poignancy of what went on inside her.

She could not speak, think or control her body. Her sheath convulsed around him in a pounding rhythm that took her breath away, her yearning nub pulsating against his agitating thumb. Her back arched and her head fell back as it overwhelmed her, blotting out everything in the world save for the man on top of her—turning her inside out and exposing all her nerves to the elements.

After what felt like an eternity, the storm within her began to abate, though it didn't cease all at once. The tension curling her toes and making her fingers clench so tight around the lapel of his waistcoat went first, and she fell beneath him in a boneless heap. Then, the soul-wrenching spasms within her eased into aftershocks that had her shaking and gasping for breath. Only then did David achieve his finish, one hand slapping against the headboard as he seated himself deeper and spilled, groaning and panting, head lowered so his hair obscured his face.

Regina could only lie there beneath him at first, stunned by what had just happened and still unable to speak. The world seemed to tilt on its axis, making her feel as if she fell through open air with nothing to hold onto, nothing to keep her from plummeting into some unknown hell.

David's harsh, ragged breaths began to slow as he lifted his head, glancing at her with heavy-lidded eyes. He looked like some wicked, pagan creature, even fully dressed—his long lashes casting shadows over his cheekbones, his lips parted and reddened as if he'd bit at them in the throes of his pleasure. A trickle of sweat glistened on his brow. His broad chest heaved beneath the layers of his clothes, making her wonder how he would look without them. How he would feel beneath her palms.

"No," she ground out, squirming to be free of him. He was still lodged inside her, softened but an ever-present reminder of what he was and why she should never have let him touch her that way.

He blinked as if awakening from a dream and gave his head a little shake. "Regina?"

"Get up," she rasped, pushing against his chest, her legs scrambling against the bedsheets as she tried to crawl out from under his bulk. "Get off me, now!"

David's movements were sudden and a bit clumsy as he pushed off her and crawled toward the foot of the bed. The slash of moonlight from the window illuminated his confused face and the unsteady hands that swiftly did up his fall. Regina pressed herself back against the headboard, jerking her nightgown over her knees as she curled them into her chest. She choked down hysterical sobs and tried to make sense of what was happening to her. Never had she known such feelings were possible during the act of intercourse. She had known what to expect every night before this one, and had even come to find the predictability of their sessions comforting. David had proven he was willing to play by her rules, and her crushing fears had eased just a bit. But now ... now she was uncertain and shaken as she tried to understand the things David had just made her feel, and what it might mean.

Still kneeling on the other end of the bed, David watched her as if she were a cornered animal about to lash out.

"Regina, what's wrong? Talk to me."

"Leave."

He flinched as if she had struck him. "I beg your pardon?"

"Get out. I do not want to talk about what you just did to me."

Sliding to the floor, he braced his hands on his hips and scoffed. "And what did I do to you exactly? Fuck you, like you are paying me to? Or maybe you're referring to the fact that you actually *enjoyed* it this time?"

Regina reared up from the bed, hands shaking as she balled them up at her sides. "How *dare* you? I am not paying you to contradict me or to force unwanted attentions upon my person!"

Running both hands through his mussed hair, he let out a frustrated growl. "If they were so unwanted, why didn't you say anything?"

She parted her lips to offer a retort, but no words were forthcoming. Why *hadn't* she protested? David had complied with her every request without question, and she'd never felt as if she were in danger with him. If she had asked him to stop, Regina was certain he would have.

But she hadn't, and she was angrier with herself than him for not knowing why.

"You stepped over the boundaries of what I have asked you to do, and you know it," she protested, the words feebly whispered.

He paced away from her, snatching up his coat from the back of a chair. "What else would you have me do? It might come as a shock, but I don't actually relish bedding you while you lay there like a corpse. I can literally *see* you counting the seconds until it's over. Forgive me for thinking that this might all be a bit more tolerable for us both if you actually derived some pleasure from it!"

Stabbing one arm into his coat, then the other, he grunted while trying to wrestle it on without assistance. His flailing might have been comedic if not for the confused muddle of her mind and the nauseating roiling of her gut.

"Whether or not I appreciate your ministrations is none of your concern. It isn't why I hired you."

His footsteps came to an abrupt halt, and she found him standing at the door with his hand on the knob.

"Madam, if you gave me half the chance, I could have you climbing the walls of this bedroom ... and I could do it blindfolded with both hands tied behind my back."

"Your arrogance is astounding."

He smiled, the impact of it devastating. "It's too bad you'll never know if it's actually arrogance, or irrefutable truth. Good evening, *Mrs. Hurst*. Send word when you are ready for me to return."

Without a look back, he jerked the door open and left without bothering to shut it behind him. Powell appeared a few seconds later, his face expressionless. Still, Regina could see in his eyes that he'd heard every word.

Mortified, she ran a hand over her face. Had he also heard her keening like a deranged lunatic when the pleasure had overtaken her? The thought had her cheeks burning hot with embarrassment.

"Want me to break his arms?" Powell offered.

A little laugh bubbled up from her throat, though she was certain the man was only half-joking. Nevertheless, his quip had broken through some of the tension clogging the room.

"No, let him go. He didn't do anything wrong."

Saying it aloud only made her feel worse, because in truth David had been trying to give her something. Dare she even say his efforts were those of kindness?

What a foreign concept. No man had ever given her anything out of the goodness of his heart, save Powell. Randolph had certainly never gone out of his way to ensure she enjoyed herself in the marriage bed. Her mother had insisted that Regina was wrong to require attentiveness and care from Randolph. Her job was to produce children and please her husband. Marital relations were a duty to be taken seriously and endured, full stop. Her father and brother had chided her for complaining to them about the man who owned her per the law.

Before marriage to Randolph, life had been simpler and Regina had understood her place in the world as a young woman, a daughter, a sister. Her mother had doted on her, and while her father hadn't been particularly attentive, neither had he been cruel. He praised her for her ladylike comportment—the results of years of governesses and an expensive seminary school education.

That all changed in the months leading to her eighteenth birthday, when she began hearing arguments between her parents over money. Her mother often came to breakfast with red-rimmed eyes, avoiding Regina's gaze. Not long after her birthday had passed, Regina was introduced to Randolph. She'd been so enchanted by his handsome face and charm that she hadn't realized what her parents had done until it was too late.

Her hand in marriage in exchange for the money to set their own affairs right, like some perverse reversal on a traditional dowry—that was the price her parents had been willing to pay. Regina's father had been determined she fulfill her part of a bargain she hadn't even realized she'd taken part in. Her mother had shown sympathy, but followed her husband's lead, becoming cold and distant. To this day, she wondered if that was her mother's way of coping with what she had done. If she pretended her only daughter didn't exist, she would not have to face the fact that she and her husband had made a deal with the devil and given up one of their children to do it.

A pounding began between her eyes, and Regina was suddenly very tired. She felt as if something inside her were being pulled in several different directions at once. Nothing made sense, and she couldn't begin to figure out how to work through her convoluted thoughts.

"I am going to bed now, and I suggest you do the same," she said, turning away from Powell. "Tomorrow will be soon enough for me to smooth things over with Mr. Graham."

She paused in the midst of straightening the bedclothes, looking up to see that Powell hadn't moved. He was watching her intently, eyes narrowed as if he were trying to see past her words and her feigned composure.

"You ... want him back?"

She frowned. "Of course. He's already been coming for weeks, understands my rules, and doesn't strike me as being weak enough to quit me just because we had a little spat. There is no need to go looking for someone else. It will only prolong my mission."

Nodding slowly, he never took those dark, penetrating eyes off her. "I see."

Regina cleared her throat, staring from him and back to the bed. When she raised questioning eyebrows, Powell nodded and reached for the door.

"Right then. Good night, ma'am."

"Good night, Powell."

She climbed into bed once he had left and burrowed beneath the bedclothes. The phantom twinges of her recent paroxysm made themselves apparent with a lingering ache between her legs. As she sank into the dark comfort of her solitude, Regina recalled the urgency of the moment before her world had exploded like a shower of stars, and shivered.

David hadn't seen anything wrong with what he'd done, and perhaps Regina might not have either—before Randolph's cruelty had made it necessary for her to protect herself. She'd done that for years by mastering her emotions and managing things that were within her power to control. That included being in command of her own self, and maintaining her sense of safety. David's wandering hands and skillful plying of her body had shattered that so easily it frightened her.

For, if he could break through her façade so easily, what else might he be capable of? How badly might she be hurt if she gave in to the overwhelmingly powerful sense of vulnerability that had swept through her in the moments following their coupling. Even now that he was long gone, Regina felt turned inside out and exposed. Weak. She had vowed never to let anyone else make her feel that way again.

But then, just before she drifted off to sleep, Regina was forced to admit—even if only to herself—that something deep within her craved more. That part of her pulsed and yearned for pleasure and satisfaction.

For David.

CHAPTER 7

"Your bath is ready, ma'am."

Regina turned away from the window, where she stood staring listlessly out at the horizon. Her lady's maid hovered near the steaming tub. She'd been so lost in her disconcerting thoughts, she hadn't even noticed the footmen trailing in and out with buckets.

"Thank you, Mary," she replied, moving away from the window. "You may go."

The maid retreated, leaving Regina alone with the specter of David Graham. Despite knowing she would eventually have to mend the rift caused by her reaction to last night's events, she had spent most of her day trying to avoid the inevitable. That proved more difficult as the hours passed, making it impossible to think—let alone read, or reply to her correspondence, or lose herself in the mindless task of needle-point. Every time her mind began to wander, it settled on David and the bewildering encounter that had left her feeling wrung dry.

After shrugging out of her dressing gown, she paused to face the mirror pushed into a far corner of the room. The reflection that met her was a pitiful one, and Regina had to force herself to confront it. During their courtship, Randolph had often waxed poetic about her beauty, leading her to believe he found something worth lingering over when he looked at her. Over the subsequent eight years, her husband had done everything within his power to tear that assumption to shreds. If his derisive remarks about the way she dressed or the style of her hair hadn't been enough to destroy what little confidence she'd had in her own allure, then his many affairs would have done the trick. Regina had lain eyes on several of his lovers, seeing in them all the things she lacked. Hair that wasn't such a garish and eye-snaring color. Eyes that sparkled with promise and the kind of joy Regina hadn't possessed since girlhood. Faces that weren't cursed with the smattering of unfashionable freckles.

Pressing a hand to her chest, she noted the collarbone that had begun to protrude too far after the first few years. Even her taste for food had been dimmed, and eating had become more about survival than enjoyment. Before she could lose her nerve, Regina pushed the chemise off her shoulders and let it fall to her feet. She had hardly ever allowed Randolph to see her nude, preferring to let him hitch up her nightgown and take what he wanted from her, keeping the fabric between them like a shield. Not that he had ever shown interest in doing anything other than penetrating her with his prick. Her gaze fell to the thatch of fiery curls between her thighs, and she shivered as she recalled David's intent gaze on that most secret of places.

Even in the dark she had registered the interest and curiosity in his eyes, as if the challenge of her body intrigued him in some way. Dare she allow herself to think there had been something else in those glittering blue depths? Desire, maybe? Need?

It was so odd, this idea that a man could look at her and want to do more than take and take until she had nothing left to give. She cupped a heavy breast with one hand, shame washing over her in a crushing tidal wave as she strummed her thumb over the nipple. Regina fought it back, determined to solve this mystery, to herself, as well as the man she had taken into her bed. A tingle of sensation flared where she touched herself, the nipple furling taut and protruding as if begging for more of that touch. Both nipples had felt like this last night when David was inside her, the tight buds rasping against her nightgown and begging for ... something. She gave the nipple a light pinch and sucked in a sharp breath at the resulting twinge that shot through her, striking deep in her belly and ending in a pulse between her legs.

What would it feel like to have that intense gaze stroking all over her bare skin, seeing her in a way no one ever had? Would he touch her the way she touched herself? Could she endure it if he did?

Regina turned away from the mirror and retreated to the bath. Resting her head on the lip of the tub, she closed her eyes. Her right nipple still tingled from the pinch of her fingers, and that feeling in her quim had yet to abate—like a shadow of what David had stoked within her last night.

Keeping her eyes shut tight, she spread her knees until they touched the sides of the tub. Embarrassment flooded her face and neck with heat, but she was alone, she was curious, and she had to know. Resting a hand on her belly, she took a deep breath and gathered what pitiful courage she possessed and allowed it to travel.

Her skin was smooth and soft beneath the water, a sharp juxtaposition to the abrasion of hairs at her groin. For a long while, she could only lie there with her palm cupping her mound, her breath coming in short rough spurts. Regina had never touched herself in any way that was not practical. If she wasn't in the bath, her hands never strayed to those womanly bits, the ones she'd come to realize could produce enjoyable sensations. She had learned everything she knew about inter-course from her mother and her husband, and neither had told her anything about *this*. The heat of her felt different than the warmth of the water, the tender flesh within her seam unlike the skin anywhere else on her body.

Finally, she began to explore, tracing the opening of her sheath and the delicate folds ... and then the tiny knot which created a burst of breathtaking sensation. She pressed the tip of her first finger against it, her belly clenching as the feeling became sharper. This was where David had touched her, where he had produced those limb-shaking tremors that rocked Regina to her core. The memory of him flooded her mind, and she mimicked the movements of his thumb, circling and pressing, learning herself. Her own touch was nothing like David's, but it was enough to awaken those secret parts of herself. It was enough to make her pinch her lips around a soft whimper of delighted shock. Her legs became restless beneath the water, and her quim pulsed and throbbed as if with its own heartbeat.

Had her body been capable of this all along? Had she simply suffered for lack of knowledge and the callousness of a husband who hadn't bothered to show her that copulation could be pleasurable for a woman?

Regina wrestled with sudden anger as she wondered whether Randolph had been different with his mistresses. Her husband had drawn women like bees to flowers, and Regina never understood how any of them could willingly offer him their bodies. She knew firsthand what it was like to be subjected to his attentions. But perhaps she hadn't been privy to the entire truth.

Releasing a frustrated huff, she withdrew her hand, leaving herself yearning and annoyed. Thoughts of Randolph had ruined the experience for her, making it difficult to hold fast to the memories that had prompted her explorations.

Regina took up a cake of soap and began scrubbing herself with rough, furious motions, jaw clenched so hard it ached. She had made herself into everything a wife should be—quiet and demure, modest and willing to please. It had not been enough. Lacking the patience to coax her into learning how to enjoy the marriage bed, Randolph had simply used her when no other woman was about, and then discarded her when he was finished.

By the time she finished washing and left the tub, Regina had worked herself into a state of determined resolution. Randolph's death had opened a world of possibility to her, and thus far she had thought only of her financial freedom and the opportunity to have the child she wanted. But, what if there could be more? What if she could take delight in the conception of her babe, as David suggested? The assertion seemed preposterous at the time, but it now filled her with hope.

Regina had no delusions about a happy future with a man who cared about her, or lasting love. But, if she could experience passion and pleasure, why shouldn't she seize that opportunity with both hands?

Wrapped in a length of toweling, she marched to her dressing room to select a gown and send for her maid. She had an apology, as well as another proposition to make. She needed to do both before she lost her nerve.

D AVID TRUDGED TOWARD HOME AS THE SUN BEGAN ITS DESCENT ON the horizon, limbs heavy with exhaustion. Never in twenty-eight years had he imagined he might labor alongside his tenants, even knowing he was set to inherit a massive farm and estate. He'd been raised knowing there were men a gentleman could hire to do the work, but desperate times called for desperate measures. Before and after his journey to London, he had spent a great deal of time in the company of Mr. Stone —who introduced him to several of the men who had worked for his father. Their advice led to his decision to slaughter half his herd of sheep. They hadn't enough feed in their stores to last them through winter, most of the enclosures were in shambles, and the sale of meat and wool would further fill his coffers and provide the money for other much-needed improvements.

Of course, since so many men were busy making important repairs on their homes, and others simply refused to labor until that work was done, they were short on manpower for the task. Stone's offer to teach him how to shear, slaughter, and butcher sheep had been made in jest, and David's reluctant agreement had taken the man by surprise. Never one to back down from a challenge, he threw himself into the task— and had become sick at the sight and odors of animal innards only twice.

He now returned home much the way he did every evening— sweating despite the cold, his shirt stained with blood and gore. He had washed at a water pump, so at least his hands, face, and neck were clean.

He supposed he ought to make quick work of cleaning himself up and taking a quick dinner if he wanted to arrive at Regina's home on time. David's mouth turned down at the thought of his client, who probably wouldn't be very happy to see him. Hell, he doubted anything had made that woman happy in a long time. As much as it disturbed David, it also annoyed him that he was left to navigate his way through her eccentricities in the dark.

He reminded himself for the umpteenth time that it wasn't his concern. If Regina wanted him to treat her like some inanimate object during their sessions, he should do so without complaint or second thought. Only, it simply wasn't in his nature. It *bothered* him to treat a woman that way, and he found it increasingly difficult to arouse himself to the task. Weary as he was tonight, David didn't know how he would manage it. But manage it he must, and the shabby state of the house he approached reminded him of that. When he came face to face with Regina tonight, he would apologize and carry on as she requested—no matter how much it disturbed him. Anything to keep her from tossing him aside and hiring another courtesan.

Resolved, he squared his shoulders to mount the front steps ... and drew up short.

A woman in black had just raised her fist to knock, and whirled at the sound of his footsteps, eyes wide in her alabaster face. David blinked, certain he was imagining things. But no, it was Regina, standing at his door looking lovely and frightened. Glancing over his shoulder, he realized he had walked right past her carriage and driver without noticing them.

Had she come to terminate their arrangement? His heart dropped at the thought. What would he do if she had?

"Hello, David," she murmured, tucking a loose strand of fiery hair back into her hat. "I stood here for a long while, too afraid to knock. I think I must have gone up and down those steps three times, and I ... well, your arrival certainly took the decision out of my hands."

Glancing down at his soiled garments, he then set disbelieving eyes back on Regina. "I had planned to come to you within the next hour. Is everything all right?"

Biting her lip, she backed away from the door as he approached. "I had hoped we could talk. If now is an inconvenient time, I can go home and await your arrival."

"No," he insisted, standing back to allow her entry. "You came all this way. Come in. I'll send for tea, and if you wouldn't mind giving me a little time to wash and change—"

He found Mrs. Moffat approaching, her smile stiff and uncertain as she eyed their visitor. "Welcome home, Mr. Graham. Can I get anything for you and your guest?"

"Tea would be wonderful, and a little something to eat. Please see to Mrs. Hurst's comfort until I return." He faced Regina, who remained in the middle of the dimly-lit entrance hall, curious eyes roaming what she could see of the house. He fought not to wince at the reek of tallow candles, used to light the house out of economy, and the pitiful state of the floors. Forcing a smile, he backed toward the staircase. "I'll return shortly."

Once out of sight, David set off at a run, curiosity and the need to keep his mother and sisters from discovering Regina propelling him along.

Fresh energy spurred his every step as he tore into his room, startling his valet. The man had anticipated his arrival and had hot water and fresh clothes waiting. David scrubbed himself from head to toe, until he no longer smelled like a butcher's shop.

When he returned downstairs, he noticed Mrs. Moffat lingering outside the drawing room, peering through a crack between the parted doors. At the sound of his cleared throat, she flinched and whirled to face him, a hand clapped over her mouth and guilt in her eyes.

David chuckled. "And just what are you doing, Mrs. Moffat?"

Lifting her chin, she sniffed. "Just wanted to lay eyes on the lady, is all."

"And? What do you think?"

"I'd begun to think she was a ghost, what with the way people speak of her and hardly anyone even knows what she looks like. Pretty little thing, even with that hair."

He wanted to argue that it was Regina's hair and those adorable freckles that made her so alluring. However, the last thing he needed was for Mrs. Moffat to go running to his mother, mentioning that David found their neighbor attractive. Especially since everyone in the county knew how wealthy she'd been made with the death of Mr. Hurst. His mother would begin talk of courtship and marriage once it was appropriate, and David didn't have the energy or patience to talk his way out of *that*.

"Please see that we are not disturbed."

Ignoring the raised eyebrows of Mrs. Moffat, David strode inside, quickly fastening the door behind him. Regina graced an overstuffed, high-backed armchair as if it were a throne, even though her feet just barely touched the floor. Her starched skirts were neatly arranged, her posture impeccable, her expression serene save for the uncertainty in her eyes as she looked up at him. She had taken off her hat, exposing the neat order of her titian hair, the stray coil kissing her cheek making him want to kiss that cheek himself.

Which was ridiculous. This woman had very clearly marked herself as one who did *not* wish to be kissed, or touched, or have someone grace her with a thorough and satisfying fuck. More was the pity.

"I hope I did not keep you waiting too long," he said, easing onto a loveseat near her chair. "I didn't think you would tolerate my presence with a day's worth of work making a mess of me."

Setting her teacup in its saucer, she gave him a bewildered look. "I don't know many gentlemen who set their hands to actual work."

"Yes, well, extenuating circumstances and all that. Why ask others to do what I will not?"

Her eyes narrowed just a tick, her gaze becoming more pensive as she set her cup aside and reached for a fresh one. "May I pour for you?"

Pleasantly surprised at the offer, he nodded, though it was the tower of cakes and biscuits that caught his eye. The fare was simple, but not so embarrassing as what might have been offered had Regina called a fortnight ago. To David they looked like manna from heaven. He hadn't eaten a thing since breakfast.

They exchanged banal remarks while she poured. David watched her all the while, intrigued by her graceful motions and the delicate movements of her slender hands. They were as pale and unblemished as the rest of her—or, at least the parts of her he'd been allowed to see —a sharp juxtaposition to her stark black attire. Her cheeks were pink, and David wondered if she might be too embarrassed to broach the subject hanging between them. While he piled a handful of biscuits in his saucer and took his first sip of tea, she began to chatter about the drive here, and how glad she was for a break in the rain. David took that opportunity to devour three of the biscuits, which helped take the edge off his hunger. But then, he could take no more. If he didn't push them toward the matter at hand, he had a feeling they would sit here all night.

"Regina ... what are you doing here? While I would certainly never turn you away, I'm sure you understand how your visit might be perceived while we are both in mourning. As well, the more ignorant we keep people to our association, the better for the sake of your reputation. But, I do not think I need to tell you that. Which makes me think you came all this way for a reason, not just to gawk at me while sipping tea."

The pink blossoms in her cheeks deepened to red and she stared down at her hands. "In truth, I wasn't certain you would come tonight. I owe you an apology, David."

He sat up straighter, the tea and biscuits forgotten. "Actually, I think I am the one who should apologize. You were very clear—"

"But I was not. I confess, I told myself we could get through this arrangement without such a conversation, but you aren't what I first made of you. I think I rather misjudged you."

She could not have shocked him more had she flung her tea in his face. Clearing his throat, David set his cup aside and leaned forward, holding her gaze. She held herself as she always did, with rigid, cold poise. But her eyes always gave her away. Just now she seemed to battle fear and anxiety, but there was something else. The glimmer of determination. Whatever she wanted to tell him required a great deal of fortitude on her part.

"I told you when we met that my job as your courtesan can be multi-faceted. If you need to confide something in me, you should feel free to do so. Your secrets are safe with me, Regina. *You* are safe with me."

A small smile edged her lips, then vanished. "I know that. At least, I do now. All my precautions were born of a fear that you might take advantage of my vulnerability. They were also born of experience. You see, my marriage to Mr. Hurst was not a happy one."

"I gathered as much. I am sorry to hear it."

She gave a slow shake of her head, eyes becoming unfocused as she stared across the room. Clenching her shaking hands in her lap, she took a deep, slow breath before replying. "I did not know him well before we married, but thought I had learned all I needed to know. He was handsome, well loved by his peers, charming. My parents were in favor of the match, my father in particular. He was very wealthy, you see, and our circumstances were dire. I was to be the salvation of our family, but I didn't mind so much if Randolph was to be my husband. On the day he proposed marriage, he told me he loved me. I was young and had little experience with men. I believed him."

David tried to imagine her as she might have been, that sweet rosebud mouth of hers more prone to smiles than frowns, the green of her eyes glittering with hope and life. Something within him reacted to the image with soul-stirring force, as he realized she was still quite young. Too young to be such a solemn, lonely creature.

"The night before the wedding, my mother came to me to explain how things should occur between husbands and wives in the bedchamber," she went on, twisting and pulling at her fingers and avoiding his gaze. "A wife should obey and seek to please her husband, and never turn him away when he asks to be allowed his rightful attentions. It would be a very unpleasant task, but such was the price a woman must pay for the security of someone to care for her. If I wanted it to be over quickly, I must lie perfectly still and let him do as he pleased. This would make him happy, and all the better if I bore him a son as soon as possible. It would hurt the first time, but would become less painful eventually. She terrified me, but I told myself it would not be that way with Randolph. He had been so kind, and even kissed me a time or two. He was always gentle, so of course our wedding night wouldn't be so horrifying as Mother had made it out to be."

David swallowed, but couldn't wash his mouth free of the bitter taste of foreboding. He knew where her story was going, and the realization made him cold with dread.

"Our wedding was small and simple, the breakfast attended by our families and closest friends. I spent the day both nervous and excited about what would happen when I was alone with him, though my mother's words were never far from my mind. When the time came, I ..."

"You do not have to do this," he insisted. "Regina, you don't have to tell me if you cannot bear to speak of it. I think I understand it well enough."

She blinked, and a lone tear fell, her chin trembling as she finally looked at him, going on as if he hadn't spoken. "He was *not* gentle or kind or patient. He became like a different man altogether. When I cried and told him it hurt, he insisted I would simply have to bear it. I was a virgin, it was supposed to hurt, and he had waited too long to have it ruined by my reticence. I tried my best to do as Mother told me, and lay very, very still, but it hurt too much. It seemed to go on forever, but could not have lasted more than a few minutes. Afterward, he told me it would get better and I would learn to enjoy it. I cried myself to sleep, alone. He'd gone back to his own bed."

"Selfish ass," David muttered under his breath, anger flooding his veins with heat. "A woman's first time doesn't have to be so miserable, Regina. He simply did not care to make it good for you."

She sniffled, another stream of tears wetting her cheeks. "I had no idea, truly. I told myself it had been my fault. After all, Mother said I should lie still, and I hadn't done that. I vowed to do better next time, and perhaps try to find some joy in the act. But it never got any better. The pain was never like it was that first time, but it was always the same aside from that. He would come to me, tell me to lie down, and climb on top of me as if I were a brood mare. I came to dread his arrival in my bedchamber, and was relieved when he would depart Lancashire on business. So relieved, that I said nothing when I learned of a mistress here, an actress there, an affair with a widow. If he took his pleasure with those women, he would not need to come to my bed. But, when he was at home, he came to me often ... I think simply to remind me that he had the right. He knew I derived no satisfaction from the act. He didn't care."

David ran a hand over his face to smooth it of the rage tightening his features. For her to have trusted that bastard with her body and her heart, only for him to abuse them both ... it defied all decency. David might be considered a rake, and he had freely slung his cock about for the sake of a good time, but he never preyed on the innocent. He had never treated a woman as if she were nothing more than a vessel for his own use. What kind of man was gratified by a bedmate who wasn't enjoying herself?

"I understand," he said, once certain he was calm enough to respond. "It cannot have been easy for you to let another man near you after eight years of that. And there hasn't been anyone since to show you that it isn't supposed to be that way."

"I haven't wanted that... until you. Even the consideration you took to make sure I was ... that I was ready to receive you was more than Randolph ever gave me."

Amusement curved the corners of his mouth over the way she had blushed at the mention of 'receiving' him. Married eight years, and the woman was as innocent as a maiden.

"Tolerable shouldn't be the best you hope for," he said, reaching out to rest his hand atop hers. "You deserve more. You deserve pleasure and comfort, and to feel safe."

"I think I can feel safe with you. Last night, I was so overwrought because I could not understand how you managed to push past my disgust and make me feel something else. I thought there was something wrong with me, and perhaps that was why Randolph took lovers."

Regina didn't resist when he urged her onto the loveseat beside him, though she was still quite stiff. Refusing to be daunted, David kept hold of her hands, making it clear he wouldn't touch her anywhere else unless she asked him to. He now better understood her requirements, as well as her standoffish reticence. Of course she hadn't trusted him. He was a man, just like the one who had betrayed her trust and hurt her. She had every reason to be wary of him.

"There is nothing wrong with you. I daresay there was something wrong with *him*. I cannot enjoy myself if the woman in bed with me isn't having the time of her life."

She furrowed her brow as if he had just spoken Ancient Greek. "Does that not take away from your own ... exertions?"

The honest guilelessness in her question made him chuckle. Draping one arm along the back of the couch, he kept his other hand entwined with hers and leaned in close—just enough that he registered that clean, slightly-floral scent of hers with every inhale. She didn't move, eyes wide as she stared at him.

"It *enhances* my exertions, as you called them. You see, I simply refuse to sink my cock into a woman until she's begging for it, until she cannot stand to wait a moment longer. Until I have found all the places on her body that make her moan when I put my lips on them. Until I have learned the feel of her, the scent of her, the taste of her. Until she's panting and writhing and pleading with me to take her. And it does please me, Regina. It pleases me to see her trembling and clutching the bedsheets, to feel her grow so wet and hot just from the touch of my lips and the stroke of my tongue."

Regina sucked in a sharp breath, a shiver tearing through her as her eyes went heavy-lidded. "Oh ..."

"I don't take my own pleasure until yours has been achieved. It is a rule I lived by even before I became a courtesan, and it's one I take very seriously. I understand your reasons for this arrangement are practical, but that doesn't mean it cannot also be enjoyable. You have endured a great deal, and were so brave to reach out to take what you wanted for yourself. Why not allow the making of your child to be an unforgettable experience?"

She flushed to the roots of her hair, though her lips twisted in a wry smile. "I stand by my earlier assessment. You are very arrogant."

David grinned. "Let me prove to you why my arrogance is well earned."

Her voice was low when she replied, but David hung on her every word. "It will not be easy, but I would like to try. I do not think I could bear it with anyone else, but you've tempted me enough to try to lower my guard. Will you be patient with me?"

"Haven't I been thus far?"

That made her laugh, but the sound was raspy and hoarse, as if she hadn't used it in a long time. "I suppose you have, and I thank you for it. It never occurred to me that my stipulations might be distasteful to you. I honestly assumed you would prefer it that way."

"Now you know better."

Her lips parted on a breathy sigh, and David felt as if all the air had been squeezed from him. He was suddenly struck with the notion that he might find his next breath somewhere within the seam of that lovely, pouting mouth. He leaned in, compelled by forces beyond his own comprehension, beyond his own will. His hair brushed her forehead, the bridge of his nose slid along hers, and his eyes remained riveted upon hers, unblinking.

"Wh-what are you doing?"

"Kissing you. At least, that's what I'd like to be doing."

"But we aren't going to ... not here. Are we?"

David felt torn between amusement and exasperation that she thought of kissing as nothing more than a prelude to copulation. What the devil had been wrong with Randolph Hurst?

"No," he replied. "And the first lesson I'm going to teach you, my dear, is that very often kissing is done simply for the enjoyment of the act itself, not as a precursor to anything else."

"Oh," she said, as if his words were a sudden revelation. "I think that would be lovely."

David wasted no time. Her consent freed him to close the space between them and lightly brush his lips over hers. He was seized with so many urges that he shook with the willpower it took to keep from overwhelming her. The need to consume and bite and lick were pushed aside, his trembling hands gently cradling her face as David drank from her mouth in slow, tortuous sips. His efforts were rewarded as Regina eased into his hold by degrees, meeting each brush of his mouth with tentative presses of her own. He angled his head to go deeper, opening his mouth to taste her plump lower lip. She whimpered against his mouth, inching closer on the loveseat and offering him more, her head tilting back in the brace of his hands. Only then did he dare to run his tongue along the curve of her upper lip, delving in so slowly and carefully. Regina gasped into his mouth but did not retreat. Her hands rested over David's and she clung to him, tentatively pushing her tongue against his.

The gentle innocence in the gesture had his blood firing hot in his veins and rushing straight to his cock. A sound of pure, raw need flowed from his mouth and into hers, originating from somewhere deep in his chest. Intense hunger clawed at him from within, as if that first taste had set off something instinctive.

"Open for me, Regina ... yes, just like that."

She parted her lips wider, her fingers tightening around his as he pushed his tongue deeper, feeding off the sweet taste of her. The velvety rasp of her tongue meeting him, playing with him, learning how to do it right, made the tension in his groin nearly unbearable. The way she trembled in his hold, the soft sounds she made without realizing it, the subtle arch of her back ... all of it tore him to pieces and exacerbated his desperation. If they were in her home instead of his, he'd likely have Regina on her back by now, well on his way to discovering if the rest of her tasted as good as her mouth.

David pulled away before he lost control, and not just because they could be caught by his mother or sisters. He would never allow himself to forget that he couldn't simply pounce on Regina the way other women paid him to in the past. She required slow and gentle handling, and for him to keep his own desires tightly leashed—at least for the time being.

"How sweet you are," he murmured, punctuating his statement with one final, short kiss.

Regina whimpered and chased his lips, prompting a chuckle from David. He doubted she realized what she had just done, or how she looked just now—lips swollen and slick, eyelids heavy, cheeks flushed. That stray strand of hair rested against her cheek, a flame-red coil of temptation. He'd never witnessed a more delectable sight in his life.

"I ... um ... thank you."

It seemed like the most natural thing in the world to plant another kiss, this one on the tip of her adorable nose. "Don't thank me yet. There is so much more for me to teach you."

"Tomorrow night," she said. "By the time we returned to my home the hour would already be quite late and I have taken up much of your time this evening. You must be in dire need of dinner and rest."

David wanted to argue that he was more than up to the task, but his belly and his aching head told him otherwise. A night of respite would better prepare him for her. "Tomorrow night it is."

Regina's lips twitched with a small smile. "If that kiss was any indication of what I can expect, consider me already intrigued."

She collected her hat on the way to the door, and David walked her to her waiting carriage. The driver had lit the lamps, illuminating them in a circle of yellow light.

"Thank you for listening," she said. "I was terrified to face you, and you somehow made our conversation bearable. I am grateful, David."

"There is no need to thank me. Remember what I said. It is no more than you deserve."

She allowed him to hand her up into the vehicle, peering down at him with one of her soft, rare smiles. "Good night. Until tomorrow."

"Good night."

David backed away and watched the carriage depart, though he lingered for a long while once it was out of sight. His earlier hunger, exhaustion, and irritation had been forgotten and now there was only anticipation. Tomorrow night couldn't come fast enough to suit him.

Turning back to the house, David looked forward to a warm meal and his bed. It wasn't until he made it halfway up the stairs that he realized Regina had come to him without the hulking shadow of Powell looming at her back.

CHAPTER 8

Regina was certain if she paced much longer she would wear a hole in the rug. Anticipation of David's arrival made her flinch at every sound, her pulse swift and unsteady. Powell had been instructed to see David to her door, then take himself elsewhere for the night. The footman's presence was no longer needed, as her courtesan had gone out of his way to prove she had no reason to fear him. Besides, she'd been mortified enough at the things Powell had overheard the last time. If David's touch between her legs for a few minutes was enough to have her cries echoing from the walls, there was no telling what reaction he might elicit once she gave him permission to do more.

The footman hadn't been content to leave her alone with David unless she agreed to accept his knife, which he had slid into a tear he created in the side of the mattress. Once Regina had demonstrated that she could quickly retrieve it if need be, Powell had agreed to her request for privacy.

Goose bumps prickled along Regina's arms as her gaze wandered to her neatly-made bed, and she imagined what might take place there in a few short minutes. Truly, her imagination was sorely lacking, but it was Regina's hope to see that change by the end of the night.

Clutching at the folds of her nightgown, she took a peek at her reflection in the mirror. In an effort to stop avoiding her reflection, she had given it a more prominent place in the bedchamber. Was her effort at tempting David to desire too gauche? She hoped he would not think her pathetic, but after the weeks he had spent with a cold, rigid version of her, Regina hoped to make amends. Reason told her it shouldn't matter. She was paying him, and that meant he was required to do as she asked and nothing more. But some secret part of her longed to know what he would think of the way her hair hung loose down her back, a startling splash against the gossamer white gown draping her body. The design of the nightgown was simple enough, but it was the sheer fabric that made it decidedly sinful. The pink shadows of her nipples were visible, as well as the red triangle of curls between her legs. The firelight shined clear through the fabric, outlining the flare of her hips and shape of her legs.

She turned away from the reflection, debating the matter of changing into one of her demurer gowns. This one had been part of her wedding trousseau, though Randolph never laid eyes on it. Nor had he ever seen the other delicate garments meant to entice a husband to lust.

Running a hand over the costly, thin material, Regina smiled. She would keep it on, and perhaps she could wear some of the others on the nights David came to visit. After all, she had stepped into a new phase of her life—one in which she experienced all the things she had been deprived of. Randolph would surely have disapproved of her in the scandalous garment, much as he had detested gowns he claimed had indecently low necklines or skirts that were too thin. But David ... perhaps he might find her alluring. Maybe he would even think her beautiful.

Her heart stuttered at the sound of a knock on the door, and she had to take a deep breath before calling out in a high, breathless voice. "Come in."

Thankfully, Powell didn't so much as peek into the room, the heavy tread of his departing footsteps indicating that she was completely alone with the man standing on the threshold. For the first time, Regina had lit every lamp and taper in the room, flooding it with golden light. And, oh, how that light loved David. It seemed to arc and strain to reach him, its facets gleaming off the black of his hair and highlighting the classical perfection of his features.

He paused halfway across the room as the light revealed her state of undress. His lips parted on a rushed exhale, fingers twitching at his sides as his gaze traveled over her from head to toe. Regina could not move, or so much as draw a single breath as she waited for him to speak, to act, to do *something* other than stand there and stare at her.

"My God," he murmured, his gaze snapping up to tangle with hers. "And here I was under the impression that *I* had come here to seduce *you*."

Her lips split in a smile she was helpless to stifle. "You ... like it?"

David started toward her, running a hand over his jaw. "If I liked it anymore, I might not survive it. Consider me thoroughly captivated."

Her legs began to shake as he neared, that enticing scent of sandalwood emanating from him as if he'd washed and shaved just before coming to her. There was something savage in his eyes that shook Regina to her core; something that inspired both fear and intrigue in her at once. The fear was calmed as she realized he was in complete control. His eyes spoke of conquering lust, but his every motion was slow and careful, calculated.

David cupped her face in his hands. Their bodies did not touch, yet a palpable energy thrummed in the space between them, making Regina feel as if invisible hands touched her everywhere.

"Before we begin, I need you to understand that you can tell me to stop at any time. There is no point of no return here. Comfort first, pleasure second. Agreed?"

"Agreed," she whispered, overwhelmed by the security his words provided. It went a long way toward easing the anxiety twisting and writhing in her belly like a nest of snakes. It also rendered Powell's knife an unnecessary safeguard.

His lips brushed the bridge of her nose, then pressed to her brow. "Will you go to the bed?"

A sudden memory stabbed through her mind—Randolph standing in this same room, face hard and unsympathetic. *Go to the bed.* A command, not a request. David's question put the control in her hands, giving her permission to accept or deny. What a novel concept.

"Yes."

Her voice had come out stronger that time, and her steps were sure as they guided her toward the place where she would begin to erase the trauma of her past. Regina had been deflowered in this bed. The sheets had been stained by both her blood and her tears. Tonight, she was determined for all of that to be washed away.

Perching on the edge of the mattress, she watched him shrug out of his coat and lay it in its usual place. Then, he was coming toward her, one hand braced at the top button of his waistcoat.

"Should I stop here ... or keep going?"

Regina dragged her gaze over the width and breadth of him, seized yet again with curiosity over how he was shaped beneath those clothes. She wanted to see it all.

"Please ... keep going."

David flicked the buttons loose without breaking eye contact, letting the garment hang open while he snatched at his cravat. The waistcoat fell to the floor and then he was moving faster, jerking the tails of his shirt free of his breeches and attacking the buttons. Regina's breath hitched at the sight of his throat—a strong, thick column of flesh revealing the thump of his pulse.

She could only watch in stunned silence as the garment came off over his head, her rapt attention fixed on the expanse of his torso as he bared it to her. A thick mat of black hair covered the swells of his chest, arrowing down into his breeches in a sleek line. He represented a duality of hard and soft, strength and gentle beauty. The contrast left her breathless and weak. No wonder he'd needed her to sit down before he started taking his clothes off. Had all his past lovers felt as if they might faint from simply looking at him?

He crouched to yank off one boot, then the other, and his stockings followed. Before he could go to work on his breeches, Regina reached out a tentative hand.

"Wait. Let me?"

One dark eyebrow winged up in pleased surprise. "Of course."

She stilled her shaking hands to work at the buttons. The first proved hardest to slip free, but she grew steadier with each one, until the breeches sagged around his hips and the fall dropped to reveal his cock. Seeing it with her own eyes was a different experience than feeling it inside her. He took her breath away, straining and swelling as if in reaction to her stare. He bent to release the buttons at his knees, then helped her ease them down. The sight of him completely unclothed took her breath away, so beautiful that it almost hurt to look at him. It didn't seem natural for someone to be so utterly perfect, but Regina's roaming eyes couldn't find a single physical flaw.

The deep olive coloring of his face and hands extended everywhere, proving that the hue was one he had been born with, not caused by time spent in this sun. He remained still and silent as if understanding her need to look her fill, everything about him radiating ease except for the growing shaft of his cock.

He looked as if he'd been carved of marble, yet there was nothing cold about him. He gave off a heat she found enthralling, making her want to place her hand against his chest. More of the inky black hair graced his arms and legs, the plane of his groin. Regina had been repulsed by everything about her husband, and because of that she could not fathom the way David's nudity made her feel. On a basic level, the two men had all the same parts, the same anatomical structure. But David wasn't just a bundle of parts sewn together to make a man. He was almost godlike in his beauty, yet his actions toward her—his patience, gentleness, and grace—balanced him out with a much-needed dose of humanity.

The sudden movement of his hands snapped Regina out of her stupor. They came to her shoulders, running down the length of her arms in a soothing gesture. She hadn't realized how tense she was until that touch suffused through her, allowing her to draw steady breaths. David stared at the powder blue ribbon threaded through the eyelets between her breasts, ending in a bow at the base of her throat.

"May I?"

He hooked his finger in one of the loops of the bow, but didn't so much as tug until she had nodded to grant her permission. The gown loosened, David's deft motions revealing her sternum inch by inch. His fingertips whispered over her skin as he pushed the gown down her arms to pool at her waist. The rise and fall of his chest quickened as he locked eyes on her bared breasts, making her nipples pucker as if begging for his touch. He urged her to her feet, sinking to one knee with his hands wrapped in the flimsy fabric of her gown. It slid along her hips and legs as he eased it down, gazing up at her from beneath his lashes. Regina held deathly still as he ran his hands lightly over her calves and thighs, pausing to cradle her hips.

His dark head lowered, and he rested against her leg with a heavy sigh. "You are so beautiful. Have you any idea?"

The earnestness in his voice stirred her, leaving her with no doubt that he spoke the truth. How could she do anything other than meet him with the same honesty?

"No," she whispered, squeezing her eyes shut. "I've never felt beautiful. My hair is unfashionable, I have freckles, my body—"

"Is perfect," he murmured against her skin, his breath warm and teasing. "Your hair is perfect, your freckles are perfect. Never let anyone make you feel as if they aren't. You *are* beautiful, Regina. If it's the last thing I do, I will make you believe it."

Regina lacked the words to respond, because then he was lifting her foot and bracing it on his thigh, his lips pressing to the inside of her knee. It struck her as a decidedly odd place for him to kiss her, until his mouth began to move. Her mind quieted, her head falling back and her eyes sliding closed as he skimmed his lips along the inside of her thigh, leaving a trail of foreign, tingling sensation. Regina leaned against the bed for purchase as he kissed his way up, up—until his mouth rested right over the core of her. She panted, head spinning as he planted a short kiss right against her mons, his breaths tickling through her curls. Then, heat and wetness flared at her lower belly, the hot, rough stroke of his tongue around her navel forcing a shocked cry from her lips.

Dear God, he was kissing her in places she never knew possessed such sensitive nerve endings. She jolted and quaked with each press of his mouth, each sweep of his searching tongue, her back arching as he worked his way up her body. Her leg wrapped around his hip as he inched upward, gliding his tongue up the center of her abdomen and along her breastbone in one long, hot drag. His hands braced her back just before she collapsed, as if he had expected her reaction to the befuddling things he was doing. It was all so unexpected that Regina could only go limp in his arms and try to anticipate what might be next.

His wicked tongue stroked at her pulse now, lapping and swirling as if he'd found some sweet delicacy there and wanted to savor it. She whimpered and clung to him, fingers wrapping around biceps that bulged and hummed with barely-contained power. Yet, despite such hardness his hands at her back were so tender, the press of his body against hers light and yielding, as if to show her that she could part from him at any moment. He lit a trail of fire along her neck, then his teeth nipped the line of her jaw, and she nearly swooned.

What sorcery was this? The man had battered his way through her defenses already, and he wasn't even inside her yet, had barely touched any of her most intimate places. It was coming, she could feel it in the slow, excruciating build of his kisses, growing more wicked by the second as he found a tender hollow behind her ear. She would never again be able to dab perfume there without thinking of his tongue, his breath teasing her toward this state of squirming, desperate arousal. He bent her back to lie on the bed with her legs dangling over the side, hands tangling in her hair as he aimed his mouth at hers. She met him with a desperate moan, lips already parted to accept the invasion of his tongue.

This kiss wasn't like the sweet one they had shared last night, navigated with caution. This was wrought fiery with need on both their parts, and Regina pushed her tongue against his with artless fervor. Her senses were so starved for taste and touch, she would have done anything—allowed him to do anything to her—to feed such ravenous desire. It was as if another person had inhabited her body; or perhaps, this was who she'd been all along. The part of her that had nearly been smothered to death by her vicious husband was emerging, tasting light and air and freedom for the first time ... and it liked what David was doing to her very, very much.

"You see?" he mumbled between light, playful nibbles at her lower lip. "I told you there was nothing wrong with you. You're coming alive in my hands. Open your eyes and look ... watch me ..."

Regina forced her heavy eyelids up just in time to see his dark olive hand cupping the pale curve of her breast. She gasped when he circled his thumb over her nipple, a shockwave rippling through her. He palmed the other, gently kneading and lifting them, eyes flashing up at her with swirls of blue fire as he parted his lips over one yearning nipple. The tip of his tongue flicked at the pink bud, making it tingle and tighten to a painful point. He did it again, the lick swift and soft, but somehow melting her limbs. She shuddered as he went on lapping at her, his tongue strokes growing stronger. He circled the edge of her areola, then closed his mouth over it, making Regina writhe and twist beneath him as the pleasure almost became too much to bear. He sucked at her with increasing force, each pull of his lips darting sensation straight between her legs.

It made no sense. He wasn't even touching her there, yet that bundle of nerves between her lower lips pulsed and throbbed as if he did. The sensation grew more unbearable as he moved his attentions to her other breast. There was no easing her in as he had with the first nipple. He attacked, moaning around the taut bud. His thumb and forefinger played with the other, leaving Regina feeling as if she were being pulled taut between two very different worlds—one in which his strong, nimble fingers twisted and pinched, and another in which the wet heat of his mouth drove her wild. The pulsing between her legs grew stronger, telltale flutters hinting at a release hanging just out of her reach.

"David," she whispered hoarsely, shock rippling through her as she realized what was happening. "David?"

His only response was an incomprehensible murmur, deep and throaty and sending another flash of aching delight through her. Then, he pinched at her left nipple at the same moment his teeth clenched around the right, and she spiraled. Her thighs clenched tight and her back arched, and the little spasms grew in strength, producing a flood of heat and wetness from deep in her core. Regina tried and failed to muffle her stunned exclamations as he teased her until she broke apart, going limp and breathless beneath him. David's gaze never left her, even as he released her nipple from his mouth, wet and red and glistening.

"Did I just ... but I couldn't have!" she managed, in startled disbelief.

He chuckled, pressing a featherlight kiss to the tip of her breast. "You did, and you will again before we are finished. I don't have to be inside you to make you come, my dear. You have been starved for this, aching for it. It's no wonder you respond so beautifully to my touch."

She reached out to cup his jaw, awe widening her eyes. "More, please. I need more."

"Yes ... yes, you do."

David's mouth was traveling again, traversing the expanse of her belly, this time on a downward trajectory, his eyes still holding her captive. She trembled from the aftershocks of her orgasm, but used the last of her strength to prop herself up on her elbows. He wanted her to watch, and despite the niggling in the back of her mind telling Regina this was unseemly, she could not look away. She wanted to see him explore those parts of herself she had stroked in the bath, wanted to know what he was capable of.

A soft whimper of distress emitted from her as he spread her knees, going off the edge of the bed to crouch on the floor. The insides of her thighs were glistening, smeared with the evidence of her climax. She'd never been this wet, not even when he prepared her to take his cock. It was mortifying. It was hypnotizing.

"Christ," he growled. "So wet already."

His gaze was now rapt upon the juncture of her thighs and the thatch of red curls, his lips parting as he dipped his head.

"David ... what ..."

"I know what you're thinking," he purred. "Yes, I am going to taste you. No, it isn't decent. No, I don't give a damn if it isn't ... and you will not either."

Yet again he robbed her of words and breath when he darted his tongue at her, swirled it at her entrance and then thrust it inside.

"David!"

His lips were pressed against her, his teeth lightly rasping that yearning, pulsing bud at the heart of her. David's grip tightened on her thighs, spreading her scandalously wide, exposing every bit of her to his lascivious gaze and wicked mouth. His tongue reached into her, invading her with velvet wetness and foreign heat. She had never felt anything more sinfully decadent ... until he moved upward, licking along the delicate folds of her cunny. Then, as his tongue pressed against the swollen, throbbing nub, she experienced true ecstasy. This man wasn't a god or an angel; he was something far more sinful yet just as otherworldly. No heavenly being could ever be capable of something so lewd, so obscene. So perfect.

"The taste of you," he groaned between licks, depraved hunger wrapped around every word. "So delectable ... glorious ... God, Regina ..."

Her response came on a wild and wanton cry as he flattened his tongue against her, rubbing and abrading the tender bud with a precision that had her seeing stars in the periphery of her vision. In the midst of it all was David, using his fingers to spread her and expose the part of her he'd been teasing with his tongue. And then ... God, help her, he latched onto it with his lips and sucked. His cheeks hollowed and his tongue worked her with slow, tormenting circles, and Regina thought her soul might fly free of her body. He held a hand over her belly as if he knew—could sense her about to fall apart and be propelled straight up into the heavens.

David spoke to her without words, the sounds he made against her wet, tender flesh arousing as well as reassuring—letting her know she was safe to fall apart, that he would catch her when she fell. She couldn't keep her eyes open any longer, nor could she quiet the sounds of bliss spilling from her parted lips as her womb seized and twisted, her inner channel clenching and rippling with waves of explosive pleasure. Her hands clawed for purchase, landing on his head, tangling in his hair and holding fast as her entire world splintered like shards of broken glass. Her first climax was a mere shadow, eclipsed by the magnificence of this one. It tore through her with the force of a raging storm, stiffening her limbs until they ached, and curling her toes.

The sudden plunge of two fingers inside her intensified the flagging orgasms with fresh waves of renewed exhilaration. He shot to his feet and leaned over her, his fingers thrusting in a swift, steady rhythm as his mouth fastened over hers. She squeezed and clenched around his invasion, and shared in the surprising taste of her own essence lingering on his lips and tongue. She should be ashamed, embarrassed by her wantonness. Instead she felt liberated and set free, at one with him and herself, with the feel of his fingers pressing against some elusive part of her and the slick, piquant flavor of her own juices.

David licked and sucked on her lips as if chasing the dregs of her. A twist of his fingers had Regina spiraling again, clawing at him like a madwoman as yet another climax seized her in its grip.

Regina's world went dark and she sank, going limp and weak beneath him. She faintly registered the soft kisses David pressed against her mouth, her cheek, her ear. His murmured words came at her as if through water, comforting and compassionate—telling her how lovely she was, how much he wanted her, that she was safe with him.

"David." Her voice cracked on the utterance of his name, and she realized for the first time that she'd begun to weep. "David."

Soft fingers banished the tears from her cheeks, tracked affectionately along her face, stroked her hair. "It's all right. Whatever you feel right now ... don't hold it back. I'm here. Let yourself go."

The need for closeness overwhelmed her in an unforeseen rush, and Regina wrapped her arms around him, burrowing her face in his neck. His scent was tangled with hers now, a harmonious duet of sandalwood and flowers, masculine musk and feminine arousal. She registered the heavy weight of his cock against her thigh, a steady pulse thrumming insistently through it.

"Don't stop," she whispered, nuzzling into the soft, springy hairs of his chest. "I want the rest. I need to know how it should be. I need you."

"Yes," he groaned, easing a hand between them to take hold of his cock. "Yes, Regina."

She felt no trepidation at the press of him at her opening, no fear or revulsion. There was only a deep hunger for the unknown. Years of neglect and ignorance had left a deep and visceral longing that must be satisfied.

He filled her with ease, guided by the wetness and eagerness of her body. His forehead fell against hers, their panted breaths tangling together as he slowly withdrew and plunged. She was full and aching, pulsing with a renewed need that demanded more friction, more pressure, more of *him*.

She braced her feet on the bed and arched into him, producing a rough moan from David, who stared down at her with heavy-lidded, unfocused eyes.

"More," she begged, not fully understanding what she was asking for, but needing it all the same.

David knew. He cupped her buttocks and held her up, his next stroke coming with more force behind it. The impact of his pelvis against hers radiated through her entire being.

"Yes?" he rasped, going still and waiting.

"Yes ... yes ..."

Skin slapped against skin, the heated drag of his cock against her inner walls driving her eyes up into her head. Each stroke came faster and faster, until he drove into her so swift and hard, she could barely draw breath between the battering thrusts of his hips. She reached up to take hold of the counterpane, though it offered her no purchase. Her body rocked against the mattress, a slave to his primal cadence, his wicked whims.

He had given her control, but now wrestled it back, taking her, branding her in a way she knew to be irrevocable. For the rest of her life, Regina could never forget this moment, when she no longer cared who was in control or what rules were being followed, or whether she was doing the right thing or the wrong thing. There was only this, only them, coming together in a joining of flesh and a something that went deeper than her understanding.

David trembled, his rhythm becoming less precise. "Come with me. Touch yourself ... take your pleasure."

He gritted his teeth as if in agony, and he seemed to fight the urge to chase his own gratification. He wanted her to have hers first, just as he had promised.

Without second thought, she slid a hand between them, pressing tentative fingers against hot, slick flesh. Sensation exploded at the point of contact, heightening the pleasure of him inside her.

"Just like that," he rasped, his stare fixated on where they were joined, where she stroked herself just the way she had in the tub. "Oh, my God … yes … that's it …"

She felt herself unraveling again and feared she wouldn't survive it, yet nothing would stop her from pressing and circling herself. The sight of it seemed to have enraptured David, which in turn fed fuel to her own desires. He looked as if he had never seen anything more riveting than the press of her fingers between her legs.

They tangled together, flying high and crashing simultaneously, David's hips jerking and his cock pulsing inside her. The hot flood of his seed bathed her insides, and his cries echoed from the walls, husky and hoarse. His eyes remained open and fixed on her through it all, glimmering with an amalgamation of truths she could not avoid.

She was desired. She was wanted.

She was, in the eyes of the most captivating man she had ever laid eyes on, beautiful.

And as he collapsed atop her, gathering her close with his body still connected to hers, Regina was undone.

CHAPTER 9

"It has occurred to me that there are still a number of ways in which you have been squandering the talents of your courtesan," David murmured.

Regina glanced at him over her shoulder, a brush held over a lock of mussed hair. He lay in repose beneath her counterpane, still nude and in no hurry to leave. If she had asked him to, he doubted he would have the strength. His legs were boneless, his eyes heavy-lidded with drowsy satisfaction. She had left the bed minutes ago, stumbling on unsteady legs behind her privacy screen—where David assumed she had cleaned herself. Reappearing dressed in a prim nightgown buttoned to the throat, she had then seated herself at her vanity and attempted to set her hair to rights.

"Is that so?" she asked, the corner of her mouth twitching with amusement.

Stretching with a groan, he then clasped his hands behind his head and made himself more comfortable amongst her pillows. "Indeed. You see, most courtesans—myself in particular—are built for comfort as well as pleasure. If you were still in this bed with me, you might discover that for yourself. Observe the expanse of my chest, upon which you might find a most convenient pillow. Then there is the length of my arms, perfect for cradling you in a variety of soothing ways. But, alas ... you leave me here devoid of purpose to brush your hair. I am wounded, my dear."

Regina's shoulders quivered, but her pinched lips held any laughter at bay. David could see the humor dancing in her eyes even from this distance. Combined with the soft pink glow to her cheeks, she left him thoroughly enchanted. Even covered in that matronly nightgown of hers, she heated his blood, making him forget that barely a quarter of an hour had passed since he'd been inside her.

"Forgive me," she said, setting the hairbrush aside. "I have never had a courtesan before, as you well know."

Neither had she been treated properly by the only man to come before him, but that did not bear saying aloud. While it irked David to know she had gone so long without knowing true passion or affection, he was gratified to be the one to teach her.

"All will be forgiven if you get back in this bed with me. No, don't braid your hair. Leave it."

Regina came to her feet, her expression shy and uncertain as she slowly approached the bed. David never took his eyes off her, the brilliance of fire and candlelight putting the outline of her body on full display through thin white cambric. The brilliant splash of her unbound hair captivated him, and even the peek of bare feet and dainty toes were enough to tie him in knots. It was the most ridiculous thing. He had a healthy appreciation for women and always had. That was all this was.

Yet, as he turned back the coverlet to let her climb in beside him, David couldn't ignore the intensity of his attraction to this particular woman. It went beyond his usual, indiscriminate love of all things feminine. Perhaps it was merely the novelty of something new—something pure and bright and lovely in the midst of his life, which had become rather difficult as of late. He decided there was nothing wrong with enjoying it while it would last. After all, he'd made it his personal mission to ensure Regina had the time of her life while in his care. Why shouldn't he also benefit? There had been so little enjoyment in anything for him in a long while.

David wrestled with keeping a straight face as she propped herself up on the pillows beside him, hands folded over her abdomen, eyes fixed on the ceiling. She held herself as rigid as a slab of steel, fingers clenched so tight he doubted he could pry them apart if he tried. The poor thing was so out of her depth.

"Hmm," he murmured, slipping one arm beneath her shoulders and gently easing her toward him. "Not quite what I had in mind. A few minor adjustments, and ... yes, that's better."

He arranged her to lay on her side pressed against him, her arm slung across his middle. Regina's breath grew unsteady, but she didn't pull away. She eventually relaxed, letting David hitch one of her thighs up to drape his.

"Did I mention that a courtesan's hands have many uses which have nothing to do with intercourse? Allow me to demonstrate."

David sank his fingers into the mass of her hair, gently kneading her scalp. Regina made a sound that reminded him of a cat's purr, her heavy sigh tickling his bare chest.

"Oh ... well, that ... that's quite good."

He smiled. "It is my job to ensure you enjoy the full experience. How am I doing thus far?"

"Even with no basis for comparison, I have to admit to being impressed. It's a wonder some woman hasn't shackled you to her bed to keep you as her prisoner."

"Well, I *have* been shackled, but never for more than an hour or so."

Her head tipped back and the look she gave him was priceless in its astonishment. "Never tell me you actually enjoyed that."

A wicked grin spread across his face. "Would you like me to bring a set of irons for my next visit so you can see for yourself? Being completely at your mercy sounds rather appealing."

Her face pinked just before she burrowed back into his chest, seeming too embarrassed to look him in the eye. It was amazing, the transformation he had witnessed—from timid innocent, to greedy wanton and back again.

"Will you ever cease shocking me?" she murmured, one hand hovering tentatively over his chest.

David gave a little hum of approval when she finally laid her palm against him, fingers tangling in the dark tangle of curls. "Not if I can help it."

She fell silent for a little while, becoming bolder in her explorations, tracing his contours and sinews. David closed his eyes, content to let Regina have her fill of him in whatever way pleased her. He liked the feel of her hands on him, the soft breaths tickling his skin, the little sounds of contentment she made without noticing.

"It's intriguing," she murmured, running a fingertip down the center of his belly.

"What is?"

"Your skin. I thought you were so dark because of the sun, but ... you're the same color all over."

Opening one eye, he glanced down to find her swirling her fingers through the trail of hairs leading to his groin, and prayed she wouldn't stop on her downward path. His cock was already stirring at the mere suggestion.

"My mother is Greek," he replied. "My father went on his grand tour, lingered in Athens longer than he did anywhere else, and came home with a wife. Apparently, she needed convincing to leave her home and family to be with him. I inherited my coloring from her."

"And your eyes?"

"Another gift from her. She is an uncommonly lovely woman. My sisters are pretty, too, but they look more like Father did."

She sat up, staring down at him with her eyebrows drawn together. "You refer to him in the past tense."

"He died just a few weeks before I met you."

Her gaze swung to where his clothes lay in a heap on the floor. "You've been in mourning all this time. I had no idea."

He shrugged, absently toying with a ruffle of lace on her sleeve. "It isn't as easy to spot a man in mourning. My wardrobe did not require nearly as much adjustment as my mother's and sisters'."

"I'm so sorry. How awful for your poor mother. It sounds as if theirs was a love match?"

"It was. My family fell on hard times during the last years of his life, but even then they seemed happy with one another. I have done my best to care for her, but there are some things even I cannot make right. To have spent so much of her life with someone only to have him taken away ... I cannot pretend to know how much that must hurt."

Regina didn't respond right away, staring across the room as if deep in thought. When she did speak, her words came out on a low whisper.

"I do not know how that feels. Randolph's death came as a relief. I felt as if shackles had been struck from me when he took his last breath. I am sorry that your mother is in pain, but I am glad for her all the same. At least her marriage wasn't a prison. When her grief has lessened, she will be able to look back on their time together with fondness."

David wanted to offer some form of solace, but found himself at a loss. There was nothing he could say to erase what Regina had endured. Any words he spoke now would be hollow and without real meaning. The impotence of it left him feeling as if a heavy weight had dropped into his chest. It bothered him to see her standing in the remnants of destroyed dreams and have no notion of how to fix it.

"What of you?" she asked suddenly, meeting his gaze again. "I hope you don't mind me asking such a personal question."

"What's a simple question between us after what we just did?" he interjected.

"The hard times you mentioned ... I assume they are the reason you became a courtesan. Or, is it a matter of actually enjoying the profession?"

David urged her to resume her position lying against him. "I will not pretend not to enjoy it immensely. But, yes, the condition of the estate and the mismanagement of my father's steward are the main reason for my decision. I've spent the past three years sending money home to my family, thinking it was being put to good use. Unfortunately, the steward was a thief, and most of it has been lost. I may as well have dumped it all into a privy."

"That's despicable," she exclaimed, her sprite-like features hardening with fury. "You must have been so distraught."

"That would be putting it mildly. There was nothing for me to do but work to set it all right. It will take time, but the responsibility is mine, and not just for the sake of my own future. I have my sisters to consider, as well. They are both twenty-one years old—identical twins, by the way—and unwed. They will make a better match with dowries I cannot yet afford. But I will. There isn't a thing I wouldn't do to see them happily settled."

She reached up to push a heavy lock of hair back from his brow. "Including making a baby with a virtual stranger?"

He huffed a laugh and took hold of her hand to kiss her fingertips. "You aren't a stranger anymore. I know plenty enough about you by now. I know how you smell and how you taste. I know that your face flushes about five different shades of red depending upon whether you are angry, embarrassed, or aroused. I know you have a tiny little beauty spot in a place even you wouldn't be able to see without a mirror."

She sucked in a sharp breath and followed David's gaze downward, before her eyes snapped back up to meet his. "You cannot be serious."

He grinned. "Oh, but I am. Remind me to bring a hand mirror to bed next time so I can show it to you. Of course, after that I won't be able to resist putting my tongue there and ... I have quite forgotten what we were discussing."

"The fact that you are attempting to get a not-so-virtual stranger pregnant," she said with a giggle.

"Ah, yes. If you must know, it wasn't only the money that drove me to my decision. Honestly, I was set on refusing you, but then ..."

"Then?" she prodded, as he kissed her palm and then the inside of her wrist. The skin there was so translucent he could make out the tiny blue veins.

"I saw how desperately you wanted a child. Even before knowing what you had been through, I saw your pain and your loneliness. You made me want this for you, almost as badly as you seem to want it for yourself. Yes, I need the money you are paying me, and the bonus I stand to gain once you are with child is an added incentive. But I can honestly admit to being disturbed by the version of you I met on that first day. If becoming a mother will change that, how could I have refused?"

"I am glad it was you Mr. Lyons sent and not someone else. I don't think I could have endured the attentions of anyone different. I appreciate what you have done for me, even when I have already demanded so much."

"You know how I will reply to that, my dear," he replied with a grin.

She returned his smile, and the weight in his chest eased the slightest bit. This. This was how he could attempt to soothe what had been broken—by making her smile as much as he could. By making her feel worthy and beautiful and desired. How could any man do less with a woman like Regina in his care? It confounded understanding to know that Randolph Hurst had such a chance and chose instead to inflict pain and heartache.

"It is no more than I deserve," she recited.

"Precisely. Don't ever forget that."

"May I ask you another question?"

"Of course."

"Why haven't you married?"

Alarm prickled his skin as it always did whenever someone mentioned marriage. He wasn't necessarily opposed to the idea, but neither was he in a hurry to settle down and begin begetting heirs. The irony that the purpose of his presence in her bed was conception of a child was not lost on him, but these weren't ordinary circumstances. He would not technically become a father to Regina's babe.

"I'm sorry," she blurted when he didn't promptly respond. "I should not have asked."

"No, it's all right. The answer is complicated. Just now, I cannot think of marrying until I have the means to support a wife. I can barely keep myself and my family clothed and fed, let alone someone else."

"You could marry for money. I find it difficult to believe London isn't overrun with heiresses who would be happy to part with their fortunes to be able to call you their husband."

He wrinkled his nose in distaste. "I suppose the need of a fortune might be enough to tempt me to the altar. Don't think I have not considered it."

"And if money was not something to be considered? What then?"

"That was true when I was younger, and I still avoided the matrimonial trap. I think, for a long time I avoided marriage because I knew I wasn't ready to devote myself to one woman. It is hardly fair to expect someone to give herself to me, to be faithful, if I knew I could not do the same."

"Then you've … had many women? Even before becoming a courtesan?"

He did his best not to squirm under her scrutiny, feeling reluctant for the first time to give voice to his numerous conquests. "Yes."

"That explains quite a lot, actually."

"Does it?"

"One would have to assume there is a reason you know your way around a woman's body the way you do. Though, I do wonder what Randolph's excuse was for being such an abysmal lover. He had a new mistress every few months, and some actress or other waiting in the wings."

"Apparently practice did not make perfect in his case," he muttered drily. "As for me, I suppose you are right. You would have my first handful of lovers to thank for my expertise. Older, seasoned women know what they like and how to get it. They were also very patient teachers."

"I find myself wanting to thank these women for the gift that is you," she said with a playful smile.

David chuckled, pulling her tighter against him and inching her nightgown up her thighs. "It doesn't bother you to know? Most of my clients prefer to think I fell from the sky and they were the first woman I clapped eyes on."

She laughed, and David realized the more she did it, the richer the sound became. Her unused laugh was being finetuned, the harshness chipped away to produce the most pleasing sound.

"I prefer to understand the makings of a person. What business is it of mine how many lovers you've had? As long as you don't currently have another, there is no reason for me to be jealous."

She gasped when he inched his fingers up the inside of one thigh, her gown bunching around her waist to allow him access to the hollow between. Her gasp melted into a moan of surrender as he inched a finger into her.

"As far as I'm concerned, you're the only woman in the world right now," he murmured against her lips before taking them in a kiss. "Are you sore? I don't want to hurt you, but—"

She cut him off by returning his kiss, her lips demanding and eager. "I am a little sore, but I don't care. If you stop now I might be forced to do you bodily harm."

He joined his first finger with a second, pushing her onto her back and nudging her legs wider. "Then I must continue, mustn't I? As an act of self-preservation if nothing else."

"Oh, yes," she moaned, raising her hips as he slowly pumped his fingers in and out, his thumb pressing down on her clit. "Yes, please."

David wasted no time giving in to her demands, spending what was left of the night showing her a variety of ways in which a courtesan could be employed. He collapsed atop her just as the sun began its ascent with sweat slicking his forehead, replete and drowsy. Regina slept like the dead, a soft smile curving the corners of her lips.

David didn't see Regina again until after the New Year by mutual agreement. Understanding how difficult this time would be for his mother, he had wanted to remain at home. The holiday passed quietly, with far less cheer than usual. As they sat to their modest dinner, trading stilted remarks, shame had fallen heavy on David's shoulders. He had rarely bothered to visit over the past few years, finding it difficult to remain in the dispiriting environs of the crumbling family home. His selfishness had cost him valuable time with his father. It had also left him blind to the realities awaiting him. He deserved to inherit a crumbling pile of complications, problems, and debt. The quandary, of course, was that his mother and sisters certainly did *not* deserve to suffer such consequences.

He told himself that this was why he was so eager to return to Regina, a little over a week after their last encounter. Servicing her enabled him to care for his family, and he would have done anything to set matters right. However, following a day's work, David found himself whistling while washing and changing his clothes. His reflection showed a mouth curved into a knowing smile and a pair of eyes glittering with anticipation.

His most recent night with Regina was never far from his mind, and David had called up the memories with pitiful frequency in the time since. Whenever he let himself linger over it, his fingers itched to touch that smooth porcelain skin and his mouth watered for a taste of her. His cock stirred, as if eager to repeat the performance. While it was typical for him to revel in the novelty of a new arrangement, David couldn't avoid the obvious truth. This client was different, and so was his reaction to her.

However, lingering over such thoughts was dangerous. David had witnessed firsthand just how sticky such a situation could become when a courtesan fell prey to softer emotions. He toed a fine line between having affection for the woman in his care, and infatuation. If he had inched just a bit over that line ... well, surely it was not too late for him to retreat back into safe territory. Seeing her again and performing the physical duties stipulated in their contract would reaffirm everything. It would serve as a reminder that what they shared was born of a contract and his keeper's desire to experience pleasure for the first time in her life. There could not be more to it than that.

The ride to Regina's house seemed to take forever, during which he succumbed to an uncharacteristic anxiety. What if everything had changed during their time apart? Regina had proved from the beginning to be a complicated woman, one with hidden facets and depths. He had a feeling the revelations she had shared about her dead husband were only the tip of the iceberg when it came to her past. Not understanding the whole of it, David was left fumbling in the dark and worrying over his every move. She certainly seemed to enjoy his attentions—not just that first time, but the several others that had followed into the night. It was his hope that she wouldn't retreat back into herself again and shut him out. Considering her disconcerting notions concerning intimacy and intercourse, it should not surprise him to discover she might be wrestling with shame.

No matter. If she erected fresh defenses, David would simply dismantle them. He refused to go back to rutting on her in the dark while fully clothed, feeling sullied and wrong despite her insistence that it had been what she wanted. His mission to show her how enjoyable conception could be had not changed. His determination to earn the promised bonus was as strong as ever.

Those were the forces propelling him up her front steps as fast as his legs would carry him—not some desperate need to lay eyes on her after time apart. Because that would be ridiculous.

Powell greeted him at the door, his craggy face drawn and tight. "My mistress is in her chambers."

David halted on his way to the stairs, noting the edge of something uneasy in the footman's voice. It was their custom for the man to escort him straight to Regina's chambers without so much as a word. Only during the most recent visit had Powell left them to their own devices, on Regina's orders, David assumed. However, the man seemed reluctant to move from his place near the door. Hands clenched behind his back, he gave David a significant look—one that wasn't easily interpreted.

"What's wrong?" David asked, unable to suppress the alarm ringing through his words. "Is she all right?"

Powell's frown deepened. "Her maid informed me she isn't feeling well."

David was halfway up the stairs before the man finished, taking them two at a time at a near run. Worry spiked his heartbeat and his stomach churned as he contemplated all that could be wrong with her.

He knocked on Regina's door but did not wait for a response before throwing it open. The small lump of her body under a pile of bedclothes snared his attention, and as his eyes adjusted to the low light he detected the spill of Regina's unbound hair across the pillow.

"Mr. Graham, please," called a voice from the other side of the room. "She's resting ... you shouldn't—"

"It's all right," Regina's voice called out, muffled and small. "He can stay, and you may go."

The slight form of Regina's lady's maid left on silent feet without a look back. Now that he was in the room, his limbs had grown heavy and sluggish—which was odd, considering the urgency of the situation hadn't abated in the slightest. Regina was unmoving and silent as he drew closer, finally making out her face. She lay on her side, curled into herself. David sank onto the edge of the bed and touched her brow, relief stealing over him when he found her without fever.

"Regina, my dear, what's the matter? Are you ill?"

He was taken aback by the lone tear that streamed down her cheek as she gazed up at him. Her lips twisted in a wry half smile.

"No," she whispered. "I am not. Oh, it's so silly. I don't even know why I'm crying."

Sweeping the tear away with his fingers, he then tucked a lock of hair behind her ear. "I am certain you have good reason. If you are not sick, then it must be something else. Will you tell me what the matter is?"

She sniffled and eased up onto her elbow. "You will think me so foolish."

"I highly doubt that."

"My courses began this morning. I ... I am not with child."

Her voice had cracked on the words, a fresh wave of tears wetting her face and ripping a fissure along David's heart. His deep, powerful reaction to those words and her grief left him feeling turned inside out. Though, along with the sinking feeling of disappointment on her behalf was a quiet sense of relief. He could hardly untangle such conflicting emotions just now, and wasn't certain he wanted to.

Cupping her face, he forced a comforting smile. "I am so sorry. It's still early yet. We will simply resume trying again when you're ready."

"I knew it might be premature to get my hopes up, but I want it so badly."

"I understand. You are permitted to be disappointed."

Was he allowed to be glad she hadn't come up with child just yet? Even if it would put that hefty bonus in his hands, David was not ready for her to be done with him yet. The nights behind them notwithstanding, their last encounter had felt like the true first taste of what they could share. It had to end, as all his arrangements inevitably did, but it was too soon. There was still so much for him to teach her.

This isn't about her, some nefarious, inner voice argued. *If it were, you would want her pregnant as soon as possible, you selfish bastard.*

That voice sounded an awful lot like his own, making it difficult to ignore. Shaking it off, David told himself he wasn't selfish to want more time with her. He knew how desperate for affection and kindness Regina was. It was not wrong for him to want to be the one to give her those things.

"I'm so sorry you wasted the trip," she said. "I ought to have sent word for you not to come, but I thought you should know I'll be requiring your services a bit longer."

"I would not call the opportunity to see you a wasted trip," he argued, leaning down to begin prying off his boots. "I'll stay, if you like."

Dropping one boot to the floor, he glanced up to find Regina leveling a questioning look at him. "Why would you, if we cannot ... oh."

Her eyes went wide as he began working on his other boot. "Surely it hasn't been so long since we have seen one another that you've forgotten the many functions of a courtesan. You are upset, and I am here. Let me lie with you."

Regina returned his smile as he removed his coat and waistcoat. His cravat followed, landing on the pile of his discarded clothes. She turned down the coverlet for him, then turned to give him her back. Easing in behind her, David slid an arm around her waist and drew her into him. She shivered, likely in reaction to the lingering chill of the night still lingering on his clothes. But she was soft and sweet-smelling, and he sank against her to absorb her warmth. Burying his face in her hair, he closed his eyes and realized how tired he was. The prospect of bedding her had renewed his energy, but simply lying with her had pushed him in the opposite direction. He was now boneless and relaxed, lulled toward drowsiness by her nearness.

Laying a hand over her belly, he kissed the back of her neck. "It will happen."

Her hand came to rest over his and she sighed. "I hope so."

Not another word was spoken between them, but she seemed to require nothing more from him than his presence. It would seem he was just as content with her nearness, because he fell asleep in short order. He didn't awake until morning.

. . .

THE FOLLOWING AFTERNOON, DAVID RETURNED TO CALL ON HER. Typically, the first few days of Regina's courses proved the most miserable, forcing her to take to bed until the weakness and discomfort abated. Today, she felt marginally better and was eager for the nuisance of her monthly terror to end so she and David could pick up where they'd left off. Of course, her keenness had everything to do with a desire to have another taste of pleasure, as well as her need to resume trying to get pregnant. That was all.

If she told herself that enough, perhaps she would believe it. Regina's mind argued it was true, but when a footman entered the drawing room to inform her that David had arrived, her heart rebelled. It fluttered and flipped, a phenomenon that only grew once he appeared before her.

Setting aside her book, she stood. "David! What are you doing here?"

Her gaze slid to Powell, who rose from his place in the corner, his own tome set aside. He offered no comment, but his gaze was curious as he set it on David.

"I mean ... I wasn't expecting you today," she added with a sheepish smile.

He returned her smile, hat in his hands as he approached. "I finished my work early and thought to look in on you. Feeling better? Your coloring is good. You seem ... well."

Nodding, she braced a hand against her belly, noting that David's eyes followed the gesture. "I am, thank you. You needn't have come all this way, though I do appreciate your thoughtfulness."

David shifted from foot to foot, glancing to Powell. For the first time in a long while, Regina began to think of the footman's constant presence as intrusive. Her courtesan seemed to want to say more, but was reticent because they weren't alone.

When she raised her eyebrows in question, David gave his head a slight shake. "Right. I ... well, would you think it odd of me to confess that I wanted to see you for myself? I have worried about you all day."

Warmth sparked in Regina's chest at his words, and she closed the distance between them. She stood near enough to make out the lighter striations of blue at the center of his irises, to smell his enticing scent.

"That is very sweet of you."

He made an exaggerated grimace of shame. "Egad, woman, I do have a reputation to uphold, you know."

Regina giggled. "It is too late, you've revealed yourself already. I shall find it quite difficult to go on thinking of you as a debauched rake."

"I'll never be able to show my face in London again. The Society of Rakes will revoke my membership."

"Is there a such thing as a society of rakes?"

David shrugged. "I would not be surprised if there were. Now, if I discover them, I won't be allowed to join."

Her shoulders quivered with laughter she couldn't contain. Suddenly, the disappointment of her empty womb didn't seem quite so devastating, because it meant more of this—more time with her courtesan. She couldn't take David to bed for another day to two, yet found she did not want him to leave. He'd come all this way just to see to her welfare after all.

"You have just arrived around the time I typically take an afternoon walk. Would you care to join me?"

Surprise flickered in his gazed, but he quickly recovered. "Of course."

That settled, Regina sent for a hat and coat. Within minutes they were setting off with Powell trailing them from a substantial distance —far enough that he could see them but not overhear their conversation.

They conversed about nothing in particular at first, and Regina clung to his arm and enjoyed the pleasant weather. The air still held the chill of January, but a near-cloudless sky allowed the sun to shine down on them, stealing the cold's biting edge.

They took the footpath snaking over the picturesque grounds of the estate, before arriving at a tree she often sat under to read. David insisted they linger as their position gave them the best view of the manicured lawns and the distant garden.

She helped him out of his coat, and he laid it on the ground for her to sit on before lowering himself beside her. Powell wandered, remaining within sight but pointedly giving them his back.

Certain they wouldn't be seen by anyone else, she removed her bonnet and set it aside, tilting her face up toward the sunlight with a happy sigh.

"This place," David remarked after a while. "It's beautiful."

"I thought so, too, at first."

"Christ, you must think me such an idiot. I shouldn't have—"

"It's all right. I was going to say, I had forgotten that over time. I spent so much time hidden away inside. These past few months have been a revelation on many fronts. This place *is* beautiful, and it is mine." A sudden thought struck her, and she gave him a flirtatious smile. "And ... it is no more than I deserve."

David returned her smile and reached up to stroke a stray lock of hair back from her face. "Indeed, it is. But, let's talk about something else. Tell me something happy. A memory from before ... him."

Regina mimicked David's posture, encouraged by the casual way he leaned back on his elbows as if not caring about soiling his sleeves. "When I was a little girl, my mother would take me for long walks. Our home wasn't nearly this grand and our land wasn't much, but it was ours. There was this charming little meadow where we would go to pick wildflowers. Mother would put them in my hair and tell me I looked like a sprite. We made daisy chains and picnicked and ... I miss that. I miss *her*. After—"

David clicked his tongue, cutting off her ramblings. "No talk of after. That's a nice memory. Perhaps you can make memories like that someday with ..."

Regina tensed when he fell silent, following his unspoken words to their conclusion. Perhaps she could make memories like that someday ... with her child. The child he would give her.

A well of longing opened within her, one she knew would someday be filled by a babe that did not yet exist. And yet, there was something else, too. Something she didn't want to examine too closely.

David seemed lost in thought, his gaze locked on some distant point.

"It is your turn," she blurted, desperate to change the subject. "To tell me a happy memory."

The corner of his mouth ticked with a smile that never fully formed, and he continued staring out at the horizon as he spoke. "My father told the most outrageous bedtime stories. Made them all up as he went along, and never told a tale the same way twice. A pirate ship might be lured to its doom by sirens the first time, but on another night it would be dragged to the depths by a kraken."

"You and your sisters must have found him enthralling," Regina said.

This time, his lips parted in a full smile, and a chuckle rumbled up from his throat. "I was, more than the twins, I think. Father's stories took on an adventuresome bend, and Petra and Constantia weren't always fond of the bloodshed. Mother often teased him over his dramatic voices ... told him that he might have been a famous actor if only someone could get him on a London stage."

The note of sadness in his voice made Regina's chest ache, and also filled her with a shameful jealousy. How fortunate he was to have had a father who was loving and attentive. She felt terrible for envying him what she'd never known.

"He must have been a wonderful man," she murmured, laying a hand on his arm.

He blinked as if coming out of stupor and frowned. "Now I'm the one turning this conversation morose."

"No," she protested. "You clearly miss your father and his loss is so fresh. If you want to talk about him, you should."

He took her hand and laced his fingers through hers. "It is difficult to think of him at times, because when I do, I am reminded that the memories grow fewer and farther between when I recall the last few years of his life. When someone dies, it seems natural to lament that there wasn't enough time. He wasn't terribly old, but neither was he a young man. The past seven years or so ... well, there was plenty of time but I wasn't here. I did not want to be."

"Why not?"

David issued a dry snort, and shook his head. "I was young and bored. Lancashire was too sedate, and I wanted excitement. I wanted parties and the company of scandalous people. I visited often at first. Christmas, Easter, Mother's birthday, the twins' coming out."

Regina tightened her hold on his hand. "You couldn't have known time was so short."

"No, but I should never have let myself forget that he wasn't immortal. There was a time I couldn't wait to pack my things and run back to London—to my friends and the life I had made for myself there. Now ... I would give anything to hear one of his stories. Even just one last time."

Glancing up from their joined hands, she was stunned to find a tear tracking down his cheek, then another. As if he sensed her perusal, he dropped her hand and swiftly wiped them away. Once they were gone there was no evidence of his grief, no lines of sorrow marring his face.

"Tell me more about your mother," he murmured. "Another happy memory."

There was almost a pleading edge to his voice, prompting Regina to recall one of her favorite childhood past times. Taking hold of his shoulder, she gently urged him onto his back, then lowered herself beside him, gaze focused upward. Her hand brushed his, and she hooked her little finger around his.

"Sometimes we would go to that meadow and lie in the grass. We would watch the clouds for hours. Mother would tell me that if I looked long enough and hard enough, I might see an angel. It was the hope of my life to one day lay eyes on one."

David's finger twitched against hers, but he remained otherwise silent. When she turned her head to look at him, she found his gaze riveted to the sky. His face was serene, with not a trace of his earlier tears. There weren't many clouds today, but he still watched as if searching for something.

"Do you miss London?" she asked.

"I did at first," he admitted. "Being home was bittersweet and the problems awaiting me there only added to the strain."

"Will you return after your affairs here are in order?"

He closed his eyes, but a palpable energy thrummed from him and into her, jolting and powerful even through the minimal contact of their joined fingers.

"I cannot speak for the future, Regina. But just now ... I wouldn't want to be anywhere else."

CHAPTER 10

Regina glanced up from the book laid across her lap to where David stood in the doorway of her bedroom, hair tousled by the wind, smile wide and eyes bright. She had just taken a hot bath, dressed in another one of her scandalous nightgowns, and every lamp and taper lit in the room. Her menses had ended yesterday, and she'd sent for David to resume his visits.

The morning after she related her failure to conceive to David, it had disconcerted her to awaken beside him. It wasn't the first time she had passed an entire night with him in her bed. But there was, she had discovered, a difference between sleeping beside a man she'd spent the night fucking, and one who had spent eight hours simply holding her. It wasn't as if she had experienced either situation before David. Randolph had always promptly taken himself off to his own chamber after using her. Her courses had been an aggravation to him. It hadn't mattered that there was always some other woman stashed nearby. Randolph had wanted her when he wanted her, and any complaint or denial on her part would send him into a fit. She shuddered to think of the times he'd made her submit to him anyway, his depravity knowing no bounds.

It had been one thing to sleep beside David after a vigorous night

151

of working to conceive. She could tell herself it was all about their contract, a necessity. But what was she to think about how good it was to simply exist in the same room with him? There had been no expectation of either of them; no demands or thought of their arrangement—though in the back of her mind, she knew they were fast running out of time. There was only so much time left for her to get pregnant if there was any hope of passing this baby off as Randolph's.

Perhaps that was why she had been so distraught to discover she wasn't pregnant after the first few weeks of effort. Nevertheless, David had been content to comfort her. Such niceties were not a part of their contract, despite David's insistence that his role as a courtesan could and should include them.

He was quite convincing, and it was difficult to think of practical matters in his presence.

And then, there had been their afternoon spent walking and talking and lying about in the grass if they were friends as well as lovers. There was no reason for him to have called upon her, and they'd both known that. Yet, she had asked him to stay, and despite knowing it was a bad idea, Regina had reveled in every moment. The memories of her mother hadn't been dredged from the depths of her mind for some time, and now they were fresh again. What had she been thinking to share them with a man she intended to eject from her life once he'd served his purpose? Why had she comforted him and delved so deeply into his life?

It now occurred to Regina that she ought to set him straight. While she certainly welcomed the delights of bedsport, they teetered on the edge of taking their connection too far. It shouldn't be too difficult to mend, keeping their arrangement strictly about the business at hand. Otherwise, parting ways in the end would prove too difficult.

Yes, that was it. Pleasure and conception of the babe, only. No comfort or intimacies. No falling asleep in his arms and waking up to the thought that she might gladly do it again the next night. No giving in to the idea that she might have more of what she had been missing.

Strictly business.

Her determination was promptly shattered when David

approached the bed without removing his coat as was customary. "Get dressed, we're going to spend an evening out."

Frowning, Regina glanced down at her book, then at the transparent fabric draping her breasts. The coverlet hid her from the waist down, but surely he hadn't failed to notice what she was wearing. The pale lilac netting was so light he must be able to see everything.

His raised eyebrows as his gaze slid downward told Regina he did, yet he remained where he stood, expectantly waiting.

"I beg your pardon?" she replied.

David rounded the bed, swiftly divesting Regina of her book and yanking the bedclothes off her legs. Grasping her hands, he urged her to her feet.

"That ... that is nearly enough to convince me to stay in for the night. God's blood, you are ravishing, my dear."

Regina grappled for words, torn between thanking him for the compliment, and pulling him to the bed and tearing off his clothes to force them back to safer territory. Before she could decide on a course of action, David was leading her toward her dressing room.

"It will have to wait until we get back. I am determined to get you out of this house."

Pulling her hand out of his grasp, Regina clutched the skirt of her gown with anxious fingers. "But ... why?"

He turned to face her, his expression incredulous. "Why not? When was the last time you left this house for any reason that wasn't an errand or related to your inheritance?"

"I'm in mourning."

"So am I."

"You are a man."

"Yes, but you're hardly ever seen about the county. My sisters even told me they didn't know what you looked like ... only that you had red hair."

Regina snorted. "That's usually enough to give me away."

"Not where I'm taking you. I promise, no one from our circles will be nearby. Trust me."

He was holding his hand out to her again, patient but resolute. Regina hardly knew what to make of all this, but could hardly refuse him. He seemed so pleased with himself, practically bouncing on his heels with excitement. It occurred to her that their circumstances weren't very dissimilar. While her financial future was secured by her inheritance, she was in mourning just as he was, and barred from socializing with others. He had also come to her most nights with exhaustion pulling at the corners of his mouth and furrows in his brow. She had seen the evidence of how hard he worked when they weren't together, on the day she'd visited him at home. Between his daily labors and his evening visits to her, he must be exhausted and worn thin.

Regina did not fault him for wanting a respite. Even his visits to her would be considered work, an obligation he could not escape even if he wanted to. She didn't want to examine too closely the idea of him thinking of bedding her as an obligation.

"Very well. Will you tell me where you're taking me?"

"A place where we can indulge in a few hours of freedom from the worries of everyday life," he hedged, lighting a lamp and holding it up to inspect the contents of her dressing room. He studied rows of dresses before selecting a plain, long-sleeved gown of forest green velvet. It had minimal trim and flounces, and would keep her warm with the added layer of the matching pelisse. "This should do nicely."

"But, it isn't black," Regina protested, though she did not resist when he began helping her out of her nightgown.

"Which makes it the best disguise. Everyone would expect to see the Widow Hurst in black. Really, they wouldn't expect to see you at all. Besides, we both know you only mourn Hurst due to propriety and not because you actually wish to. When was the last time you wore a gown that complimented your figure and coloring? When was the last time you enjoyed yourself?"

He fired these questions at her while easing a chemise over her head, then urging her to sit on a cushioned stool so he could help her into a pair of stockings. Watching as he went to one knee, Regina noticed he knew his way around a woman's dressing room and clothing quite well. Not a surprising trait considering his secret profession.

"I cannot recall," she murmured as he tied off one of her garters. "On either front. Randolph controlled every aspect of my life. He hated for me to call attention to myself, and if any man set eyes on me for longer than was seemly, it was always my fault. Eventually, I stopped accompanying him to parties and dinners and such. It was simply too difficult to figure out how to act in a way that would please him.”

David paused with one hand braced on her thigh, his gaze lifting to meet hers. Regina had expected to find pity in his eyes, but realized that he seemed more angered than anything else.

“What an insufferable ass he must have been.”

Her lips quivered with a suppressed laugh. It was refreshing to hear someone speak so baldly about Randolph, when no one else seemed to want to admit the truth. It was uncouth to speak ill of the dead, but just now it felt good to have someone share in her feelings.

“Yes,” she said with a little giggle. “He *was* an insufferable ass. I ... I am glad he’s gone.”

It surprised her to realize how easily the words had fallen from her lips. Especially considering the lack of regret or remorse making her feel lighter than air. It was such a relief to be able to admit, out loud, that Randolph’s death had freed her.

Regina suddenly wanted this night out with David more than she had ever wanted anything. She was alive and in control of her own fate for the first time. It felt like an occasion to be celebrated.

“So am I, for your sake,” David remarked, going back to his work. A pair of boots followed the stockings, which he tied with swift, deft movements. “I have a hard time imagining that a man could have a wife as sweet and lovely as you and not want to flaunt her like the jewel she is.”

Regina took a deep, slow breath, reeling from the impact of those words. He uttered them so casually, as if he hadn’t given them a second thought before opening his mouth. He finished her boots but remained on his knees, hands resting on her ankles.

“Were you mine, it would gratify me to watch other men make fools of themselves over you and be secure in the knowledge that none of them could have what’s mine. It would delight me to gaze at you from across the room and watch your cheeks flush at the memory of what I'd done to you hours before, and what I plan to do to you when I get you alone again."

"David … oh!"

Her fingers tightened around the seat of the stool as David pushed her legs wider, urging her chemise up to her hips. His gaze was fixated between her thighs, where she was already slick and wanting. Their one perfect night together had not been enough. David had awakened something in Regina that she feared could never be put back to sleep. The yearning was tearing her apart, eating her alive, consuming her entirely.

"I cannot help myself," he whispered, lowering his head to nuzzle at her mons. His tongue flicked at the seam, and Regina shivered with anticipation. "It's been too long, and I missed you. I missed *this*."

A startled gasp flew from her lips as he put his mouth on her. He made an appreciative sound as if tasting something sweet, both hands bracing on her thighs to keep her open. Regina's back arched and her arms shook with the strain of keeping upright as he licked and sucked her as if starving for every last drop of her resulting wetness. Her legs were trembling within seconds, heat and ecstasy erupting in her womb and expanding out to encompass her entire body. The artful movements of his tongue were precise and purposeful, lacking the playfulness of their last encounter—almost as if he were in a hurry to get to the matter at hand.

This was no leisurely exploration giving her room to grow accustomed to the intimate invasion of his tongue. It was an onslaught, one that grew more intense with each passing second. One of his hands crept up her body, snatching Regina's chemise off one shoulder and baring her breast. She threw her head back and moaned when he cupped it, his thumb and forefinger teasing the nipple. Each tug and squeeze sent waves of sensation washing through her middle, exacerbating the pleasure of his tongue rubbing her clit in the perfect, exquisite rhythm.

She climaxed in mere minutes, shaking and sighing, thighs clenched on either side of his shoulders as he slid a finger inside her and heightened the finish with swift, precise strokes. He came up on his haunches, licking his lips and covering her legs as she struggled for air and composure. She was quite out of sorts, uncertain how he had gone from helping her dress to being on his knees with his head between her legs.

David stood, revealing the swollen ridge outlined at the front of his breeches. Moisture pooled in Regina's mouth at the sight of it, her cunny clenching for want of him inside her. Following her gaze downward, he laughed, then urged her to her feet.

"I think not. You have distracted me enough tonight, and I will not be swayed. We are going out, and you will simply have to wait until we return."

It was difficult to feel disappointed after the explosive orgasm he'd just treated her to, so Regina bowed to his wishes. They made quick work of her stays and petticoat, and before Regina knew it, she wore the gown and its matching coat, her hair pulled into a simple knot.

"Perfect," David declared, before taking her hand and leading her from the room. "That shade of green is stunning on you, by the way."

Regina's cheeks heated, but she offered no response as they descended the stairs. It was odd, being the recipient of such praise. She hadn't been offered such treatment since her courtship with Randolph. Her husband's effusive compliments and gestures of affection had dried up after the wedding, and Regina had not realized how starved she was for kindness of any sort. For someone to tell her she looked well in green, or that she was lovely, seemed so trifling. And yet, just now they felt like a gift—one she had been anticipating for years and years.

Powell awaited them in the entrance hall, a pair of Regina's kid gloves held in his meaty hands. He traded a wary glance with David before giving her a questioning look. "Will you require my presence this evening, ma'am?"

She gave him a smile and accepted the gloves. Regina heard the question he did not ask aloud and noticed his perusal of her attire. He looked pleased to see her out of black, yet also uncertain about her leaving in the company of David. Leaving him alone with her in the bedchamber was one thing. Allowing Regina to depart in his company was quite another, and they both knew it.

It felt like a massive weight had been lifted off her shoulders as she shook her head. "No, Powell. I think perhaps you ought to take the rest of the evening off and rest. I'll be perfectly safe with Mr. Graham."

Powell's stunned look told her he could hardly believe his ears. Regina had to admit she had shocked herself, but in a good way. She trusted David as she had only ever trusted Powell. Her courtesan had earned that with his patience and persistence.

"Very well," Powell replied, though he was now looking at David with a clear warning in his eyes.

Regina knew that look. The man could promise violence and mayhem without even speaking a word—one of the reasons she suspected her husband had kept him around for so long. If she were being honest, it was one of the reasons she felt safe with him. It was difficult to be afraid of anyone or anything with Powell nearby.

Tucking her hand into the crook of his arm, David gave the footman a nod, as if acknowledging the silent threat.

"I'll see her home safely. You have my word."

With a grunt, Powell opened the door for them, revealing that her carriage had been readied and stood waiting for them.

"I hope you don't mind," he said while guiding her down the front steps. "My own carriage is in need of repair, and I want you to be comfortable for the drive into Preston."

She waited until he had settled her on the carriage squabs and climbed in after her before offering a reply. "Preston, at this time of night? Whatever for?"

The carriage rocked as her driver set off, clearly having been given his orders by David already. He smiled, his teeth a brilliant flash in the dim interior of the vehicle.

"My dear, I am taking you to a public house."

David was far too amused at Regina's wide-eyed shock when he ushered her through the door of The Crimson Dove. He might have never brought a gently bred lady into such a place if not for the fact that tonight, this particular public house was hosting an assembly. He had gotten wind of it through one of his tenants, and it occurred to him that he hadn't been to a dance in months. The last few routs he attended in London had been frightfully dull.

There would be no observance of the social niceties of the *ton* here, and it was exactly why David had wanted to come. Like him, Regina had no true connection to the nobility, but neither was she of the class of people currently filling the public house from wall to wall. This lessened the likelihood of her being recognized, and he hoped it would also prove enough to allow her to unwind and enjoy herself.

It didn't take much prompting to urge her to stay close to him as they weaved their way through the crowded taproom. A partition that usually separated this main room from another had been pushed open, widening the space for dancing. The tables that typically sat clustered in the center of the room were pushed to the perimeter, many of them laden with platters of food. The aromas of fresh bread and ale mingled with those of several bodies—some sweetly perfumed and others unwashed, all cloistered together in the humid box of a room.

Near one of the hearths, a trio of musicians plied their trade for coin. As long as the hat resting at the feet of the fiddler was kept filled with shillings, they would play to the delight of those who wished to dance. Mingling with the music were dozens of raised voices in a tangle of accents and inflections.

Pressed against his side, Regina took it all in with wide eyes and parted lips. She had handed her pelisse, hat, and gloves off to an attendant upon entering, and David had removed his coat, as the heat of the room demanded fewer layers. The lighting seemed to embrace her, making the deep red tones of her hair gleam and brightening the translucence of her skin. It made the forest green she wore even more of a delight. Her eyes sparkled with curiosity as she glanced about before finally turning her gaze up to him.

"There, you see?" he murmured, wrapping an arm around her waist. "No one is paying us the slightest bit of notice."

She stiffened at his open display of affection, but then seemed to notice he was right. The center of the room teemed with dancing couples. Others stood in shadowed corners, sweat glistening on brows and bosoms as they flirted shamelessly, laughed too loudly, and generally acted as if they hadn't a care in the world. Everyone was so intent on their own amusement that no more than a few pairs of eyes had flicked to them upon their entry.

"Do you come to many of these assemblies?" she asked, raising her voice to be heard over the din.

"Not since I took up residence in London," he replied, shouldering his way toward the bar and pulling her along with him. "But in my youth, I lived for them. They were a nice distraction from what I thought of as the tedium of country life."

He quickly maneuvered them into an empty space created by two men wandering off with their drinks and leaned his elbow on the counter, facing her. They were met with a barmaid wearing a thread-bare gown and stained apron. He ordered ale for them both, yet another development that took Regina aback. At the incredulous look she gave the amber brew filled to the brim of a pewter mug, David chuckled.

"Just try it. The Crimson Dove has some of the best ale in the county. I wouldn't take you just anywhere to have your first taste."

He did not have to ask if she'd ever had anything stronger than champagne or the occasional cordial. Considering how controlling her husband had been, perhaps she hadn't even sampled that much.

Taking a deep breath, she raised the cup to her lips.

David halted her with a hand over her arm. "Wait. This is a special occasion."

He raised his mug between them and she followed suit.

"What shall we toast to?" she asked.

"To new experiences, and leaving the past behind us, where it belongs. And to you, my dear."

Her smile faded as their cups clinked, and she held his gaze while he took his first sip. Seeming encouraged by this, she drank, eyes flaring wide as she stared at him over the rim.

"Oh!" she exclaimed, staring into the cup and licking foam off her lips. "That is far better than I expected."

"Only the best for you," he murmured. "Careful not to drink that too fast. Though, if you become soused I'll carry you out of here. However, I cannot promise not to take advantage of your lowered inhi-bitions."

Regina laughed, sending one of those perplexing pangs of feeling through him. His reaction to her laughter was unsettling, yet he still craved more of the sound.

His cock twitched in his breeches as she dipped her fingers into the front of his waistcoat and pulled him closer. Ale sloshed over the sides of his mug to wet his hand, but he could pay that small aggravation no heed while drowning in her eyes.

"It wouldn't be taking advantage if I wanted it."

"Christ," he muttered, squeezing his eyes shut and battling down a raging cockstand.

It had taken a great deal of effort to restrain himself in her dressing room, though he hadn't fought the need to taste her, to feel her climax against his tongue and hear her moan his name. By the end of the night, he would find his way inside her ... but it was too soon. She would enjoy it so much more if he dragged the matter out and made her wait, if he teased and wooed.

Switching his ale to the other hand, he lifted the wet one between them and promptly licked the sweet, slightly fruity, slightly bitter liquid off his knuckles. Her breasts swelled against her bodice with a sharp inhale, and her eyes grew heavy-lidded. Was she remembering the way he'd tongued and sucked her clit not an hour ago? God knew it was all David could think about at present. The scent of her was still on him, and it seemed sharper just then.

"Noted, my dear," he said with a raised eyebrow. "Duly noted."

He downed half his ale in one long swallow and then glanced about the room. The fiddler and his friends had just struck up a new song, and space opened on the dance floor as a few couples stepped outside to cool off.

Offering Regina his hand, David inclined his head toward the remaining dancers falling seamlessly into a country dance. "Shall we?"

She hesitated only a moment before nodding, setting aside her half-finished ale and letting him lead her onto the dance floor. Conversation was impossible with such a racket going up from the other occupants of the public house—voices raised in song, laughter, cheers and groans from those gathered around tables where men tried their luck with cards. But David couldn't have found the words even if she could hear him. It became difficult to think of the steps of the dance when all he wanted to do was observe her in an environment that wasn't her dimly-lit bedroom or some other stuffy chamber of her mausoleum of a house.

Her steps were timid and reluctant at first, but at the encouragement of several women around them, Regina began to loosen up, a soft smile curving the corners of her perfect mouth. That little smirk grew by the minute, turning into a broad smile as she seemed to realize this dance wasn't like any she'd have attended in the past. Half the people in this room didn't know the proper steps but were pleased to improvise. Even knowing she had not danced in public in a long time, she put even his own skill to shame. She was light on her feet and graceful, which should come as no surprise to David. Even the slightest fluttering of her hands had struck him as poised and refined. Why shouldn't she also dance like a veritable angel?

From that first dance, time seemed to move past them with undue speed. They alternated between turns about the dance floor and respites at the bar, where Regina proved more than capable of holding her drink. After her third mug, all her sense of propriety seemed to have fled, and David watched her down the fourth one with all the relish of a sailor fresh home from sea. He goggled at her in disbelief as her throat worked with every swallow, head tipped back and deep, noisy breaths echoing through the hollow inside of her mug.

Their gazes met as she slammed the mug down, lips glistening and eyes bright. A tiny belch emitted from within her chest, and the startled look on her face sent David into peals of laughter. She stared at him for a moment, face flushed and one hand pressed over her mouth. Then, she burst into a fit of giggles, bending at the waist as she clutched the edge of the bar as if for dear life.

When she straightened, Regina wore a wide grin, her shoulders and chest heaving as she tried to catch her breath.

"Another dance?" he asked. "Or have you had enough?"

She practically fell into him when he took her hand, still giggling and snorting. "I could dance with you all night, Mr. Graham."

"And what a fine dancer you are, Mrs. Hurst."

"Before my marriage, it was my favorite part of attending any event. Of course, all that ended once Randolph and I wed. I was only ever allowed to dance with him, and he was barely passable. Before I stopped accompanying him to soirees, I would spend my evenings on the edge of the ballroom, watching everyone else enjoy what I longed to do. I have missed it so much, you know ... dancing, being in the company of others. Laughing."

"Then you shall dance and laugh with me."

Yanking her against him once they stood on the edge of the throng of dancers he positioned her for a waltz—though there was nothing courtly or sensible about this form of the dance. The fiddler sawed the rhythm several times faster than what one might expect in a ballroom, sending the dancers into a dizzy tailspin of stepping feet and swirling skirts.

Regina clung to him, her expression at once surprised and enchanted as she glanced around to find they weren't the only couple dancing indecently close. A boisterous laugh tore from her as he spun her, using a hand against her waist to guide her into a wild turn before reeling her back in.

As the world beyond them faded into a meaningless blur, David's heart dropped into the pit of his stomach. He was locked in Regina's gaze, falling headlong into a trap of his own making and realizing he could do nothing to stop it. A cold tendril of fear snaked its way through the warm haze of drink and revelry as he realized what he had allowed to happen—what he had *made* happen with his damnable need to please. He'd wanted to give Regina the child she so desperately craved, then he had wanted to give her pleasure. That hadn't been enough, though. He had gone from wanting to make her climax to wanting to show her the joy in life's little pleasures—like being held while one slept, drinking a fine ale, and dancing in a room full of people who weren't criticizing their every move.

But, as the dance came to an end and David stared down at the woman in the circle of his arms, the realization that he wanted to give her so much more struck him like a club to the back of his head. It wasn't enough, and never would be. He wanted to give her all of him, everything he had.

David acted without thinking, momentarily oblivious to his

surroundings and desperate to know he wasn't alone in his feelings—sudden and frightening as they were. His forehead fell against hers, and he closed his eyes as their lips brushed. Regina's hand tightened on his shoulder as her head fell back, eyes wide and questioning when they met his. Had she asked him aloud what he was doing, David doubted he would have an answer for her. He was out of his depth here, with no notion of what to do or say.

So, he deepened the kiss—just for a second, just long enough to register the taste of Regina and ale, and to feel regret when he was forced to pull away.

Swallowing past the painful knot in his throat, he cursed himself for the fool he was. David Graham, connoisseur of women, untamed rake, irreverent debauchee who wore the status of 'courtesan' like a badge of honor, had been brought to his knees by this tiny slip of a woman. The tragedy of it all was that not only had she not been trying in the slightest, she likely wanted nothing from him beyond their arrangement. He knew that, had known it from the start. Why, then, had he allowed himself to develop feelings for her? Feelings he was too afraid to name or even consider—but that made themselves more apparent with each passing day.

He was a fool. He was an imbecile.

He was doomed.

CHAPTER 11

David spent the four weeks following his outing with Regina wrestling with the notion that he was falling in love. At first, it felt like a trick of his drink-addled mind. After all, he'd had quite a lot of ale that night at The Crimson Dove, and it wouldn't be the first time drunkenness had filled his head with nonsensical ideas. He was simply caught up in having a good time, seeing Regina in clothes that weren't shapeless and black, watching her smile and knowing he had been the one to make her happy. A frenetic, wild fuck in the carriage on the way home had only further muddied the waters. He clung to her afterward, panting and trembling with the aftershocks of what had just passed between them, a voice in his head telling him he could be this way with her forever and die happy.

A good night's sleep would be enough to cure him of such melodramatics. Regina Hurst was beautiful, sweet, and compelling. That wasn't enough for him to up and decide he loved her. However, his feelings became no less true in the harsh light of the following day, or the day after that, or the day after that. Difficult to think of it as a ridiculous lark when it greeted him with each new day, persistently and without fail.

There was nothing to be done about it, of course. It was against the rules for him to even entertain such thoughts. Aside from that, there was Regina's part in all this. She had made herself quite clear from the beginning that he was a means to an end and nothing more. What did it matter if she had come to like him during their time together? He couldn't forget that she was his employer in a transaction of flesh and seed. That she liked and trusted him did not mean she loved him. He would be foolish to delude himself into believing otherwise.

And so, his days took on a painful sort of routine, with him very much aware that time was running out. They were together nearly every night of the week, their attempts at siring a babe many and vigorous. For David, their sessions had become less about conception and more about enjoying what pieces of Regina he could have while they were still his. Nothing seemed to have changed for her. She never said anything to him aloud, but David could see the lingering glances she gave herself in the mirror, pulling her nightgown tight and turning this way and that as if searching for even the minutest changes in her shape. He observed the glimmer of hope in her eyes after he spilled inside her, the wistful sighs as she used cushions to elevate her hips, one hand resting over a belly that hadn't yet begun to swell.

He still wanted to be successful, for the money as well as for Regina's own happiness. Yet, it became increasingly clear that her success would ultimately damn him. The thought of being sent away once he'd gotten her with child now left a bitter taste in his mouth, and not only because the idea of a person walking around with his hair, or eyes, or facial features unnerved him. He didn't want to admit exactly *why* he felt this way, so David continued along the path of denial and avoidance, reminding himself why it had to be this way.

"It will pass," he told himself. "It only feels so intense because it's so new. Surely once the arrangement is over, you will be able to move on."

Glancing about as he walked home from visiting tenants, he rolled his eyes at his own ridiculousness. He had taken to talking to himself aloud, perhaps in hopes that hearing his own voice raised in opposition to this idea would help him combat it. Benedict wasn't here to remind him how messy an arrangement could be once softer feelings got involved, so he had to take matters into his own hands.

"Just look at Hugh," he reminded himself, boots crunching over the frost-covered ground. The air smelled and tasted of coming snow, and the sharp prick of an intense chill propelled him along faster. "He's become so dreadfully dull and uninteresting since getting married. He's practically an old man now."

But then, David could remember the last time he'd seen his friend. Despite cracking a few jokes over his insistence that he couldn't join the other courtesans because he wanted to get home to his wife, David had witnessed Hugh's happiness. It was obvious how marriage to Evelyn had improved Hugh's mood, as well as the quality of his art once his painting of her had launched him to fame.

Hugh was also about five months away from becoming a father, yet another thought that soured David's disposition even more. He would get to hold his child once it was born, and perhaps even have a hand in naming it. Hugh would be present for the appearance of tiny baby teeth and those first clumsy, toddling footsteps. He would introduce the child to watercolors and pastels, and discover whether his offspring possessed any of his natural gift for the arts. He would get to watch Evelyn cradle the tiny little bundle of plump cheeks and downy hair they had made together. He would have everything David would be denied because of the parameters of an arrangement he had readily agreed to.

"You don't want any of those things," he growled, combing restless fingers through mussed hair. "You only think you do because of Regina. It's ridiculous, and you need to snap out of it!"

A few months ago, he'd been terrified at the prospect of creating new life, even if he wouldn't be the one helping raise the babe once it was born. In fact, it had eased his mind to think of leaving his offspring in Regina's care so he could go on rebuilding his family holdings and caring for the people who needed him. So, what had changed? Why had he now decided that perhaps Regina and her baby—no, *their* baby —could become part of that family?

You fell in love with her. That's what changed.

Shaking his head to try to dislodge that thought, David grunted in frustration at his own idiocy. He wasn't a man who fell in love, got married, and sired brats. Hugh had been cut from a different cloth from the beginning, already filled with notions of romance and all that rot. But then, there was Dominick, the only man of David's circle who could be called a bigger rake than him. He was the last person anyone might have pegged as the sort to marry for love. Not only had he done that, he'd created the hell of a scandal in the process. How was this unexpected twist of fate to be explained away?

It couldn't be; not in any way that would make David feel better about his own situation. In fact, he could too easily see himself mirrored in Nick's downfall, and that was more frightening than it was comforting.

"Pull yourself together," he groused, stomping up the front steps.

The waning light of dusk usually filled him with energy and excitement. Most days, it hurried him through his evening toilette and a hasty dinner so he could get to Regina. Tonight, David dragged his feet through the entrance hall, shoulders slumped and a frigid weight heavy in his chest. Even the pleasant aroma of new beeswax candles and lemony floor polish—a sure sign that matters were starting to improve in the Graham household—couldn't lift his spirits. The closer he came to setting things right around here, the closer he also came to losing Regina for good.

"Welcome home, Master David," called Mrs. Moffat's cheery voice. She glanced to the half-open door to the blue salon. "There's a visitor, but you needn't worry. Your mother and sisters are entertaining her."

David's gaze darted toward the room, head tilting as he listened to the murmur of female voices from within. One was clearly his mother, and then the tangled tones of the twins as they spoke as one and finished one another's sentences. Then, a pause after a question, and a fourth voice that made his chest constrict.

Regina. She was alone in a room with his mother and sisters, who were likely regaling her with embarrassing anecdotes of his childhood or trying to pry into their relationship.

His panic must have shown outwardly, because Mrs. Moffat patted his shoulder. "Not to worry. Mrs. Graham made the twins promise not to put their little noses in your affairs. They simply wish to show her kindness. She hasn't any friends in the county at all, you know. Except ... well, there's you, isn't there?"

Clearing his throat, David tried to smooth his expression into a serene one before meeting the housekeeper's questioning gaze. "Indeed. Thank you, Mrs. Moffat."

"Hmm," she murmured, eyes narrowing as she seemed to try staring straight through him.

Ignoring her probing look, David made his way toward the salon. He didn't think his mother would be able to hold Petra and Constantia off for much longer without his interference.

Four pairs of eyes landed on him as he lingered in the doorway, now feeling like an unwanted intruder in his own home. Regina stood out as the only one not wearing stark black, a becoming gown of deep burgundy velvet enhancing her flawless complexion. It made David want to help her out of it—a disturbing thought to have while standing under the scrutinizing eyes of his mother and sisters.

"Oh, David," his mother murmured with a smile. "There you are. Mrs. Hurst arrived half an hour ago, and the girls and I thought it would be the perfect opportunity to make her acquaintance."

"Besides, we haven't had a visitor in ages," Petra chimed in, giving David a teasing grin over the rim of her teacup. The little minx was clearly enjoying his discomfort. "And Mrs. Hurst is ever so lovely, isn't she, Con?"

"Oh yes," Constantia replied. "Why have you been hiding her from us, David? How wicked of you not to introduce us yourself."

"It wasn't my intention to keep you from meeting," he said, doing his best to keep his voice level. "There just never seemed to be a good time."

He met Regina's gaze, and found she looked far more comfortable with this turn of events than he was. Perhaps she thought nothing of it because she was simply meeting her neighbors, women she might encounter again once they were all out of mourning and able to be social again. They would never know about her affair with David, or that her child had been sired by him. They would never truly know Regina, because as he well knew, she allowed very few people to get close.

"It is wonderful to see you again, Mrs. Hurst," he added with a slight bow, finally regaining hold of his senses as well as his manners.

"Forgive me for not being here when you called. I had a matter of business to tend to before I could return for the night."

"Not that you're ever here for long before you go dashing off to do God-knows-what," Petra muttered into her teacup before taking a long sip.

David glared, wondering if she even realized how her voice carried. What had been meant as a whisper to Constantia had carried across the room to him, which meant his mother and Regina had heard it.

Wonderful. Now he would have to suffer his mother's questions about whether his evenings away from home had anything to do with Regina. If she hadn't been suspicious before, she certainly must be now. For a widowed woman to indulge in an affair wasn't unheard of, or even particularly scandalous. But if Regina's baby were born with any distinguishing features such as his bright blue eyes or swarthy skin, and his mother caught wind of it ... Christ, why hadn't he thought of this before?

Because he needed the money. Because he never intended for Regina to ever come face to face with his mother.

Because he was a bumbling idiot. It was a wonder he'd survived as long as he had without wandering off the edge of a cliff or walking into the path of a carriage and team.

"Mrs. Hurst will be joining us for dinner," his mother said. "I insisted, and she accepted my invitation."

"Your mother was quite convincing," Regina added with a shy smile.

There was a silent question in her eyes, as well as a bit of reticence—almost as if she worried he wouldn't want her here. David wanted to laugh as he was forced to admit he wanted her to stay more than anything, and not just for dinner. Even as her immaculate dress and beauty put the drab environs of the faded blue salon to shame, David was seized with the urge to drop to his knees and beg her to stay forever. Not just to brighten this room, but his entire world and everything in it.

He was going stark raving mad.

"I am glad to hear it," he mumbled, running a hand over his jaw, which had begun to sprout a fine spray of stubble over the last several hours. "If you will excuse me, I should go make myself worthy of sharing a table with four such lovely women."

Petra and Constantia shared communicative looks, while his mother reached for the teapot to refill her cup.

"Of course. Mrs. Hurst will be just fine in our company until you return. Won't you, dear?"

"Just so," Regina agreed. Her head dipped in a slight nod when she met his gaze again, and he took that as reassurance.

Leaving without a longing glance back was difficult, but David managed it. His toilette seemed to drag by, though David's valet moved with his usual swift efficiency. What felt like an hour seemed an eternity, until at last he was clean, shaved, and dressed for dinner. By the time he returned to the salon, dinner had been announced and the ladies had risen to trek to the dining room. David discovered them on his way down the stairs, his sisters flanking Regina with their arms linked through both of hers. Regina was smiling and laughing as the twins chattered about something or another. David could hardly hear them, so entranced was he at the sight of her walking the corridors of his home as if she belonged here. What had felt like a cold and dismal place became something more with her here—not a place to be escaped, but one to be nurtured and shaped and made worthy of her.

"I like her."

He started at the sound of his mother's voice, mortified to be caught gaping at Regina's retreating back.

Raising one dark eyebrow, his mother pursed her lips. "It would seem you like her, too."

"Mrs. Hurst has been gracious and kind," he hedged, though he wouldn't avoid her gaze. She knew him too well, and would see that for the avoidance it was. "Despite being a woman, she is very knowledgeable about the running of an estate the size of ours."

"Is she?" Taking his arm, she let him lead her to the dining room. "That is not at all surprising, though I do find it odd that she would come to call so late in the day if her business with you were pertaining to the farm."

David nearly tripped as his mother's words had the intended effect. Her teasing smirk put him on edge, telling him he was doing a terrible job hiding his feelings. Once he registered that thought, another more pressing one, took its place at the forefront of his mind.

Why had Regina come? She must have expected David to visit her as he did almost every night. She'd only needed to wait for him to arrive to speak with him.

Was something the matter? Had she begun her courses again? It had been just a little over a month since her last menses, which meant they were due again. Unless ...

He made a choked sound of distress that had his mother grabbing his arm and halting him just outside the dining room. Blinking out of his stupor, David glanced down to find her watching him with a furrowed brow.

"Forget I mentioned it," she said, patting his shoulder. "You've been working so hard, and have done such for this family these past months. Whatever is going on between you and Mrs. Hurst is none of my affair, as long as you are certain you know what you are doing."

No, he wanted to tell her. *No, I don't know what the bloody hell I've gotten myself into, or what to do now.*

"I just wanted you to know that I do like her, if it means anything to you."

Odd, he wouldn't have thought it would matter, but knowing his mother approved of Regina made him hopeful. But ... hopeful of what, exactly? It wasn't as if this were a conventional situation. He was not courting Regina; he was fucking her. And perhaps that would soon come to an end if she'd come to tell David what he suspected.

"It means a great deal," he said, forcing a smile for the benefit of his mother. "Thank you."

They entered the dining room, where his sisters had taken up their usual places side by side, with Regina across from them. She would sit at his right, with his mother on her other side. As he took his place and motioned for Caruthers and one of the footmen to serve them, David felt Regina's eyes on him. He met her gaze, and what he saw there brought him no comfort. He had become too familiar with Regina to miss the subtle glint of both excitement and sadness in her eyes.

This was it. She'd come to give him her good news. Which meant she had also come to say good-bye.

REGINA PEERED THROUGH THE WINDOW OF HER GUEST CHAMBER, watching as flurries of powdery snow danced on the wind. She could see nothing beyond those white flashes in the dark, though the chill of the night reached out to her through the pane. It had been foolish of her to intrude on David's home, and now was all but forced to remain for the night. She'd been in such haste to get to him, she had paid no heed to the impending weather. The snow began sometime during dinner, and by the time Regina, David, and his family retired back to the salon, it was falling so fast and thick she could hardly see beyond the front steps.

"Oh, but you cannot attempt to drive home in this ghastly weather," Theodora Graham had said, brow wrinkled with motherly concern. "It is far too dangerous. I insist you and your driver remain here for the night. I will never sleep a wink over worrying for you. David, surely you agree Mrs. Hurst cannot make the journey home tonight."

Regina's stomach flipped at the look David gave her then. He had watched her all evening, remaining silent unless someone asked him a direct question. His perusal was unnerving, especially when it kept straying to her bodice ... and lower. Did he suspect the reason for her presence here? Was he angry with her for encroaching on this part of his life? Regina couldn't blame him if he were. She never expected to be greeted by his mother and sisters, nor had she thought to be invited to stay for dinner. What could she have done when Theodora was unwilling to take no for an answer?

"Of course," David had replied. "I won't hear of it, Mrs. Hurst. Of course you'll stay."

"And you shall see her safely home in the morning," Theodora added with a resolute nod. "Yes, I think that would be quite satisfactory."

The woman had a sharpness to her, an air of command. She was also one of the most beautiful women Regina had ever seen, and she would only become more graceful and dignified with age. Perhaps it was Theodora's kindness that made Regina see her in a maternal light. Truly, all the women of David's family were agreeable. The twins reminded her of herself in her youth—bright-eyed, slightly mischievous, filled with life and hope.

She had been nervous about accepting the invitation for dinner, but was quickly put at ease. Regina hadn't had female friends since before her marriage to Randolph. The few she'd had eventually fell away as Regina became a recluse—mostly to keep anyone from seeing her bruises. It was so nice to indulge in gossip and idle chatter over tea, to eat dinner with actual people instead of sitting alone while mulling over her own morose thoughts.

It was yet another one of those things she had rediscovered after finding David—yet another aspect of life Regina had forgotten could impart so much meaning.

When a knock sounded at the door, Regina turned away from the window with a sigh. It might be time for her to relinquish all that, for her wish had been fulfilled. Now she must abandon the man who had made it come true. Surely he was ready to get on with his life.

Regina's heart leaped into her throat as she swung the door open, but it sank when she realized it was a footman on the threshold and not David. He silently offered her a folded slip of paper with one gloved hand, then bowed and wished her a good evening. Her chest tightened when she opened it to find a note from David.

Take a left at the end of the corridor and enter the third door. I will be waiting.

-D

Regina squeezed her eyes shut and fought to get her bearings. After all, if she was right about her condition, they would only have to meet one more time after tonight—for her to give him the promised bonus. Regina told herself it was the pleasure and companionship she would miss. But then, trying to imagine some faceless lover eventually taking his place made her stomach turn. Perhaps in the future she might bring herself to feel desire for someone else, but just now David dominated her thoughts. When she considered what it felt like to be kissed, touched, and handled with such forethought and care, his face was all she could see.

But that was all she could have from now on—memories and longing. David had his own life to get back to, and had made it clear that he didn't think himself capable of faithfulness to one woman. Besides, even if he were keen to settle down, Regina was far too damaged. Her adamant stance against marriage had not changed. It would seem the time had come for them to part ways.

At the mirror over the washstand, Regina took a quick glance at her reflection before leaving the room. Her coloring was high, slightly flushed with anxiety and excitement. Her eyes looked too large in her face, but they were bright and clear. Combing her fingers through her hair, she released it from its braid.

The nightgown she had borrowed from Constantia was too long, for the other woman topped her by about two inches. Regina had to hold the hem aloft while traversing the corridor with lamp in hand. The passage remained empty and quiet, leaving Regina confident she wouldn't be caught traipsing about this time of night. She reached David's door without being accosted, and lightly rapped it with her knuckles.

"Come," David's voice called from the other side, soft and muffled.

She obeyed, and found herself in a neat study that smelled of brandy, leather, and furniture polish. David sat behind a large desk, his slouched body and the heaviness of his eyelids hinting at relaxed indolence. But as she closed the door and drew closer, Regina could see it was a façade. His eyes were sharp and unwavering when they met hers, and the clench of his fingers around a tumbler denoted thinly-veiled tension.

He had removed his coat and cravat. His shirtsleeves were rolled back to reveal the riveting sight of his forearms, taut with sinews and rippling here and there with prominent veins.

"David," she began, setting her lamp on the mantel before approaching the desk. "I need to—"

"I think I know what you've come to tell me," he said, holding one hand up to silence her. "If it's what I suspect, I am not quite ready to hear it. Not yet."

What an interesting coincidence; Regina was not ready to say it.

"Oh?" she murmured, staring down at the one hand he braced on the desk. Would her child have that same olive skin, or would he be fair like Regina? She imagined an infant with a thick cap of inky black hair and felt her throat tighten.

"Will you give me tonight?" he asked, staring down at his brandy as he toyed with his glass. "I realize what you have to tell me will put an end to what we have shared these past months. But ... I am not quite ready for that."

"Neither am I."

Regina barely managed to get the words out, but he'd heard her rough whisper. A muscle twitched in his jaw when he glanced up at her again. Then, he set his glass aside and pushed his chair back before crooking a finger to summon her closer. She rounded the desk as if pulled by an invisible tether—some unseen thing linking her to him. Soon would come the time to cut and run, but not now. Not yet.

David took hold of her waist once she was in reach, moving her to stand between his spread legs. For a while he simply stared at her. Regina took the opportunity to drink him in, committing him to memory. As if one could ever forget the magnificence of David Graham. The riveting eyes so clear and blue God must regret not using the color to paint the sky. Those sooty lashes so long and full women everywhere must despise him for what they lacked. The lips so plush and perfectly formed, capable of the sweetest or wickedest of kisses depending on his mood.

He had given her so much, and Regina could never express her gratitude. But she could show him. She could try to give him back some of what he had so selflessly offered her.

She made quick work of the buttons running between her breasts. David's eyes sparked with interest, and he sat up straighter as he watched her slip the nightgown off one shoulder, then the other. The garment fell with a soft whisper to land at her feet, leaving Regina stripped bare and vulnerable. His lips parted on a slow exhale, and he shifted in his chair to accommodate his growing erection. She could see the outline of it at the front of his breeches, calling to her with promises of pleasure and connection to the only man she'd ever desired in this way.

It was quite exhilarating to stand nude before him and realize that her desire was matched with equal potency.

There was too much air between them, too many things unsaid, so many experiences untouched. Regina closed the gap, bracing both hands on his chest and climbing up to straddle him. His eyes widened, presumably at her boldness, but Regina couldn't explain what had come over her when she hardly understood it herself.

"Regina," he mumbled against her lips, just before she kissed him, tangling her fingers in his hair.

His hands skimmed her thighs to grip her hips, pressing her down onto his rigid cock as he returned her kiss. He tasted of brandy and the cake they'd had after dinner, the rasping strokes of his tongue making her dizzy with lust and want. She tore at his shirt, ripping loose the remaining buttons and combing her fingers through the whorls of his chest hair, tracing her way up his neck and jaw, drinking from his lips with growing desperation. She whimpered into his mouth and he answered with a low groan, fingers tightening on her buttocks as he ground against her. His hardness and the rough fabric of his breeches teased the sensitive bud of her clit, and she shamelessly squirmed and rutted against him, telling him without words what she needed, wild with the urgency of it.

Tearing his mouth away from hers, he worked his way down her throat. Regina threw her head back, eyes sliding shut as he nibbled and licked his way up to her ear. The man ought to be knighted for the deadly precision with which he wielded that tongue of his, never failing to find the places that curled her toes or forced moans of delight from between her lips.

He reached toward the desk and lifted his tumbler, salacious purpose gleaming in his eyes as he tipped it toward her. Regina gasped at the first splash and trickle of brandy over one breast, but then she moaned her shocked delight as his tongue chased the rivulet toward her nipple. He lapped and sucked, bathing her clean before going back for more. Wantonness held her in its thrall, and she arched her back to offer herself up as his chalice, another cool splash preceding the warmth of his tongue. He doused both her breasts and her belly, then braced a hand at her back and devoured her, drinking the brandy from her skin.

Regina clung to the edge of his desk and tried not to collapse when his mouth closed over a nipple, his teeth scraping the tip. She was far more sensitive than usual, a sure sign of the truth that lingered between them unsaid. The changes in her were subtle, but very much real and impossible to ignore. He seemed to notice the increased tenderness of her nipples, lingering there to hungrily suck and lick and nip, driving her closer and closer to the edge of her tolerance.

David grunted when she pushed against his chest, forcing him back in his chair so she could yank his shirttails free of his breeches. His chest heaved with every breath, and his hands shook as he helped her open his fall. His eyes were wild and glassy when he met her gaze, as if he'd lost complete control of himself and now acted purely on animal instinct. They slid closed when she took him in her palm, stroking her thumb over his swollen tip ... but then flew open again when she began sliding down his body. Their gazes met and held, surprise lighting in David's as she went to her knees on the floor, her mouth poised over his cock.

He stroked her cheek, then his thumb traced the curve of her lower lip. "You don't have to do that."

The note of sympathy in his voice set her teeth on edge, though not because of anything he'd done. She had confided in him that Randolph forced her to suck him off a few times and she had found it off-putting. David had never asked such a thing of her, and when she'd mentioned it he simply shrugged and reminded her that their arrangement was about her needs anyway, not his. But, she would not let Randolph ruin even this for her. In the past, thoughts of intercourse had made her ill because of memories of him. Now, she knew what it was like to feel someone inside her and take pleasure from it. Why shouldn't David also replace these other horrid memories? Now, when she thought of performing such an act on a man, she would remember the naked desire in David's eyes as he stared down at her, the restless twitch of his fingers against his thighs as he waited for her to press her lips to him.

"I want to," she insisted. "I *need* to."

Regina acted before she could lose her nerve. Angling his cock toward her lips, she surged her tongue against the head. His sharp intake of breath preceded a rough groan as Regina took him as deep as she could, determination driving her. She kept her eyes open and fixed on him, resolved not to let the ghost of someone she hated encroach upon her moment of triumph. His flesh was rigid and unrelenting at the back of her throat, the taste of him salty and pleasantly male. Funny, how her perspective on all things 'masculine' had been changed by this man.

He shook with what she assumed was a great deal of control as she bobbed her head, taking him in and out, her tongue sliding along the underside of his shaft. Pushing his shirt farther up, she noted the tension in his abdomen as he kept from thrusting his hips. His hands curled into fists, the tendons in his wrists pulled taut as if he wanted to touch her, to guide her with his hands.

Fear spiked in her at the thought of a fist clenched in her hair, ruthless and dominating. But all it took was a look at David for her to remember who she knelt before and the choice she had made. She refused to regret it.

His fingers were a featherlight whisper on the shell of her ear and the side of her neck—questioning, tentative, and seeking. She sucked him harder in response, moaning around the thick length of him in encouragement. And still he held back, gritting his teeth and grunting at the pulls of her mouth around him.

"Yes?" he asked while gently threading his fingers in the hair at her nape. When she nodded and circled her tongue around his head, David shut his eyes and tightened his hold, surging his cock deeper into her mouth. "Yes!"

Regina's eyes watered with the effort it took not to blink, for she couldn't look away from David. His pulse thundered beneath his jaw, and his lips fell open on the sounds of his pleasure. The dark fans of his lashes left shadows on his cheekbones, the vulnerability of his expression at odds with the sheer size and strength of him. But even the hand guiding her head and tangling in her hair was reverent and worshipful, as opposed to harsh and forceful.

She luxuriated in being the source of every sigh and groan, every shiver that wracked him. It became so potent, so powerful and all-consuming, Regina couldn't stop even when she tasted the first hint of his coming seed. He gazed down at her in shock, lips moving with words that never emitted as she intensified her efforts, determination driving her to bring him to his finish.

His entire body went tense, and his cock jerked against her tongue before the wild, salty cascade of his seed flooded her mouth. Regina swallowed and released him, gasping for air as she dropped her head to rest against his thigh. For a while, only their harsh breaths rang out through the room. David's fingers remained, lightly stroking along her scalp as she caught her breath.

David urged her back onto his lap, holding her tight against his chest as he kissed her brow. "Not ... finished with you ... yet."

She smiled against his chest. "I certainly hope not."

His fingers tilted her chin, and then their mouths met in a slow, thorough exploration—as if he were searching her depths for traces of his own spend. Regina closed her eyes and opened herself to what this kiss made her feel, understanding that she might never feel this again. If he did nothing else but kiss her for the rest of the night, Regina would have been content. She never imagined someone else's lips on hers could be so soul-stirring, so life-changing.

Suddenly, David tore his mouth from hers and urged her to her feet. He turned her and used a hand against her back to bend her over. Hands braced on the surface of his desk, Regina panted and arched at the stroke of his fingers down her spine, coming up on tiptoe and spreading her legs wider. All sense of modesty or shame disappeared, as they always did whenever he touched her, awakening these secret, base parts of her.

His fingers continued their downward path, and Regina held her breath while waiting for him to touch her where she wanted it most. Her inner thighs were already damp with arousal, her cunny clenching and pulsing with desperate need. A finger slid into her, then another, and Regina's head fell to the desk as he began fucking her with them—first with slow, precise thrusts, then with faster ones that made her sheath clench and squeeze around him. Just when she hovered on the edge of climax, he withdrew and then dipped his thumb into her.

Before she knew what was happening, his first two fingers were back inside her and the thick tip of his thumb pressed against another part of her ... a place he'd never before touched. She opened her mouth to ask him what he was doing and why, but then he gained an inch into her rear passage, and then another, and words failed her.

"Oh," she whispered, the tension melting from her spine as she registered the foreign sensations of him breeching both her entrances at once. "David ..."

His lips skimmed her shoulder, his fingers steadily teasing her back toward climax. His entire thumb was lodged in her now, adding a sense of fullness and wicked, vulgar pleasure to his steady caresses inside her quim.

"Didn't I tell you?" he whispered, kissing his way along the back of her neck. "There is so much left for me to teach you ... so many things I could do to make you melt for me."

She had melted minutes ago, and was now a weightless, formless bundle of nerves at his fingertips. Climax unfurled from within her in what felt like an instant, tearing through her with unrelenting intensity. She clawed the desk and bit her lip around a moan, hips bucking and legs quivering as he quickened the strokes of his fingers, his knuckles slamming into her with a savagery she welcomed with every backward sway of her hips.

Only when she'd gone still did he remove his fingers and position the head of his cock at her entrance. He was aroused again, full and thick and demanding as he pressed into her. Regina gasped when he paused halfway in, withdrew, and then plunged, his hips battering her buttocks and pushing her into the edge of the desk. He did it again, then again, one hand pressing at her lower back to hold her where he wanted as he fucked her with hard, measured strokes. The dying embers of her first climax roared to life again, and by the time he'd worked himself up to a swift, steady rhythm, she was falling apart again. The hand at her back slid under her and pulled her up, his chest pressed into her back. His arm locked around her waist and his teeth clenched around her earlobe as he pounded into her, driving her climax higher and higher until she could hardly breathe through the belly-clenching spasms.

Regina lifted her hands into his hair, swaying back into each of his thrusts, accepting everything he had to give and wishing it never had to end.

But, end it did, when David pushed her back over the desk and fell against her, head buried in her neck as he chased his own climax. His hands slid up her body and along her arms, until his hands rested over hers, their fingers intertwining. Regina clung to him as he groaned his release into her ear, hips jerking, his heart thudding against her back.

He went deathly still, though his weight wasn't so unpleasant that Regina required him to leave her. She enjoyed the solidity of him, as if he were her shield against the world. Closing her eyes, she allowed herself to hang onto the final moments they would share together, knowing the time had come to lay everything bare.

She waited until his breathing had quieted and he finally straightened from on top of her. Until he had used his cravat to clean himself, then folded it and offered it to her use. Until he had pulled his breeches back up and offered her the forgotten nightgown.

Then, she turned to face him, one hand pressed against her middle. He stared at her, one hand clenching the back of his chair and his mouth a harsh line as wide, dazed eyes fell to where her hand cradled new life.

Regina parted her lips to speak, hoping to get her words out before David could utter his.

In the end, they both spoke at once.

"I'm pregnant," she whispered, at the exact moment David met her gaze and uttered, without batting an eyelash, "Marry me."

CHAPTER 12

David squeezed his eyes shut and rested his head against the back of the carriage seat. Last night's confrontation with Regina had kept him awake through the night, and now plagued him in the bright light of day. He never intended to speak the words that had shattered what was left of their fragile connection. Before sending the note summoning her to his study, David told himself to be strong. He would hear what she had to say and accept it with grace and a stiff upper lip. He would congratulate her on becoming a mother and wish her well. He would let her go.

But then, he'd lain eyes on her and all his good intentions had fallen away. David couldn't think of anything other than having one last night with her, forestalling the inevitable and pretending this might end differently.

One last taste of her, and he could set her free. He could go on about his life pretending there wasn't a child of his bloodline walking about Lancashire, or that his heart wasn't broken at the loss of the one woman he'd ever felt more than attraction and mild affection for. Regina owned him body and soul, and David wanted the same of her. He wanted to be able to call her his, to take comfort in the knowledge that he would never have to be without her.

Which was why, after taking her across his desk, David had found himself unable to adhere to his plan. Let her go? He would rather die.

There had been no forethought, no rehearsal of the words he might have used to better explain his feelings. *Marry me*, he'd blurted like a mad fool. The horror on her face had dealt the first agonizing blow to his ravaged heart, and then had come the question he had found himself hard-pressed to answer.

"Why, David? Why do you want to marry me?"

"You've just informed me that you are carrying my child."

"As per our contract! We entered into this agreement with the knowledge that it would end in me becoming pregnant with my child."

"That was before. Everything has changed now. Can't you see that?"

God, he was such an idiot. 'I love you, that's why.' Why hadn't he been able to say those words? Why could he only stand there gaping at her as she began erecting her barriers against him, eyes growing shuttered and her demeanor freezing over like a lake hardening in winter.

"Nothing has changed. I wanted a child, and you have helped me conceive one, as promised. We were both clear enough with each other from the beginning. I never want to marry again, and you have admitted to only being interested in taking a wife for the sake of a fortune. I think the bonus you are set to earn is more than enough of my money to meet your needs. There is no need to try to shackle me to you for life."

That had hurt, but what could David say in his own defense? Those words *had* come out of his stupid, stupid mouth. How could he expect her to believe his position on marriage had changed because of her? Still, realizing that hadn't stopped him from trying.

"You can keep every penny of your own money, I won't touch it. Your inheritance isn't what I want, Regina."

"Isn't it?"

"Damn it, no! You cannot honestly think me such a cad."

"Perhaps not, but the timing of your proposal does you no credit. If it isn't my money you are after, then surely this is about the child."

"It certainly shouldn't be left out of the conversation. It's a baby, *Regina. Our baby."*

"Stop saying that! God, you men are all the same, aren't you? Even when I have made myself clear, established boundaries and required your agreement to my terms, you still try to twist the situation to fit your own wants and needs. I promised myself no man would ever own me again, that everything I had earned would remain mine ... and you somehow think planting a child in me entitles you to all the rest? You think I should give you my money, my home, my body just because you spilled your seed in me?"

"Idiot, idiot, idiot!" he growled, as her harsh words resonated through his memory. He lifted his head and dropped it against the back of the seat with each utterance of the word, as he remembered being tongue-tied in the face of her fury.

Because, damn it, she was right. Not about his intentions, and certainly not about his notions of entitlement or greed. She was right to be angry with him for trying to break the terms of their arrangement. She was right to assume the worst of him. He had signed his name in agreement of her terms and owed her what he'd promised. He fulfilled the first part of the bargain by getting her with child, but surely his clumsy marriage proposal had been in violation of the other part of the contract—the part where he was supposed to take his bonus and walk away without a look back.

David wanted to be angry with her. He wanted to think of her as frigid and unrelenting and cruel. But, try as he might, he couldn't stop feeling guilty for what he'd done. He couldn't stop wishing that if he were going to trample over the rules of their arrangement, he would have done it in a way that left her with no doubt to how he felt.

"I want to marry you because I love you," he recited to the empty carriage. "Because I cannot live without you, and because I had no idea what it meant to commit to one person until I realized I wanted to commit myself to you."

Not perfect, but true enough. Words he ought to have found the courage to say in the heat of the moment, but for the first time his tongue had failed him. Seduction and charm, he could manage. Talk of real and deep emotion, he was utterly miserable at. It was no wonder she would not have him.

Anyway, it was too late for him to try to smooth things over. He had left his bedchamber this morning to find that the snow had ceased hours ago, and rising temperatures had already begun melting it away. Caruthers reported that Regina and her driver departed shortly after dawn, with David none the wiser. He had sulked over breakfast, his expression clearly enough to keep his mother and the twins from asking probing questions. If they suspected what had gone on between him and Regina the night before, no one spoke of it.

By midday, a bank draft had arrived from Regina in the amount of five thousand pounds. There was no accompanying note, no hint that she wanted anything more than to deliver his promised funds. Of course there was nothing more than that. She had made it clear she intended to adhere to their contract without wavering. He had his answer, no matter how unsatisfactory, and there was nothing left for David to do but carry on with his life.

Thus, his impromptu trip to London. His things had been packed and the carriage readied in less than an hour. His valet had been left behind, with David in no mood to endure the company of another person. Having to tie his own cravats seemed like a small enough inconvenience for the sake of solitude with his own tormented thoughts.

He did not plan to remain for long, but Benedict had written to inform him that Hugh, Aubrey, and Nick were all back in Town. Seeing them again might offer a sense of familiarity and make him feel more like himself. The farm was far from saved, but once winter gave way to spring, the land along the east pasture would be ready for planting. The income from the sale of wool and meat had gone into the materials needed to repair their mill, building of new and better enclosures, and improvements about the house. With Regina's bank draft, they would finally find firmer footing. In the next year or two, profits from harvests and wool would be enough to restore the Graham family and their lands to their former glory. He would begin interviewing new stewards upon his return now that he could afford to pay one.

Matters had improved enough that the entire estate wouldn't crumble in his absence. He would spend a few days in the company of his friends and try to convince himself that Regina's rejection had been for the best.

REGINA FLINCHED AND MUTTERED A CURSE, BEFORE LIFTING HER pricked and reddened finger to her lips. That was the third time she had jabbed herself with the sewing needle in the past hour, as her mind wandered away from the chore of mending. Her maid typically did this work, but Regina had hoped setting herself to some mindless task might help her stop thinking about David.

No such luck.

Apparently, mending stockings and chemises was almost too senseless a job, because Regina's traitorous mind kept taking her into dangerous territory. David's words echoed in her thoughts, wracking her with guilt and giving her a pounding headache.

But, why should she feel guilty? David had been in the wrong. By asking her to marry him, he had completely disregarded her wishes. He'd used her unborn child as a tool by which to manipulate her into marriage. Whether because he wanted her money, or because he wanted the babe he had sired, it made no difference. Regina had vowed never to wed again, and she would not change her mind.

"Are you ready to talk about it now?" Powell asked from his corner of the room.

He'd been silent all day, hovering at her back over breakfast and trailing her during her morning ride. When she settled down with her mending, Powell had opened a book and taken his place in an armchair, occasionally peering at her over the pages. She had hoped he might not try to pull her into conversation, but Regina ought to have known better. Powell had not yet asked about her overnight stay at David's house, but he had to notice the dark circles under her eyes and the tight set to her mouth. She had tossed and turned the entire night, reliving her last hours with David over and over.

"No," she snapped, lowering her head back over her chemise. But then, the needle slipped and a drop of blood splashed the lace of the neckline and Regina threw everything—needle and all—to the floor at her feet. "Bloody hell!"

Powell raised an eyebrow and glanced at the little box containing spools of thread and other bits and bobs. "Haven't you a thimble or some such?"

She blinked, staring at him as if he'd just asked her to solve a mathematical equation without the benefit of pencil and paper. Such a simple question, one that should not make her feel like such an imbecile.

"I do," she muttered taking up a scrap of unused fabric from the chest and using it to apply pressure to her tortured finger. "I'm not feeling at all the thing today and forgot it entirely."

"Because you're now in a ... delicate way?"

When Regina's lips parted on a sharp breath, Powell slouched and crossed one leg over the other with a shrug. "I noticed you've been sleeping later the past few weeks. My sister slept like a corpse when she carried my nephew ... it was the first sign, even before the sickness. We'll hear the cries of a newborn around September, I'm thinking."

With a disbelieving shake of her head, she avoided Powell's probing gaze. The man was too astute by half, and his constant nearness meant he always knew even the things she tried to hide.

"You are correct. I discovered it just a few days ago and informed David last night."

"Ah, so that's it, then."

Regina had just gone back into her basket when Powell's words stilled her. "What's that supposed to mean?"

"Only that I had a feeling it might come to this once you got what you wanted. He wasn't content to walk away once you told him, was he?" At her shocked expression, Powell chuckled. "Haven't you been paying attention? The man's been besotted with you from the first."

Regina might have upbraided him for such impertinent talk, but Powell wasn't just a servant. Because of Randolph's tyrannical rule, he was the only friend she had in the world.

David was your friend. He was your lover, but he became more than that.

The thought made a well of nausea erupt in her throat and panic flare in her chest. Powell was wrong. She *had* been paying attention, so she knew David had grown fond of her. However, she hadn't wanted to believe it was true. She still did not.

"He doesn't want me, he only thinks he does," she argued feebly, twisting the skirt of her gown with shaking fingers. She wore spring green today, a fabric she had bought because the *modiste* pointed out how it matched her eyes. It hadn't been worn in years, and for some reason after her night at The Crimson Dove with David, Regina had found it impossible to go back to the widow's weeds.

"I think the man knows his own mind better than you."

"And I think it's just like you to take the other man's side in this!"

Powell's mouth turned down as he studied her, fingers stroking his chin. "I'm on your side in all things, and I think you know that. However, I also think you do your Mr. Graham a disservice. He isn't Hurst."

She shot to her feet, her injured finger throbbing as she balled her hands into fists. "I never said he was."

Powell arched an eyebrow. "Didn't you? If it isn't you he wants, then just what do you suspect Mr. Graham is after? Your money?"

"He is certainly in desperate need," she argued. "He told me himself he wasn't the marrying sort, but would possibly consider it if enough money were involved."

"And do you think a few thousand pounds would matter if you could be made happy? Not just content, or living with what small joys you think you can have. I mean actually, truly happy, as you have been these past months."

She parted her lips to insist that she certainly had *not* been as happy as Powell claimed, but the pitying look he gave her had Regina snapping them shut. To argue that David hadn't brought her joy would be a lie, and no one would see that better than Powell.

"You left this house for the first time in weeks to go to that public house, and I've never seen you as happy as you were the next morning ... when you came down to breakfast wearing a *pink* frock. You haven't been able to force yourself back into the black ever since. You hum to yourself when you think I can't hear, and you practically bounce with excitement while waiting for him to come to you at night. Until this morning you haven't asked me to follow you anywhere, or stand outside your door, and it's because he made you feel safe. You weren't afraid of him."

Her eyes began to sting with tears, which Regina found befuddling, considering her eyes had been dry through the entire argument with David. The man must have thought her so cold and unfeeling. But she'd concealed all that from him after years of practice. Randolph had only taken pleasure in her tears.

Only now, the dam was breaking, and she didn't think she could fight it anymore.

"I have been a man's wife," she rasped, her voice hitching on a sob. "There wasn't a part of myself that belonged to me. I've only just begun to rediscover myself again, to feel as if I am actually alive instead of just breathing for the purpose of existence. I ... I cannot ... you don't understand!"

Powell came to his feet. "I *don't* understand. Hurst was a bastard and a coward, but Graham isn't like him."

"He is a man like any other."

"And so am I. Yet you trust me with your life."

"You are different, Powell."

"Am I? I'm bigger than you, certainly stronger. I could strangle you with one hand right now, and you'd be powerless to stop me. Last I looked, I still have a cock, which can be its own sort of weapon and well you know it."

Despite the sinister nature of those words, Regina didn't feel an inkling of fear. "You would never hurt me."

"Why do you think that?" he prodded, taking a step toward her, then another. "I'm a man, aren't I?"

"But you aren't ..."

He gave her a significant look when she trailed off, realizing where his round of questioning had led her. "I am not Randolph Hurst. It's like I said already ... neither is Graham."

It seemed like a logical enough conclusion, yet its impact affected her differently this time. It weakened her resolve, and she crumbled back into her chair, shoulders sagging as she succumbed to the first wave of tears. Powell's big hand appeared in her periphery, a white handkerchief held between his fingers.

"There are many men in the world who would hurt a sweet, deli-cate little thing like you," he said, crouching at her feet. "I will not lie to you and say there aren't. The thought of anyone else treating you as Hurst did is one of the reasons I've stayed. The other being that I have a great deal of affection for you."

Regina dabbed at her eyes and gave him a smile, though it was shaky. "You know I feel the same way."

"Then I hope you'll excuse my impudence just this once, and listen to me. If you never want to wed again because you value your independence and want to raise this babe alone, then I am happy for you. I will serve you, and care for that child just as I care for you. But I am a servant, and there are voids in you that I can't fill. If you're avoiding a second marriage out of fear, then I cannot stand by and allow that without telling you I think you're making a grave mistake. Graham may need your money, and the child in your belly might have made him feel responsible for you, but I believe there's more to it than that. I suspect you believe that, too."

"How can I trust it?" she whispered. "It was difficult enough to trust him with my person. But ... all the rest? Powell, I'm so afraid."

"Do you love him?"

She closed her eyes, all the air vacating her lungs as she grappled with that question. *Did* she love David? Thinking back over their time together, she could see things so clearly. He put her at ease, but it was more than that. He made her laugh and smile, and had reminded her how it felt to have hope. Regina had thought herself in love with Randolph because he was handsome and charming, but she'd been young and naïve then. With all her life experience having taught her what love wasn't, it should be easy enough for her to recognize what it *was*.

She had allowed herself to be fooled once; stoicism and iciness seemed like effective defenses against ever being tricked again. So, she kept her guard up to protect herself—only, it hadn't worked. David had worked his way past her defenses, making it impossible for her to deny what had begun happening between them weeks ago.

Love. One small word that had caused her a world of hurt in her youth. She still carried the internal scars, and even a few outer ones.

"I thought I loved *him*. He told me he loved me, and I believed him."

"I'm not asking you about Hurst. Forget him. He's dead, and good riddance. Graham ... do you love him?"

Powell waited for her answer with a furrowed brow, and he leaned in slightly as if anticipating her answer.

"Yes. I do love him, and that terrifies me most of all, because ... what if he doesn't love me back?"

One large, thick finger swiped at her cheek, and Powell's mouth curved at one corner. "What's not to love? Besides, it seems fairly obvious to me. A blind man could see he's mad for you."

Was Powell right? Had he noticed what Regina hadn't wanted to see? David hadn't mentioned love when proposing marriage, but then she hadn't given him a chance to fully express his thoughts. She had been so intent on keeping him from getting too close, she never stopped to realize the battle had been lost already.

And yet, fear was still such a powerful force. It whispered nefarious warnings through the darkest corners of her mind.

"What if you're wrong?"

Powell stood and shrugged, turning to go back to his corner of the room. "What if I'm right?"

As it turned out, being in the presence of his friends had the opposite effect on David's mood that he'd hoped for. Honestly, he ought to have known better. After all, among the five original courtesans, he and Benedict were the only ones who weren't blissfully in love and newly married. Aubrey, Hugh, and Dominick were so nauseatingly happy that it only reminded David how miserable he was.

Upon arriving in London, he had been invited to take a guestroom at Hugh and Evelyn's townhouse, which he accepted for lack of his own residence and the need to conserve his funds. Two days into his visit he had been driven out of his mind. The newlywed couple—who were also expectant parents—were so adorable together David's teeth ached from mere proximity to such sweetness. Hugh doted on Evelyn in a way that surpassed even his usual attentiveness, which reminded anyone in their company of his wife's delicate condition. While the drape of her gowns hid any evidence, David couldn't help but think of Regina whenever he set eyes on his friend's wife.

How long before Regina's belly began to swell, making her unsteady on her feet? Would Powell remain nearby to make sure she didn't overtax herself, or knock into things, or go tumbling down the stairs? Who would send for the physician if something went wrong, or comfort her when she was ill? Hugh did all these things for Evelyn, taking her arm on the stairs even when she insisted she didn't need his help, forcing her to sit and prop her feet up when he felt she had been standing too long, rushing to tend her when her maid came to report that her mistress was feeling ill. He'd even waited in a line of carriages at Gunter's for two hours because Evelyn craved a specific flavor of ice, and apparently no substitute would do.

Yes, accepting their offer of a room had been ill-advised. But where else was he to go? Aubrey and Lucinda were fresh home from their wedding trip to Venice, and they had begun applying themselves to the husband hunt on behalf of their young niece. Nick and Calliope were just as giddy after their honeymoon in Paris, and Dominick was perhaps the worst of all the new husbands. He called his wife 'goddess' and acted as if the sun shined out of her arse—quite a bewildering turn of events considering his past reputation.

David might have retreated to Benedict's house, but for some reason being in the company of someone who was as bitter on matters of love was just as unappealing.

His first night in London had been marked by a dinner at Nick's and Calliope's house, over which there were toasts to the new marriages and the impending birth of Hugh's and Evie's baby. The afternoon following day Jacksons, during which Benedict had pummeled every last one of them. The women had joined them for a night at the theater, where they sat in Benedict's private box and pretended not to notice the stares and whispers. Most of the time, Benedict's and Aubrey's presence were enough to gain quite a bit of attention, but this time David suspected it was Nick and Calliope who caused the uproar.

Now, on this third night, the men had all gathered at Boodles for dinner, drinks, and cards. Benedict had yet to arrive, but Hugh, Nick, and Aubrey all shared a table with David. Dinner had been consumed, and now they were on to drinks and cigars while awaiting Ben's arrival so they could start their game. A collection of newspapers littered the table between them, though a copy of *The London Gossip* could not be found in the pile.

"Ben certainly seems to have shut her up, at least for now," Hugh remarked when the subject came up.

"A single copy of that rag hasn't been seen in London in two months," Aubrey said, shoulders shaking with laughter. "When she realized her boys had been compromised, she let them go and found new ones."

"Ben bought them, too," Nick sputtered between sips of brandy. "The mad, bloody genius. I daresay she realizes by now there isn't a person whose loyalty she can purchase in this entire city when Ben has the blunt to outbid her."

David had to admit the plan seemed like a sound one, though Benedict had yet to tell them what the next step might be. There were only so many times he could purchase the services of the Gossip's errand boys before she found some new way to spread her written words. The woman had created a successful gossip column anonymously, and she had enough dirt on half the peerage to gain herself anything she might want. The other men might find her amusing, but David couldn't help but share Benedict's assessment that she was dangerous.

"Not that there's any shortage of amusing gossip to be read elsewhere," Aubrey said, lifting one of the papers and turning it so they could all see the illustration. "Nick, they've portrayed you as a satyr in this one."

"Let me see that!" Nick exclaimed, snatching the paper from Aubrey and tilting it into the candlelight.

From where David sat, he could make out a rather humorous drawing of Nick and Calliope—only Nick didn't look himself. He had the legs of a goat with the horns to match, his grin malicious as he carried a shocked, wedding dress-clad Calliope out of St. George's over his shoulder. The drawing favored Calliope, at least, which was more than could be said for some of the others they'd seen—ones that had sent Nick into a rage and had him tearing up every copy he got his hands on. In this particular column, Calliope had been painted the poor, beautiful innocent, and Nick the notorious debauchee.

"I quite like this one," Nick said with raised eyebrows. "Look how pretty my Anni is … and the horns rather flatter my bone structure, don't you think?"

Hugh and Aubrey burst out laughing while Nick folded the paper and tucked it into the breast pocket of his coat, insisting he must take it home to show his wife. Meanwhile, Aubrey's attention had been captured by another paper, one he read while scowling, all trace of humor wiped from his face. David emptied his fourth tumbler of brandy down his throat and signaled a waiter for more.

"What's wrong?" Hugh asked.

"Devil if I know," Nick muttered, giving David an acerbic look. "He's been pouting all week."

"Not him," Hugh said. "Aubrey. He looks like he's seen a ghost."

Aubrey laid the paper down and shook his head as if coming out of a daze. "It's nothing … just a death notice. I was surprised by it, is all."

David's interest was finally captured, likely because it took the attention off him and his 'pouting.' "Who died?"

"The Countess of Vautrey," Aubrey replied. "I didn't know her well, but her husband was a friend of ours from Eton, and then Cambridge. You remember Vautrey, Nick?"

Nick frowned. "Of course. Best dressed man I ever met other than you. We attended his wedding. His countess has died, then?"

"So it would seem," Aubrey replied. "It must have been sudden. She was young and in good health."

"I am sorry for it," Nick murmured, squirming in his chair as if uncomfortable with the subject of death. Not much time had passed since his uncle's passing, and the two had been quite close. As well, David suspected the notion of a man losing his wife hit far closer to home than it might have several months ago. "What the devil has Vautrey been up to these days, anyway?"

"What's that about Vautrey?"

Benedict's sudden appearance had Aubrey sitting up straighter.

David paused with his tumbler pressed to his lips, as Ben lowered himself into the empty seat on Nick's other side.

"I was just wondering where he's been all these years," Nick said, oblivious to Aubrey's wide eyes and the slight shake of his head. "Now that I think of it, I haven't seen him in Town since his wedding. Ben, the two of you were always close. Any idea where he's been hiding?"

Ben had just accepted a filled decanter from a waiter—his usual when he frequented Boodles—and glowered at Nick as he slammed it on the surface of the table. David flinched, caught off guard by the sudden motion as well as the resulting clatter. He worked his jaw as if grinding glass between his teeth, fingers flexing tight around the neck of the decanter.

"Ben," Aubrey said, his voice low. "He asked because of this."

Benedict took up the paper and narrowed his eyes at it. His expression transformed by degrees at what he found on the page, softening to one of disbelief and shock, then hardening until his upper lip peeled back in a sneer.

"My condolences," he said, sounding as if he were anything but sorry about the death of this mysterious countess.

"Ben," Aubrey said again. "Don't."

Benedict waved a dismissive hand. "Don't what? Drink this entire decanter of brandy? Because that's exactly what I'm going to do."

Nick snatched up the waiting deck of cards to begin shuffling. "No need to get a bee in your breeches. I just thought the two of you were friends, so maybe you knew something."

"Nick, leave it," Aubrey warned.

"You thought wrong," Benedict snapped, already halfway through his first tumbler. "Bugger him."

"Nick, deal the cards," Hugh interjected, looking as if he would rather be anywhere else just now. Like David, he wasn't much for confrontation.

Everyone knew Benedict was not to be trifled with when he was in such a mood, but Nick was antagonistic by nature. He could also be oblivious at times, and often let his mouth run away with him until it was too late to stop the resulting fallout.

"Yes," Aubrey agreed. "Now Ben's here, we can start the game."

David was relieved when Nick silently dealt the cards, though there was clearly an undercurrent of silent communication happening between Ben and Aubrey, which in turn seemed to annoy Dominick more. Of the five of them, Aubrey and Ben were the closest, and David had long accepted that there were things Aubrey knew about Benedict that the rest of them might never be privy to.

Whatever was happening here, David had his own problems and was too inebriated to care about whatever had Benedict in a dudgeon. The distraction of a card game was exactly what he needed.

It only worked for about an hour, during which Benedict finished three-quarters of his decanter and surpassed David in drunkenness.

"All right," Hugh said suddenly, with an exasperated sigh. "I cannot sit here any longer and pretend everything is all right. Something is very clearly wrong with both of you."

He said this while swiveling his gaze from Benedict to David, eyebrows raised as if waiting for an answer.

Nick snapped the deck into a neat stack and laid them down. "He's right. If Ben insists on acting like an ass—"

"I do," Benedict interjected, raising his glass to them before taking another long swallow.

"Then, David, you're going to have to start talking. You haven't been yourself since you got back to London."

"For God's sake, Nick," Aubrey ground out. "The man's father died, and he's been killing himself trying to keep his family clothed and fed."

"It's more than that," Nick argued, before turning back to David. "Isn't it?"

"Leave him be," Benedict said, his words slurring as the brandy began getting the best of him. "The way you three carry on, it's almost as if you have forgotten what life was like before the clouds parted and Eros struck you with his mythical arrows. Any idiot with half a brain could see he's heartsick. Fool's gone and fallen in love with Regina Hurst."

David choked on the mouthful of brandy he'd just sipped, sputtering and swiping at his mouth with his sleeve while Aubrey pounded his back. Hugh and Nick glanced back and forth between them in clear shock.

Benedict threw his head back and laughed, brandy sloshing over the sides of his glass as he slammed it to the table. "Tell me I'm wrong. You can't, can you? I have seen that pitiful look often enough—first from Hugh, then Aubrey and Nick, and now you.

Hugh turned to David, who then became the sole recipient of his concern. "Is it true, David?"

David nodded, his head spinning from what had just occurred as well as the brandy muddling his senses. "I asked her to marry me, but she refused. Ben is right ... I'm pitiful."

"No, he isn't," Nick said, glaring at Benedict. "This Hurst woman is pitiful if she can't see what a fine catch you are."

"I own an impoverished estate," David pointed out.

"Trivial. Besides, your letters indicated things are on the mend."

"I don't exactly have a reputation as the most respectable of men."

Nick scoffed. "Last I heard that wasn't an impediment to marriage. Just ask the biggest rake in London ... oh! He's sitting right here, fresh off his honeymoon—though I'll have you know he is entirely reformed."

"He's not wrong," Hugh said with a shrug. "Perhaps you could try again. Do you have any reason to believe she might return your feelings?"

David thought back to those blissful moments right before he'd gone and put his foot in his mouth. He thought over the long nights they had spent in her bed, whispered conversations stretching between bouts of lovemaking. He remembered holding her while she slept and dancing with her in a crowded public house. The memories were colored by his love for her, by the realization that he had probably been in love with her for longer than he'd realized. But, did that mean his view of those moments had been distorted? Had he seen things that were not there?

"I'm not entirely certain," he admitted. "But then, that is probably my fault. I didn't actually tell her how I feel. I think she assumed I only asked her to marry me because she's pregnant."

Hugh groaned and braced his forehead in one hand while Nick muttered that he was an idiot. Benedict glowered at him in silence.

"You're going to have to tell us everything, from the beginning," Aubrey said, signaling a waiter for more brandy.

They drank it as David told his story, holding back the most intimate of details but ensuring they understood the whole of it. When he was finished, Nick and Aubrey were looking at him as if unable to believe what he had just heard. Hugh seemed less shocked but was still thoughtful.

"Well?" David asked. "What am I to do? I can't simply sit back and accept that I've lost her."

"No," Hugh agreed. "You're going to have to convince her to listen to you, and you have to make yourself clear this time."

David sat up straighter. "I can do that."

Nick snorted. "Can you? That pretty face of yours always does the talking. The reputation your mouth has isn't exactly for your use of words."

Aubrey choked on a laugh, then schooled his face into a more serious expression as he turned back to David. "Sorry. That was bloody funny."

David shrugged. "I'll admit it was. But what about Regina? If she will even hear me out, I assume I only have one last chance to get this right."

Hugh and Nick traded meaningful glances, before both turned back to him as if they'd come to the same conclusion.

"What you need is a grand gesture," Hugh said.

"He's right," Nick agreed. "Something big ... something guaranteed to leave her with no doubt that you refuse to live without her."

"I suppose that could work," David mused.

"Trust us, it will work," Hugh insisted. "You're looking at the kings of the grand gesture. One of us stormed a wedding to beg the bride to marry him, then fought a duel and took a bullet from the scorned groom."

"And one of us publicly exhibited a half-nude painting of a woman before the entire *beau monde*," Nick added. "After which, he issued a public marriage proposal at a ball where the most influential people in society were in attendance."

"Mine was definitely the better gesture," Hugh muttered.

"I think not," Nick fired back.

"We're talking about David right now," Aubrey grumbled.

David shook his head to clear it, fatigue and brandy making it diffi-cult to follow their back-and-forth. But then, clarity dawned, and the niggling of an idea crept onto the periphery of his thoughts. It might just work ... or it might backfire spectacularly. But David was desper-ate. He couldn't stand to wallow in such misery; not without doing everything he could to win Regina's heart.

"I think I have an idea."

Ben chose that moment to interject, making a low sound of scorn in his throat. "God, could you be more predictable? The woman threw you away, and here you are ready to go crawling back. Just like Hugh did when Evelyn wrote him off, or just like Aubrey did when Lucinda walked out, or just like Nick did when Calliope literally chose to *marry someone else.*"

"That's enough," Aubrey said, rising to face Benedict. "You're making a scene."

"So I am," Benedict said with another little laugh, this one derisive and harsh. "It's odd, isn't it? All this time I thought I was the one trying to prevent us all from being exposed. I'm the only one who gave a bloody fuck about our reputations and protecting the lot of you from ruin. And what did you all do? You ran off and made fools of yourselves over women who wouldn't have had you otherwise."

"Oh, sod off, you pompous ass," Nick snapped. "If you were any more envious you'd choke on it! Whatever the hell happened between you and the Countess of Vautrey has nothing to do with the rest of us."

Ben had been about to turn away from the table, but Nick's words halted him in his tracks. He swiveled to face them, fists clenched and a thundercloud of fury settling over his face.

"You don't know what you're talking about," he growled, his words holding a clear warning.

Nick chose not to heed it. "Don't I? You have been in your cups ever since Aubrey told you about her death. You think I didn't notice you haven't attended a wedding since hers and Vautrey's? Not until Aubrey and Lucinda, anyway. What's that about, hm? Maybe you're so angry with me, and Hugh, and David, and Aubrey because you never got over wanting someone who didn't want you back!"

David traded glances with Hugh, who looked as confused and worried over this whole mess as he felt. These revelations were news to David, but made sense when Nick laid them out that way. David glanced at Aubrey, who was watching Ben, worry creating brackets around his mouth and furrows in his brow.

Benedict remained surprisingly calm, clearing his throat and running a hand over his jaw. When he looked at Nick again, all expression had left his face, but the rage still burned in his eyes, fiery and raw.

"Fuck Vautrey, fuck his countess, and fuck you."

Nick snorted and rolled his eyes as if he'd expected such, but said nothing. Benedict whirled to leave, but Aubrey gave chase, stepping over the chair Ben had overturned in his haste.

"No," Ben said, holding up a hand to ward Aubrey off. "I don't need you … any of you. Go home to your *wives*. David, you are on your own. I'm done cleaning up your messes."

Aubrey glanced back to David as Ben made his exit, turning several heads on his way out. The club hadn't gone quite silent, but several eyes had strayed to their table once Nick and Benedict started trading verbal jabs.

Aubrey's dark eyes brimmed with helplessness and remorse as he squeezed David's shoulder. "He didn't mean that."

"Like hell he didn't," Nick grumbled. "He's been unbearable since Hugh and Evelyn married, and you know it."

"Nick, just leave it," Hugh said. "You've only gone and made matters worse."

"You're wrong," Aubrey added. "You have no idea what you're talking about. If you did, you would have kept your mouth shut for once in your life."

With that, he gave David one last apologetic look, then turned and set off for the exit—obviously intent on catching up with Benedict. No one else dared follow.

CHAPTER 13

Regina wiped her damp palms on the skirt of her gown as she followed the housekeeper to the salon where the Graham family received visitors. A fortnight had passed since she'd last seen David, though not for lack of trying on her part. After her conversation with Powell, she had spent a great deal of time alone with her own turbulent thoughts. Her fear hadn't abated entirely—really, it had hardly lessened at all. But it had occurred to Regina that fear nearly kept her from experiencing passion and pleasure in the bedchamber. Had she not pushed her trepidation aside to allow David to show her how things should be, she might still be a half-dead shell of her former self.

And, it wasn't only sensuality he had introduced her to. There had been laughter and joy and lighthearted fun, which she had forgotten over the eight years of her first marriage. She had come into their arrangement feeling old, shriveled, and lifeless. Now, she stood on the other side a new woman—perhaps not completely changed, but still in a better state than when they had begun.

The expanse of the rest of her life stretched before her, alive with possibilities she might never have considered if not for David.

That epiphany had led her to his doorstep, only for the butler to inform her David had left for London and no one knew exactly when he should be expected to return. That had been disappointing, but Regina was no less determined to see him. She returned three times more, only to be turned away. David had returned to Lancashire days ago, but he was never at home when she called.

Until now.

Mrs. Moffat gave her a puzzled look on her way out, as if wondering what she might be doing here. Surely she didn't know the truth of what went on between her and David, but the household couldn't have failed to notice that David's swift departure had coincided with her overnight stay in this house.

Once left alone, she sprang up from her chair. Even sitting still became too much of a trial, and she paced while ruminating over what she would say to David. During their time apart she'd had far too much time to rehearse various speeches, but nothing that truly encompassed how she felt. It had been Regina's hope that she would know what to say once she laid eyes on him.

Apparently, she hadn't been as prepared to see him as she supposed, because Regina's throat constricted the moment the door swung open. Her heart fluttered wildly at the sight of David, disheveled but still heartbreakingly handsome as he filled the doorway. One hand braced on the knob, he stared at her as if unable to believe his eyes.

He wore trousers and braces over a shirt, all of which looked old and worn. His hair held a layer of dust, and a sheen of sweat stood out along his brow. What had she interrupted?

"Hello, David," she said, then cleared her throat and injected confidence she did not feel into her voice. "I hope I haven't come at an inconvenient time."

Rubbing the back of his neck, he glanced over his shoulder, then stepped into the room and shut the door. "Not exactly, but ... well, I had intended to ask you to call on me, only ... I wasn't ready just yet."

"Oh. If you need more time—"

"No!" he said suddenly, lurching toward her but then coming to a halt halfway across the room as if thinking better of it. "That is, I am glad to see you, Regina. You look ... well."

His gaze traveled over her, and she stiffened, realizing he must be searching for any sign of her condition. Regina's face flushed as his gaze fell to her bodice, which stretched a bit tight over her bosom. There was definitely more flesh filling her gowns these days, and the tenderness of her breasts made her stays an uncomfortable nuisance.

"Are you?" he added, gazing down at her belly as if to indicate the baby. "Everything is all right?"

"Oh, yes. I have been seen by a physician who assures me all seems to be going as expected."

His jaw flexed as he looked away from her, and she wondered if she might not be too late. Was he still angry with her? Had he decided that perhaps he didn't want her anymore?

But then, he shocked her by offering a small smile and gesturing toward the door. "Will you come with me? I want to show you something."

She wanted to insist they continue their conversation, but the earnest longing in his eyes made her willing to follow him anywhere.

He led her from the room and to the staircase, offering his arm while bracing the other hand on the banister. Regina wanted to lean into him, burying her face in his shirt and inhale the scent of him—the light hint of clean sweat melding with his signature sandalwood. But she didn't feel as if she had the right to such intimacies. Not until she was certain he would accept her. Then, nothing would stop her from holding him, kissing him, and lavishing him with affection.

Interestingly, he led her down a corridor opposite the one her guest room had been in, leaving her wondering if this might not be where the family's rooms were located.

"David?"

He turned to her in front of one of the doors, hands folded behind his back. "The last time we spoke, I did not make myself as clear as I should have. The quarrel that followed was entirely my fault."

Horror overwhelmed her as she realized he had blamed himself for her shortcomings. Had he stayed away for so long thinking himself completely at fault?

"No, please, I cannot allow you to take the blame," she argued. "It was me, I ... I didn't understand—"

He held one hand up to silence her, then grinned. "It would seem we both share some of the blame. For my part, I did not explain myself well enough and that led to you assuming the worst. And why shouldn't you have? Experience has taught you not to trust any man who isn't Powell."

"But I do trust you. You've proven yourself to me time and again, and I am so very sorry for making you think that I did not."

"I will forgive you, but only if you come into this room and remain silent until I finish talking."

Curiosity reared its head as he laid his hand on the knob, excitement brightening his eyes as he watched her. Whatever was behind this door must be important.

"Very well."

Taking a deep breath, he let it out while pushing the door open. Regina squinted as he took her hand to lead her inside, parted curtains letting in a great deal of natural light. This time of day the sun seemed to shine directly into the space, allowing her the perfect view. What she saw took her breath away. One hand held over her open mouth, Regina gazed about, observing it all in stunned silence.

David backed away from her and held his arms out to encompass the space. "I was going to send for you when it was ready. I wanted this to be absolutely perfect, but you're here now and I will admit to being a little impatient. That smell is a combination of paint and furniture polish ... it will go away once I open the windows for a few hours."

What he had been so excited to show her turned out to be a suite encompassing a nursery. They stood in a day room just now, where white cloths draped various pieces of furniture, which David started removing under her watchful eyes. A couch, love seat, and collection of child-size chairs all appearing brand new. They were upholstered in a cheery yellow damask printed with tiny blue flowers—a perfect match for the striped wallpaper adorning the walls over freshly-painted white wainscoting. Silver sconces gleamed as if freshly polished, and pale blue curtains decorated the windows. One wall was lined with chests and bookshelves, and collections of toys caught her attention in this corner and that.

A hearth stood along the far wall, with an ancient-looking rocking-chair placed beside it.

"My mother sat in that chair to rock me to sleep," he said when he noticed her staring at it. "I gave it a polish, but left it entirely as I found it. It's a Graham family heirloom. Oh, and look!"

He dashed to one of the open doors, which Regina saw led into a sleeping chamber. Within, she found a row of three tiny beds, as well as an infant's cradle near a window seat, which had been dressed with a collection of hand-embroidered pillows. David pointed to the inside of the doorframe, upon which were scratched children's growth measurements.

"Here I am at eight," he said with a little laugh. "I couldn't have been considered tall until I was about twelve. See how much I grew that year? Here are the twins at five, and at eight, and at ten. They have always been exactly the same height. Oh, and see here?"

He crossed to another set of doors on opposite walls, opening both to show her that they led into separate rooms. One was a nurse's chamber, and the other was a bright and airy room roughly the size of her chamber at home. A room decorated in shades of magenta and rose, fit for the lady of the house.

When she turned back to David, her eyes were filled with unshed tears, her chest tight with the overwhelming emotion welling up in her.

He smiled and cupped her face, his thumbs swiping at the tears that escaped when she blinked. "I brought most of the fabric and newer decor from London, and have been working on this in my every spare hour. My home isn't perfect, Regina, and neither is my life. I still have a great deal of work to do before things are as they should be, but I needed you to see for yourself what I'm willing to do for the comfort and care of our child ... but also of you. You see, the baby was part of a contract, and I cannot lay any claim to him unless you let me. And I do hope you will let me, because I already love him ... or her, I don't care which it turns out to be. I only know that this baby will be the best parts of you and I combined, and that will make it the most perfect thing God ever created."

A small sob escaped her throat. "David ..."

"Now, now, you're supposed to let me finish talking. You are supposed to let me tell you that I love you. Not your money, or the idea of you bearing my child ... but you, Regina Hurst. I think I've loved you for far longer than I realized. You have made what might have been the worst time in my life bearable. I miss you when we aren't together, and my world seems better, brighter, and more beautiful with you in it. So, you see, I can no longer settle for the occasional night in your bed, or illicit contracts with inevitable endings. I never want to sleep another night without you beside me. I don't want to wake another morning without your face being the first thing I see when I open my eyes. I understand that there is still so much for us to learn about each other, and I know you have no reason to put your life into the hands of another man. But if you could trust me with your heart, with the child inside you, and with your future, I can promise you will not regret it."

She was a weeping mess by the time he finished, smiling and sobbing and trying her best to mop at the tears on her face. Taking her hands, David guided her back into the day room, easing her down onto the sofa and sitting down beside her.

"There now," he murmured, using the cuff of his shirt to dab at her face. "I didn't mean to overwhelm you. I meant for this to be a good surprise."

She smiled through her tears and took hold of his hands. "It's a wonderful surprise ... the most beautiful thing anyone has ever given me."

He sighed, relief making his shoulders sag and his brow smooth over. "I'm so glad you like it. It isn't finished, though. I still have to—"

"David, it's perfect, every bit of it. Now that you're finished, I have some things I must tell you. I came here thinking to take you by surprise, but you have managed to outdo me. I can only hope my words will suffice."

David draped an arm along the back of the couch, his fingertips stroking the nape of her neck as she began.

"My father urged me into the marriage with Randolph because he was wealthy. We were a genteel family and my father owned a bit of land, but it was nothing compared to what your family owns, or what I have inherited. Father wanted higher social standing, and a relative he could approach with his hand outstretched, so of course Randolph seemed like the perfect choice. None of that mattered to me, though. I thought I loved him and that he loved me. My delusion continued for the first few years of our marriage, and my own naiveté was partly to blame. I kept telling myself that it was my fault I couldn't enjoy his attentions in bed, or that he always seemed annoyed with me. The first time I denied him use of my body, he slapped me and forced me to comply anyway. I bit my tongue, and it bled for hours after. As I wept, I told myself I was to blame. My father told me it would be my husband's job to discipline me if he saw fit. If I was a good wife, I would have nothing to worry about."

David's hand tightened at the back of her neck, and he went deathly still. He remained silent, but Regina could see how difficult it was for him to control his reaction to what he'd just heard. She gave him a moment to recover and hoped he would be able to stomach the rest. Only Powell knew the entire truth, and now so would David.

"The first time he beat me with his fists, I packed a valise and fled back to my family. My brother was still a bachelor living at home. I thought he, at least, would defend me. I thought my mother would insist my father allow me to stay. Randolph hadn't just hit me with his open palm that one time. Over time, his flares of temper had gotten progressively worse. He had gone from occasionally slapping my face, to yanking me about by my hair and hurling me across the room. Once, my face smashed into a door, and it bruised my cheek and jaw. Randolph fussed over me and apologized, but he blamed me for upsetting him. The door had hurt me, not him, and I ought to mind my tongue if I did not want it to happen again. But this time ... he punched me and punched me—in my face, my belly, my shoulders, my back. I was in such pain. While I lay abed weeping, my mother asked me what I had done to force Randolph's hand. You see, it was obvious to her he'd had just cause for beating me."

"Fucking hell," David spat, lowering his head and drawing in a few deep, rasping breaths. "Regina ... surely you don't believe that."

"Not anymore, but I did then. When Randolph came to fetch me back home, I had convinced myself I could be a better wife to him. I would make him happy, and he wouldn't beat me again. Of course, I'm certain you realize it did not happen the way I'd hoped."

"Oh, Regina," he murmured, pulling her to him and holding her close. "My dear, I'm so sorry you endured that. I'm sorry no one was there to defend you."

"Powell was there," she said, clinging to the front of his shirt and drawing succor from his nearness. "But he was only a servant and there wasn't much he could do. Randolph's accident came as a blessing. It set me free ... not just from being under his thumb, but from my previous gullibility. You see, I had loved him, and he'd told me he felt the same ... and if that was how love felt, I wanted no part of it."

"Randolph didn't love you. He liked the idea of controlling you."

"I came to see that, but I was still so afraid. My heart led me to trust Randolph, and he hurt me. Thus, my heart could not be trusted. What if I let myself think I had fallen in love again, only to find myself in the clutches of another man like him? I couldn't survive it."

David stroked her hair and pressed his lips to her temple. "I understand. It's all right."

She leaned back to look into his eyes. "It's not all right. I was afraid of intimacy, but you showed me how wonderful it could be. You have made me happier these few months than I have been my entire life. I am still afraid, but I am done allowing fear to rule my life. I want to know all the joy and love Randolph deprived me of. I want that with you. So ... if you wouldn't mind terribly, I would love for you to ask me again to marry you."

He smiled, then went off the side of the sofa to one knee, taking one of her hands in both of his. "Regina ... will you marry me?"

Returning his smile, she lifted their joined hands to her lips and pressed a kiss to his knuckles. "Yes."

He stood and pulled her up with him, arms circling her waist. "Thank you for giving me a chance to propose again ... the right way."

"With such a lovely gesture, how could any woman say no?"

"My God, it worked!"

Regina started at the sudden intrusion of another man's voice, and turned in David's arms to find someone standing in the doorway. He was tall and slender, with a tumble of glossy brown hair falling into eyes that sparkled with mischief.

"It did," David replied, one arm still around her as he waved the other man in. "Come, meet my fiancée."

Regina tensed as the man entered the room, followed by three others. There was a woman with lightly-bronzed skin complemented by inky black hair and large, lovely eyes. Then came a second man who stood slightly shorter than the first, his hair dark like David's, his eyes a soft and kind brown. On his arm came a brown-haired woman with the slight protrusion of a pregnant belly showing at the front of her gown. It was so minor as to be almost unrecognizable, but when she placed her hand upon it in an unconscious gesture, Regina saw clearly she was in the early stages of pregnancy.

David guided her forward to greet them. "Regina, these are my friends—Dominick Burke and his wife, Calliope, and Hugh Radcliffe and his wife, Evelyn."

"How do you do?" she murmured.

David's lips brushed her ear as he whispered, "Nick and Hugh are former gentleman courtesans. Both have recently wed their former clients. So, you and these ladies have much in common."

Evelyn blushed and took hold of Regina's arm to pry her away from David. "Forgive him, I'm certain he couldn't resist the urge to shock you. It is true, however."

Calliope appeared on her other side, looping one arm through Evelyn's as they left the men to return to the sofa. They seated her between them, and Calliope patted her hand.

"The three of us are unique among the other ladies of society—oh, well I suppose I should say the four of us. Mustn't forget about Lucinda. She is Aubrey's wife, and I know she'll be elated to meet you."

Regina furrowed her brow. "And, this Aubrey ... he is also ..."

"A former courtesan, yes," Evelyn filled in. "Goodness, now that David is marrying you, there will be so few of them left. He's done well in his choice of bride. I can tell that already."

"She *must* be special if she could bring our dear David to his knees," Calliope added with a laugh.

"Funny," Dominick called out from where he stood with the other two men. "People often say the same thing about you, goddess."

Calliope raised her chin and gave her husband a look filled with hidden secrets and innuendo. "This is true."

"I'm so sorry to overwhelm you this way," Evelyn said, drawing Regina's attention away from the couple making eyes at one another in a most inappropriate fashion. "But Hugh insisted we must accompany David to Lancashire so he and Dominick could assist with his lovely gesture."

"So romantic," Calliope sighed, her lips parting in a riveting smile. "I am so glad for you. Dominick and I are only recently wed, but I've begun getting to know the other men and their wives, and can tell you … you've never had better friends."

"I like to think of us as more of a family than mere friends," Evelyn said. "And now that you and David are getting married, you'll be a part of it."

Regina felt her eyes brimming with tears, and she cursed her delicate nerves. She had been on edge for weeks, thinking it had to do with her uncertainty over David. But now that things were settled, she wondered if it was her condition making her so prone to tears. Calliope went into her reticule to offer a handkerchief, while Evelyn patted her hand and cooed over her like a mother hen.

As Regina dabbed at her cheeks, David caught her eye from where he stood with his friends, who were jostling him and pounding his back while offering their congratulations. He looked at her and smiled, seeming unconcerned about the tears she shed. He had to know what had brought on such an emotional response. In the span of a few months, their arrangement had filled so many of the empty places in her life. It had offered her love, and the child she longed for. Their marriage would give her a mother and sisters-in-law. It would give her the friends she'd been forced to go without for so long.

As she fell into conversation with the two women, Regina reminded herself to pull Powell aside later to thank him … and to inform him that he'd been right after all.

• • •

DAVID GLANCED UP FROM THE PAIR OF TINY FEET AND SLENDER ankles draped across his lap to find Powell hovering in the open doorway of the drawing room connected to what had once been Regina's bedchamber. As of this morning, she was now Mrs. David Graham, and would take up residence with him the moment their time of isolation from the rest of the world had ended.

They had agreed to wed as soon as humanly possible, with Regina having no care for the scandal it would cause for her to marry a mere few months after her first husband's death. She no longer wanted the world to think their child had been sired by Randolph, and was willing to let people gossip about the beginnings of her and David's relationship to keep their child from being presumed a Hurst.

They had spoken their vows in a small ceremony with only his mother, the twins, Powell, and the courtesans and their wives in attendance. Even Benedict had made the journey from London, though he remained sullen and silent after the ceremony and during the wedding breakfast. The tension between him and Nick was thicker than ever, and the two barely exchanged a word.

David had spoken to him briefly the night before, with Benedict offering an apology for his behavior at Boodles, but still giving no explanation. David hadn't pressed him for any.

He and Regina would spend a few weeks here alone before having her things moved to his residence—wanting their privacy but realizing that an actual wedding trip was going to have to wait. There were matters here that needed his attention, and it seemed he would be faced with one of them on his bloody wedding night.

"Begging your pardon, Mr. Graham. Forgive the interruption, but it can't be helped."

"What is it, Powell?" Regina asked, annoyance creating tiny lines between her eyebrows.

She had just kicked off her slippers, confessing to being exhausted after a long day of entertaining their small wedding party. David had been in the process of making her pliant so he could debauch her and consummate their marriage.

"That visitor we anticipated is here. Now."

David perked up at that. "Is he, now?"

Regina frowned and tried to sit up, but David pressed his thumb to the arch of her foot, making her relax against the cushion at her back. "Who's here?"

"Your cousin-in-law," David replied, never breaking Powell's gaze. "He knows about the wedding?"

"It would seem so, sir."

"Good. Bring him here and tell him Regina's *husband* will receive him."

Regina gaped at him as Powell left to do his bidding. "What on earth is going on? Surely you don't intend to speak with Tobias on our wedding night!"

He went on rubbing her foot, his gaze returning to the half-open door. "Oh, but I do. Today marks our new beginning, my dear. I'll not have him intruding upon our lives going forward. I am your husband now, and that means your problems are mine to solve ... or grind into dust if it comes to it."

She groaned when he found a particularly tender spot near the ball of her foot, then sighed as he circled and pressed to ease the tension. "You keep that up, I'll let you do whatever you like."

He spared her a glance and a sly smile. "Oh, I intend to the moment this matter has been handled to my satisfaction."

David and Powell had shared a few drinks a week before the wedding, and the man had filled him in on the persistence of one, Tobias Hurst. Apparently, the man had been harassing Regina for funds, and had even laid his hands on her during his last visit. David had anticipated the man's visit and instructed Powell to inform him the moment Tobias turned up their doorstep, no matter when.

Thus, the presence of her spineless cousin-in-law in this private drawing room. Regina moved to sit up and pull her feet off his lap, but David rested a hand on her ankle to keep her from going. He would be damned if Tobias Hurst disturbed her more than he already had.

"Mr. Hurst, I presume?" David said, looking the man over from head to toe and allowing his face to show the results of his assessment. He was unimpressive and obviously as much a coward as his cousin had been. "I take it you have come to congratulate Regina on her marriage.

You are a bit late, but we can forgive such a lapse in manners, can we not, my dear?"

"Perhaps," Regina said, remaining cool and composed.

Tobias sneered at her before turning his attention to David. "So, you're the pretty fop who earned himself my cousin's fortune today."

David frowned, feigning confusion. "Your cousin ... forgive me, but I was under the impression that Randolph is dead. Is he not dead some months past, my dear?"

"Quite," Regina offered.

"I did not come here to play your games, Graham," Tobias spat. "I'm sure you cannot know what a conniving strumpet you've married, but I have come to tell you—"

"Powell."

The single word from David was enough to spur the footman into action. He moved so swiftly Tobias never saw or heard him coming. One arm was wrenched behind his back at an unnatural angle, and a sweep of Powell's foot drove him to his knees. Tobias was forced to bend at the waist, howling and squirming, but Powell merely twisted his wrist and pulled, pushing the other man's face into the carpet and rendering him motionless.

"Much better," David said, as casually as if they discussed the weather. "Now, you will listen and keep your mouth closed unless instructed to speak. Powell will break your arm if you fail to follow my direction. There, you see? It would seem you *did* come to play my game. You have threatened and disturbed my wife, and now interrupt my wedding night. Surely you can imagine how vexing such an inconvenience is, so I will make this brief. Randolph Hurst's money and estate became Regina's upon his death per the terms of his will. Out of the kindness of her heart, she offered you a generous stipend to live on, knowing that the late Mr. Hurst had been responsible for your upkeep. Perhaps she did it out of obligation rather than kindness, but the point is ... the money was hers to do with as she pleased, and for reasons I cannot understand she chose to give a bit of it to you. However, all that money, all that land, everything your cousin owned ... why, I do believe it belongs to me now. It's mine to do with as *I* see fit."

Tobias flinched and opened his mouth to speak, but his words died on a gurgle and a sharp, pained wail as Powell wrenched and twisted the arm. He fell silent then, his pitiful, whining breaths the only sound emitting from him as he drooled into the carpet.

"Now, then," David continued. "I am a generous man, and am more than willing to allow the Hurst estate to continue to provide your living at the yearly amount decided upon by my wife and her solicitor. I find it to be a fair sum, and more than a wastrel like you deserves. However, there are stipulations to my generosity. Would you like to hear them? Oh, and you may speak now."

"Yes, damn you," Tobias growled, one dark eye glowering at David from beneath his tousled hair.

"It's quite simple, really. If you return to this house, or otherwise accost my wife in any way, I will cut you off without a farthing for the rest of your days. You see, Regina felt herself responsible for you because you were her relative by marriage. But you and I aren't related, are we? Which means I have no interest in keeping you supplied with horseflesh, women, and liquor. So, I suggest you keep your distance and manage your funds better. Agreed?"

"Agreed!" Tobias spat, face now the color of a plum as he grunted and snorted his rage.

"Before you go, I would request that you apologize to my wife for the inconvenience you have caused her. Make it pretty."

Tobias glowered at him, and for a moment David thought he wouldn't comply. But, one squeeze of Powell's hand at his wrist, and the man opened his mouth. "I beg your pardon for any offense I may have caused you in the past, cousin. You have my word it will not happen again."

"Well done," David murmured, turning to Regina. "Was that good enough, my dear, or would you like it a bit more poetic?"

Regina's pinched lips and quivering shoulders hinted at her amusement, but she hid it well. "It will do, I suppose."

"Very well. Oh, one more thing, Tobias. I have been generous, yet you don't seem very grateful. A simple 'thank you, Mr. Graham' will do."

"Thank you ... Mr. Graham," Tobias managed from behind clenched teeth.

At David's nod, Powell let him up, clapping a hand on his shoulder and steering him toward the door.

"All right then, time to go," Powell muttered, pushing Tobias out into the corridor, where two other footmen lay in wait. They each took one of Tobias's arms and led him out of sight, leaving Powell in the room with them.

David studied the footman, who seemed reluctant to leave as he looked to Regina. If he wasn't mistaken, guilt was clearly written on Powell's face as he cleared his throat.

"Before I go, ma'am, there's something I must tell you. It has weighed on my conscience all these months, but I did not want to cause you distress. Seems like now might be the best time for me to lay it all at your feet."

This time, when Regina sat up straight, David let her go, too curious over what Powell might have to confess to stop her.

"What is it?" she asked.

The footman flinched under the weight of her stare but maintained his quiet dignity. "You have to understand, I wanted to kill him. I almost did, truth be told. He was already dying, but some men can survive anything. I couldn't stand back and let him hurt you anymore."

"You mean Randolph," Regina whispered, her voice quavering.

David rested a hand over hers but said nothing, offering his silent support.

"Yes," Powell confirmed. "I went into his room the night after his accident, while you were sleeping, and meant to be in and out in a trice. I'd press the pillow over his face and have done with it. No one would know and all would assume he succumbed to his injuries. But then, he awakened when I was standing over him. He saw me."

Regina turned her hand over to press her palm against David's, squeezing him so hard his knuckles ached. David kept his silence and let her. He didn't like the idea of Randolph Hurst overshadowing their wedding day in any way, but this matter was between his wife and the man who had cared for her before he had come along.

"What happened?" Regina whispered.

"He told me he knew why I'd come. Said he always knew I had sympathy for you, accused me of wanting you for myself. 'Do you think she'll be yours once I'm gone?' That's what he asked me as he lay there struggling to breathe and grimacing in agony."

Regina snorted. "Randolph could never understand a relationship between a man and a woman that wasn't carnal in nature."

"That's true enough. I stood there thinking about smothering him, but then I had another thought. What if he died and left you nothing? What if, after he was gone, you were abandoned with no money or a place to live? I couldn't bear it. I had to know. I asked him what was in his will and what he'd set aside for you."

David knew what Powell would say before the words were spoken, but they still left a bitter taste in his mouth and an even stronger loathing for the ghost of Randolph Hurst.

"Not a ha'penny was meant for you," he said with a shake of his head. "Not a dower's portion, or a house ... not a goddamn thing."

Regina leaned forward, lips parting and eyes spreading wide as she seemed to register Powell's meaning. "Randolph's will ... That was you?"

Powell squared his shoulders, unflinching pride radiating from his eyes. "It was. I hurt him, just enough to remind him of his helplessness. Told him I'd make his last days on earth a living hell if he didn't send for the solicitor right away and make sure you received everything he owned. Took away his spirits and his laudanum until he complied. He spent three days in misery before he finally called for the man to see it done."

"Dear God," Regina murmured. "I knew it. I knew there was something not quite right about him leaving me everything."

Powell bowed his head then, appearing contrite for his actions for the first time. "Tobias knew it, too, and I'm that sorry for it. I just wanted to help you. I wanted you to be taken care of. It was less than you deserved, but all I could give you. Maybe it was wrong for me to take it all when it wasn't mine to give in the first place. But I'd do it again, and not be sorry. I only regret that it cast you in a suspicious light. I wasn't thinking of that when I did it. I just wanted you to be all right."

Regina came to her feet, tugging her hand away from David's and approaching the servant. He remained where she had left him, watching as she took Powell's face in her hands and pressed a chaste kiss to his cheek.

"Thank you. Right or wrong, you have always tried to protect me. I could never repay you for that."

"You aren't angry with me?"

"Of course not. Perhaps you ought to have left Tobias a little something, but there's nothing we can do about it now. Besides, he would have ruined the estate within a year, so it was probably for the best."

Powell's lips twitched with amusement as Regina released him, and he straightened, inclining his head at David. "And now, I leave her in your care. You have things well in hand, I suppose."

David stood and took hold of Regina, pulling her to stand at his side. "I have it from here, Powell. Thank you."

Powell then made his exit, leaving David alone with his bride once more. Taking hold of her hand, he graced her knuckles with a kiss.

"Are you all right? I suspect that was a lot to digest after what had already been a long day."

Regina wrapped her arms around his waist and grinned. "It was, but I am glad to have Tobias dealt with, and finally know the truth about Randolph's will. Now it feels as if we are really ready to begin our lives together."

"Indeed we are, my dear," he replied, slowly backing her toward the open door leading into the bedroom. "And now that's all behind us, I can give you your wedding gift."

Holding up her hand to study the ring he'd slid onto her finger at the altar, she wiggled her fingers so the firelight played over the facets of a diamond flanked by tiny pearls. It was one of the only pieces of jewelry his mother hadn't sold, and she had been happy to part with it for Regina to wear as her wedding ring.

"I thought this was my gift."

David released her, then went to the bed, pushing off his braces and tearing his shirt off over his head as he went. "If I have anything to say about it, you are going to become quite spoiled. Best you grow used to the idea, my dear. Now, turn around and let me help you out of your gown."

She gave him her back, goosebumps appearing on her nape as he kissed her there while unfastening her dress. Regina remained passive while he unlaced her stays and divested her of her chemise. Once she stood before him in only her stockings and garters, he took a moment to drink her in. She was as perfect as ever, perhaps even more so now that David had come to know her body so well. The subtle changes hinting at her pregnancy had already begun, and they made him desire her all the more.

Once he'd looked his fill, David went back to the bed, lifting the black length of cloth he had laid there an hour ago. "If you don't mind, I require your assistance."

Then, he was covering his eyes with the material and tying it off in a loose knot at the back of his head. Regina's confused expression was the last thing he saw before the world went dark.

"What on earth ..."

"Well, I did promise to prove that my arrogance was well-earned," David teased. "Now, if you'll just use that other bit of cloth to tie my hands, I'll set about fulfilling my promise."

A beat of silence, and then Regina erupted into giggles, her hands resting on his chest as she fell into him. "Would that be your promise to have me climbing the walls while blindfolded with both hands tied behind your back?"

"The very one."

Regina's finger played along the seam of his lips, the sensation heightened by his lack of sight. His cock swelled in response, arousal already plaguing him at thoughts of what the night would hold. He didn't need to see her to want her so badly it hurt. He could smell her, feel her ... and very shortly, intended to taste her until she begged him to stop. His mouth watered with expectancy.

Regina's hand caressed down his arm, then back up to his shoulder as she circled him, her footsteps soft and nearly silent on the thick rug. She pressed her lips to his shoulder blade before drawing his hands together behind his back to tie his wrists together.

"I must admit to being excited that I am now to spend the rest of my life learning all the other functions of a courtesan."

"You'll learn them all, and when we are finished, I shall invent new ones. Now ..."

He perched on the edge of the bed, which Regina took as her cue to use a hand at the center of his chest to push him to his back. David inched farther up the bed, adjusting his arms more comfortably beneath him. He felt the slight dip of the mattress as Regina climbed on, and then she was lying on top of him and offering her mouth for a kiss.

David snared her lips with unrestrained hunger, his tongue treating her to a prelude of what he had in store.

"My God, do I love you ... Mrs. Graham."

He felt her smile against his brow before pressing a kiss between his eyes. "I love you, too, Mr. Graham."

Giving her one last short, sweet kiss, David undulated beneath her, reveling in the drag of her naked breasts against his chest, the press of her mound against his swelling cock.

"You've situated yourself too low, my dear. Would you shift up just a bit?"

She complied, but not nearly enough for David's liking.

"More," he urged, until she sat straddling his torso. "Nearly there ... up ... up ..."

When she finally rested where he wanted her, he raised his head to nuzzle the soft nest of her curls. He could see them in his mind's eye, a fiery red splash against the pale translucence of her skin. He kissed the inside of each smooth, creamy thigh, drawing soft sighs of delight from her.

"Perfect," he murmured, lightly dragging his tongue down her slit. "Now ... down."

Then, his senses were awash in Regina—her satiny-slick flesh pressed to his lips, the swollen nub of her clit sliding against his tongue. David groaned and went at her like a man starved, losing himself to the feel of her, the taste of her, the scent of her arousal, cloying and sweet.

The scrape of Regina's nails against the headboard filled his ears, followed by the gasps and moans of her pleasure—music to David's ears.

As he fulfilled his promise to pleasure her like she'd never been pleasured in her life—all without the benefits of hands or eyesight—

David realized how wrong he had been to think being surrounded by women was some form of heaven on earth. For certain, women were marvelous creatures, but there was none like his Regina. She was light and life and joy. She was everything he'd been missing, and she would now belong to him until the day he died.

She alone was David's idea of heaven.

EPILOGUE

Benedict stared into the dark amber liquid in his tumbler, finding he had no desire to lose himself to its siren's call. The need to drown himself in excess pleasures and strong drink had faded away days ago, leaving him an empty, hollow shell. He had hardly eaten all day, hadn't slept more than a few hours all week, and was generally a very miserable person to be around.

His friends had mostly left him to his own devices—all save Aubrey, who visited every day on his way home from his linen drapery to ensure Benedict hadn't hanged himself from the rafters or slit his own throat.

In truth, he wasn't *that* miserable just yet, but he could understand his best friend's concerns. He had not been himself these past weeks, and they both knew why.

There was no explaining it to the other courtesans, who had no idea how that death notice in the papers had poked and prodded at old wounds. So, he allowed Hugh, David, and Dominick to think he was simply stewing in jealousy over having to stand back and watch each of them find happiness with the women they loved, and go on to become husbands and fathers. Honestly, he did feel the slightest twinge of envy, but not for the reasons they might think. He didn't want what they had for himself—had realized quite early in life that such things weren't possible for him.

Yes, it hurt to feel as if he had lost them all one by one, because now he was the only man of their set who didn't quite fit. The only one who wasn't someone's husband or soon to be a father. The only miserable bastard who woke every morning alone, and who went to his bed each night the same way. It had been foolish of him to think this wouldn't eventually happen, and perhaps in the back of his mind he had always known better.

However, Benedict hadn't counted on how much he would come to rely on them. He moaned and complained about the messes they made, but he secretly reveled in being the one they came to when the time came to clean those messes. Perhaps Aubrey hadn't needed him quite as much as the others, but the things making them different from the other men of their circle was what drew them together. It was what helped Aubrey understand him in a way no one else did.

Benedict had accused David of being pitiful, but the truth couldn't be clearer. *He* was the pitiful one.

However, watching David and Regina wed in their small, private ceremony had given him what he needed to move forward. All he had ever wanted was for his friends to be secure and cared for. That mission had been accomplished, whether by his own efforts or those of the women they loved. However, there were still a few loose ends that needed tying up, and it was better for them to stay away from him so he could do what needed to be done.

Upon his return from Lancashire, he'd been visited by Lady Millicent Dane. She came with news that neither surprised nor angered him … because as she related how she had uncovered the identity of The London Gossip, Benedict realized he already knew. He'd known from the moment she had overtaken him in St. Giles, and that nauseating scent of lily of the valley had wafted up his nostrils. Millicent's report had only confirmed his suspicions, making his next and final move very clear.

In the end, it would seem all had turned out as it should, because David's marriage had pushed him firmly into the ranks of former courtesans who had become respectable. All he had to do now was take the

Gossip down without allowing their past involvement with the agency to become public knowledge. And, he knew exactly how to accomplish such an aim.

What then?

The unwelcome thought intruded upon the machinations of his mind, prompting him to take his first sip of brandy all day. He hadn't wanted to drown himself in drink, but damn it, he couldn't let himself think of the future. There were some things he simply was not ready to face, such as the inevitability of inheriting a viscountcy and the years ahead that would see him grow old alone.

The taste of the brandy soured on his tongue, and he set the tumbler aside before coming to his feet. If he continued like this, he'd become slow and fat, and his next pugilist match would end with him choking on someone's fist. He needed distraction and movement. He needed to outrun the memories plaguing his waking hours as well as his dreams.

He didn't bother with a greatcoat, barreling out of his study, down the corridor and straight through the front door. The chill of the late-night air stung his face and bare hands, but Benedict curled his fingers into his palms and pressed on, walking at a brisk and purposeful pace with nowhere to go.

It doesn't matter that the countess is dead. It changes nothing.

Benedict repeated those words to himself over and over, because if he didn't, he might lose control. And he was never anything if not in complete control—of his life, his destiny, his circumstances. Things didn't *happen* to Benedict Sterling, he made them happen his way. The world didn't kick him about as it once had, not anymore. He thumbed his nose at the world and did as he pleased.

He was *not* a starving dog staring in a bakery window, damn it. There wasn't a thing in this world Benedict could want that wasn't within his reach. What need had he to pine over a lover who had decided he wasn't worth the trouble of spurning convention and the wishes of a tyrannical father? He was better off alone.

Benedict wandered aimlessly for what felt like hours, though without his watch he had no concept of time. The night grew colder, his nose numb and sore, his fingers stiff. He had wandered quite a ways from home, and picked up the pace on his way back. The walk had helped clear his head and cleanse him of all foolish notions of love.

He could rejoice in the happiness of his friends without feeling as if he needed what they had. He didn't, and he would not let the pain of the past convince him otherwise. Choices had been made—irrevocable choices. All parties involved had to live with the results, himself included. There was too much riding on his success in this battle with The London Gossip. He couldn't afford distractions of any kind.

By the time he reached home, Benedict felt worlds better. Physical activity had always given him solace, and it was easier to remember that when his mind was not addled by drink. His trainer would give him an earful over his sluggishness once he began preparing for his next match, but Benedict would work hard to undo the destruction of treating his body like a rubbish bin for the past month. He would restrict his diet and do away with rich foods drenched in heavy sauces—which tasted wonderful and brought him comfort, but were hell on his speed and agility. He would shun strong drink and return to his morning runs and afternoon sparring sessions. He would pull himself up and press on, as he had always done.

The solemn face of his butler greeted him when he stepped into the entrance hall, shivering and blowing into the cradle of his freezing hands.

"Your pardon, sir, but you have a visitor."

Following the servant's gaze to the closed door of his study, Benedict scowled. "This time of night? No ... I don't want to see anyone. Send them away."

"I'm sorry, but the gentleman seemed most insistent. He made it clear he would not leave unless ..."

Benedict raised one eyebrow and pinned the butler with a pointed look, unable to believe what he was hearing. "Unless *what?*"

The man cleared his throat and averted his gaze, face flushing. "He said ... and these were his words, sir, you should know ... um ... he said that if you wanted him to leave, you could come into that room and eject him bodily yourself."

Annoyance shot through Benedict, bringing the feeling back to his fingers as he imagined pummeling this faceless intruder into a bloody pulp. With the way he'd been feeling lately, he would relish such a task.

"I see. You are dismissed. I will handle this myself." It wasn't until he was halfway to the door that he had a sudden thought and paused, looking back at the butler—who remained where Benedict had left him. "Who did you say the gentleman was?"

"I didn't, sir, I apologize. It is His Lordship, the Earl of Vautrey."

All the heat of his fury melted away, to be replaced by a stunned iciness that seized him from the inside out. For about half a minute Benedict could not breathe, could hardly see as the world around him tilted and spun far too fast. He shook his head and took a breath, certain he hadn't heard the butler correctly. But the man had followed Benedict's order to make himself scarce, and couldn't be asked to repeat the name.

His ears rang as he turned back to the door, then began to roar with the pounding of his own blood, rushing hot and fast through his veins. He oughtn't be surprised; Vautrey had been made an earl by his father's death, which meant he wouldn't have been able to go on hiding in Kent forever. His parliamentary duties and social obligations would demand he return to London at some point. And because Benedict preferred London, it stood to reason they would have to come face to face eventually. He had hoped that by the time they came to this, his fury over the other man's betrayal would have diminished. Benedict took his time entering the room, certain he would be tempted to rearrange the structure of Vautrey's face on first sight.

As it happened, the earl's face wasn't the first thing Benedict encountered. It was his back, encased in a black coat, and a head full of thick, shiny brown hair. He stood staring out a window at the moonlit walkway leading to the courtyard off the back of the house. There wasn't much of interest out there, yet the man took his time turning to face him.

Time had done very little to change him, and when Benedict first caught sight of his face he lost the urge to bash it with his fists. Because that face reminded him of the boy who had befriended him at Eton. The boy who had dragged him off the lads he'd pounded into the dirt for calling him foul, hurtful names. The boy whose friendship had made him feel a little less alone in a world where it seemed no one else was like him. As it had turned out, there were many others like him, and Lord Alexander Osborn, Earl of Vautrey had opened his eyes to that fact.

Then, he'd gutted Benedict and left him to die. Metaphorically, of course.

"Hello, Ben," he said, voice low but clear and firm. No hesitation, no uncertainty ... just Alex as Benedict had always known him—sure of himself and filling the room with an undeniable presence.

The door rattled in the frame when Benedict slammed it. He kept the entire length of the room between them, knowing he could not be trusted to hold on to his self-control otherwise. The firelight cast its glow over Alexander from the hearth, illuminating patrician features and dark brows that shadowed his eyes.

"What ... the bloody fuck ... are *you* doing here?" The words came out clipped, between harsh breaths as he struggled to contain the overflow of emotion welling up from his middle. Rage, fury, sadness, confusion and pain. It was a toxic combination, poisoning him, killing him by degrees.

Alexander moved away from the window at a sedate walk, his fingers running along the surface of Benedict's desk as he took in his surroundings with a curious eye. The man stood an inch taller than Ben, making him a veritable giant, but Benedict outweighed him by a stone and a half, carrying more bulk across his shoulders and chest. He dressed like a fashion plate and never had a hair out of place, but no one would call Alex a fop—at least, not to his face.

He paused, rhythmically rapping his knuckles against the edge of Ben's desk and staring down at his polished boots. "I should think that was obvious. Surely you've heard the news. Katherine, she ... died."

A muscle in Benedict's cheek jerked in reaction to that statement, and the urge to tear the room down around them surged within him once again. "So I have heard. You have my most sincere condolences, though I fail to understand why her death would bring you to my doorstep."

A small smile curved the corner of Alex's lips, making a dimple appear in his cheek. "Oh, Ben ... you were never any good at hiding your emotions."

"I've changed. You'd know that if you hadn't run off to Kent with your blushing *bride*."

"Ben—"

"What did you expect?" Benedict snapped. "That I would have spent the past three years sobbing into my brandy and wishing to have back what was lost?"

"Of course not."

"Then you hoped to be welcomed back into my life as if you didn't betray me?"

"That isn't it, either."

Benedict hadn't realized he had begun closing the distance between them, until he was close enough to reach out and touch Alex—which he did. His arm shot out, one fist closing around the lapel of the other man's coat. Alex stumbled, but righted himself and did nothing to be free of Ben's grasp. He merely stared at Benedict with mournful eyes the color of cognac and sighed.

"I knew you wouldn't have forgiven me, but I had hoped we might talk. You don't even have to listen to me. You can berate me and call me every horrible name you can think of, and I will sit and listen. I just ... when I had settled my affairs in Kent, I found myself wandering around this cold, empty house and ... I had to come. Even knowing you hate me, even realizing I have no right to intrude on your life."

Benedict squeezed his eyes shut and drew in a slow breath, quickly losing the battle with his rational mind. This was madness. Every word Alex had just said was true. He had no right coming here and upending Benedict's life. And yet ...

"Say it," Benedict demanded, yanking Alex closer until they were nearly nose to nose. "Tell me why you've come."

Alex took hold of the hand gripping his coat, though he didn't pry it loose. He simply held it there, against his chest as he lowered his head toward Benedict's.

"I came for you."

The murmured words fell against his lips a second before Alex's mouth followed, pressing against Ben's, tentative and searching. With a savage growl, Benedict slammed his hands against his chest, sending him sprawling back against the desk.

Chest heaving and heart pounding, he glared at Alex while swiping the back of his hand across his mouth. Still, the taste of him lingered— sugary and sweet, laced with peppermint. Even that hadn't changed. Apparently, Alex still suffered from an incurable sweet tooth. Benedict could taste the evidence of that, but there was more, too. There was history and a collection of secrets held between them. There was pleasure and pain and wild abandon. There was a sudden clash of past and present that left him reeling.

There was the very real possibility that Benedict was going insane, because instead of taking Alex by the collar and tossing him out on his ear, he did the unthinkable.

Forgetting for just one moment that this man had nearly been the death of him, Benedict advanced. He took hold of the edge of the desk, caging Alex between his arms and using his body to pin the other man in place. Then, he searched out the source of that cloying sweetness with a pained groan. He kissed Alex with all the force of his anger and his grief, releasing three years' worth of starvation and need. Going pliant against him, Alex raised both hands to Benedict's jaw, and with a tilt of his head and sweep of his tongue, kissed him back.

BOOK 5: CHASING BENEDICT

Benedict Sterling founded The Gentleman Courtesans agency to
assure financial security for himself and his friends. Unfortunately, the

efforts of a spiteful gossip-column writer threaten to expose his secrets —including those that could see him ruined and ostracized. With everyone he cares about in the path of his enemy, he is determined to silence The London Gossip once and for all. But when a lover from his past returns seeking to make amends, Benedict is left grappling with the pain of his past as well as his present dilemma.

Lord Alexander Osborne, Earl of Vautrey, has returned to London with a singular goal—win back the man he loves. Unfortunately, their previous separation has made Benedict resistant to ever allow Alex into his life again. He'll do anything to win the other man's heart— including accept the terms of a contract that will temporarily set Benedict up as his courtesan. For now, Alex is willing to take whatever Ben is willing to give. However, in the end he will settle for nothing less than love and a future with the love of his life.

THE GENTLEMAN COURTESANS
SERIES READING ORDER

Now Available:

Tempting the Bluestocking (prequel novella)

Portrait of a Lady

What a Courtesan Wants

Making of a Scandal

Taming of the Rake

Chasing Benedict

ABOUT THE AUTHOR

Sexy heroes ... sassy heroines ... electrifying erotic romance.
Victoria Vale has written over two dozen Romance and Young Adult
novels under various pseudonyms. As a lover of erotic romance, she
enjoys nothing more than a sexy hero paired with a sassy heroine,
flavored with a dash of spice and lots of heat. A wife and mother of
three, she enjoys reading (of course), cooking, sewing ... and other
activities that aren't appropriate for inclusion in a biography.